THE
VON RITTERMANN
LEGACY

THE
VON RITTERMANN
LEGACY

Deborah Read

Published in the United Kingdom in 2010 by

Bank House Books
PO Box 3
New Romney
TN29 9WJ

www.bankhousebooks.com

British Library Cataloguing in Publication Data
A catalogue record for this book is available from the British Library

Front cover image by Andrea Stevenon
Von Rittermann family trees by Christopher Fletcher

ISBN 9781904408062

Typesetting and origination by Bank House Books

To my dear mother, who has patiently put up with Rhiannon and family for so long.

Meredith-Mayschoss Line: I. Desc

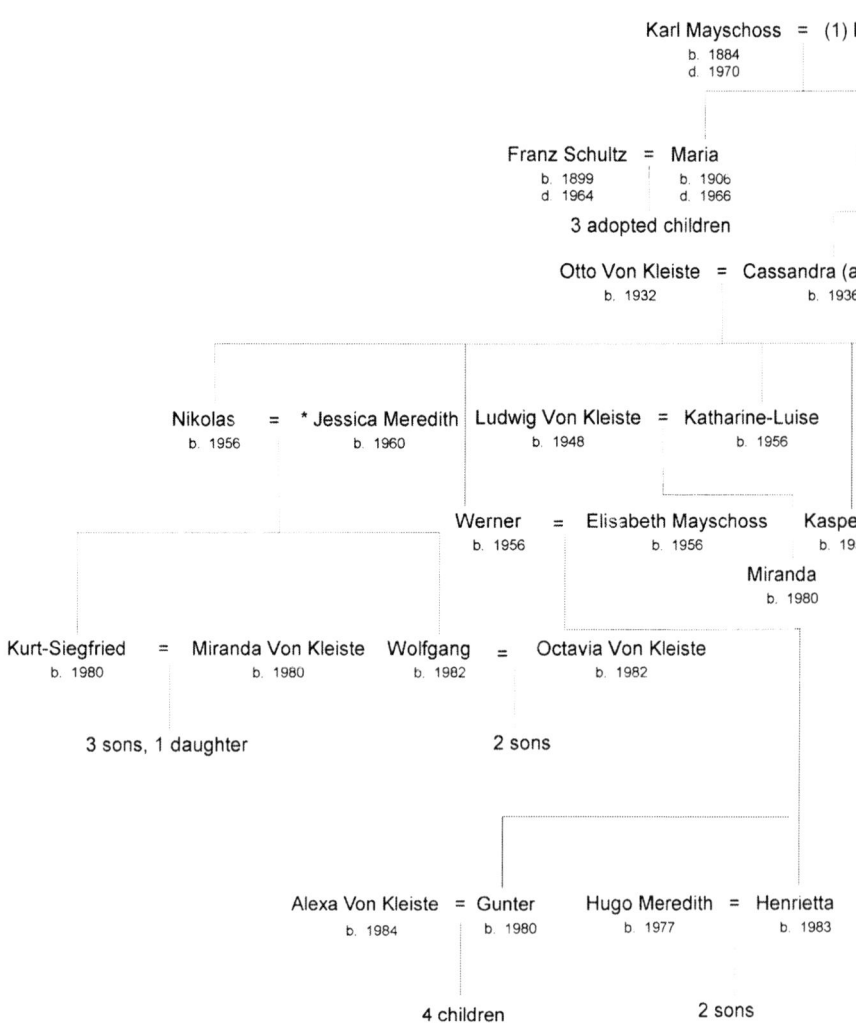

Karl Mayschoss = (1) E
b. 1884
d. 1970

Franz Schultz = Maria
b. 1899   b. 1906
d. 1964   d. 1966

3 adopted children

Otto Von Kleiste = Cassandra (a
b. 1932   b. 1936

Nikolas = * Jessica Meredith   Ludwig Von Kleiste = Katharine-Luise
b. 1956   b. 1960   b. 1948   b. 1956

Werner = Elisabeth Mayschoss   Kaspe
b. 1956   b. 1956   b. 198

Miranda
b. 1980

Kurt-Siegfried = Miranda Von Kleiste   Wolfgang = Octavia Von Kleiste
b. 1980   b. 1980   b. 1982   b. 1982

3 sons, 1 daughter   2 sons

Alexa Von Kleiste = Gunter   Hugo Meredith = Henrietta
b. 1984   b. 1980   b. 1977   b. 1983

4 children   2 sons

ants of Cassandra and Otto Von Kleiste

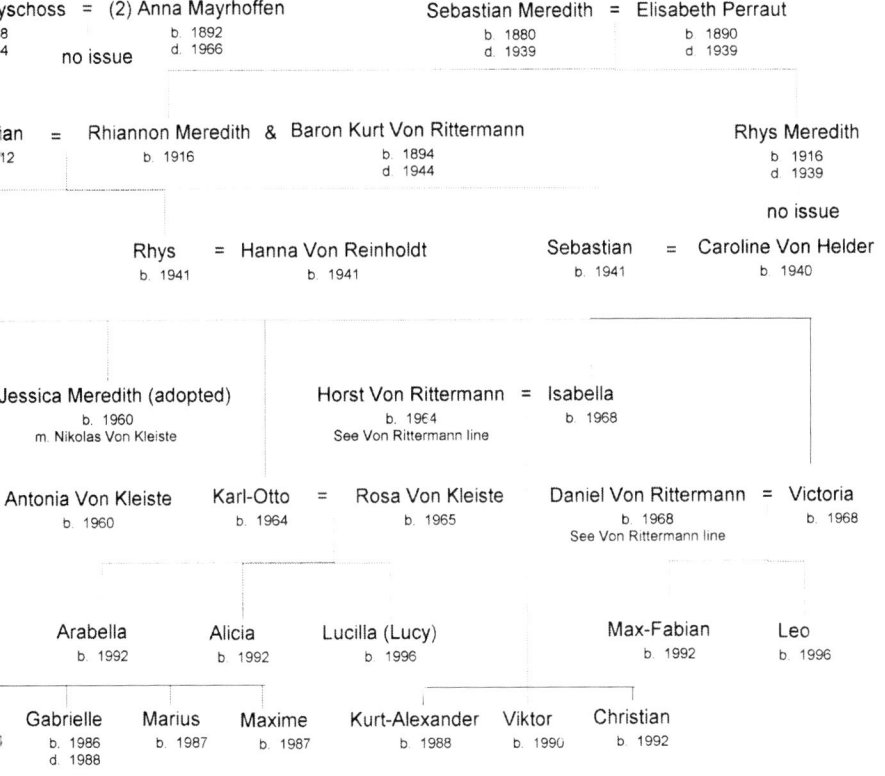

schoss = (2) Anna Mayrhoffen
8   b. 1892
4   no issue   d. 1966

Sebastian Meredith = Elisabeth Perraut
        b. 1880   b. 1890
        d. 1939   d. 1939

an = Rhiannon Meredith & Baron Kurt Von Rittermann
12   b. 1916   b. 1894
                                  d. 1944

Rhys Meredith
    b. 1916
    d. 1939

no issue

Rhys = Hanna Von Reinholdt
b. 1941   b. 1941

Sebastian = Caroline Von Helder
  b. 1941   b. 1940

Jessica Meredith (adopted)
        b. 1960
  m. Nikolas Von Kleiste

Horst Von Rittermann = Isabella
        b. 1964   b. 1968
  See Von Rittermann line

Antonia Von Kleiste   Karl-Otto = Rosa Von Kleiste
        b. 1960   b. 1964   b. 1965

Daniel Von Rittermann = Victoria
        b. 1968   b. 1968
  See Von Rittermann line

Arabella   Alicia   Lucilla (Lucy)
  b. 1992   b. 1992   b. 1996

Max-Fabian   Leo
    b. 1992   b. 1996

Gabrielle   Marius   Maxime   Kurt-Alexander   Viktor   Christian
  b. 1986   b. 1987   b. 1987   b. 1988   b. 1990   b. 1992
  d. 1988

Meredith-Mayschoss Line: II. Descenc

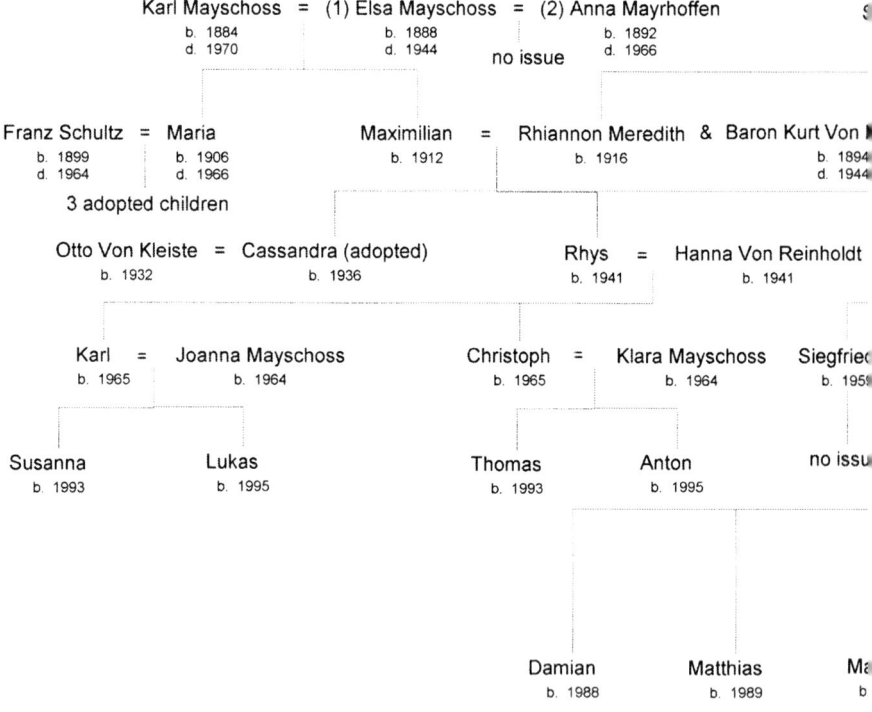

Karl Mayschoss = (1) Elsa Mayschoss = (2) Anna Mayrhoffen
b. 1884   b. 1888   b. 1892
d. 1970   d. 1944   no issue   d. 1966

Franz Schultz = Maria   Maximilian = Rhiannon Meredith & Baron Kurt Von
b. 1899   b. 1906   b. 1912   b. 1916   b. 1894
d. 1964   d. 1966   d. 1944
3 adopted children

Otto Von Kleiste = Cassandra (adopted)   Rhys = Hanna Von Reinholdt
b. 1932   b. 1936   b. 1941   b. 1941

Karl = Joanna Mayschoss   Christoph = Klara Mayschoss   Siegfried
b. 1965   b. 1964   b. 1965   b. 1964   b. 1959

Susanna   Lukas   Thomas   Anton   no issue
b. 1993   b. 1995   b. 1993   b. 1995

                                   Damian   Matthias   Ma
                                   b. 1988   b. 1989   b.

s of Rhys and Sebastian Mayschoss

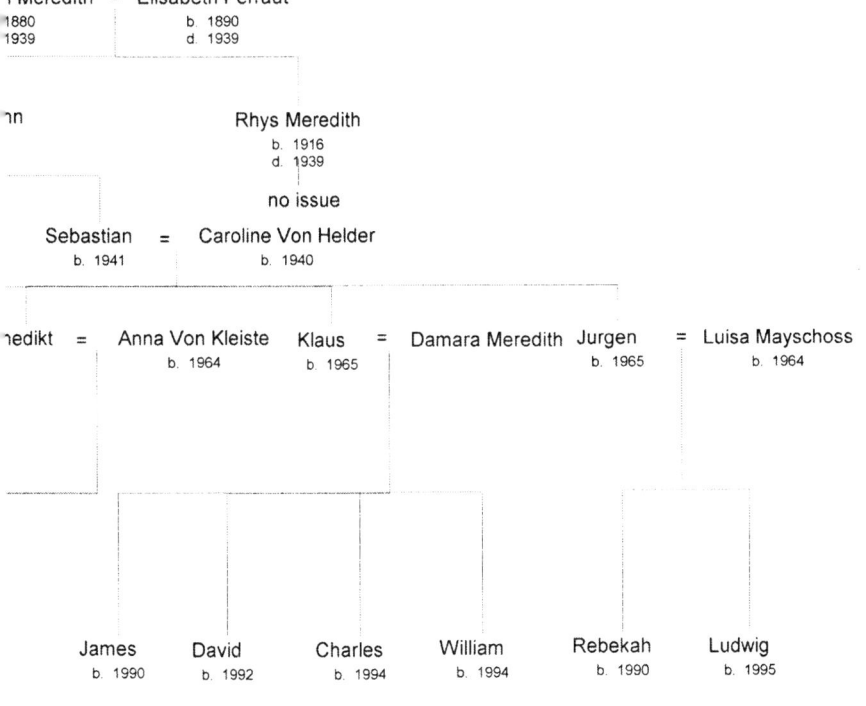

n Meredith = Elisabeth Perraut
1880   b. 1890
1939   d. 1939

nn

Rhys Meredith
b. 1916
d. 1939

no issue

Sebastian   =   Caroline Von Helder
b. 1941   b. 1940

nedikt = Anna Von Kleiste   Klaus = Damara Meredith   Jurgen = Luisa Mayschoss
b. 1964   b. 1965   b. 1965   b. 1964

James   David   Charles   William   Rebekah   Ludwig
b. 1990   b. 1992   b. 1994   b. 1994   b. 1990   b. 1995

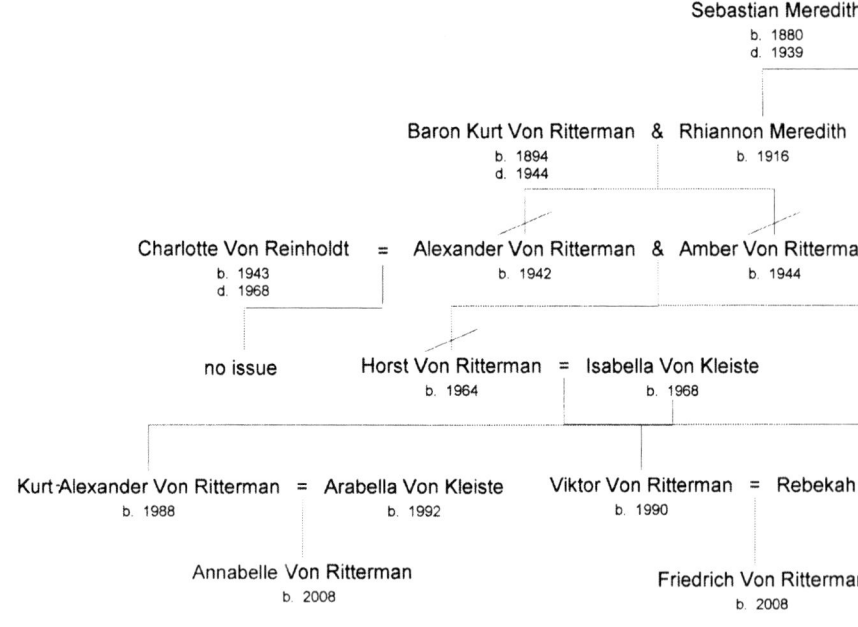

Von R

Sebastian Meredith
b. 1880
d. 1939

Baron Kurt Von Ritterman & Rhiannon Meredith
b. 1894   b. 1916
d. 1944

Charlotte Von Reinholdt = Alexander Von Ritterman & Amber Von Ritterma
b. 1943   b. 1942   b. 1944
d. 1968

no issue   Horst Von Ritterman = Isabella Von Kleiste
b. 1964   b. 1968

Kurt-Alexander Von Ritterman = Arabella Von Kleiste   Viktor Von Ritterman = Rebekah
b. 1988   b. 1992   b. 1990

Annabelle Von Ritterman   Friedrich Von Ritterma
b. 2008   b. 2008

nann Line

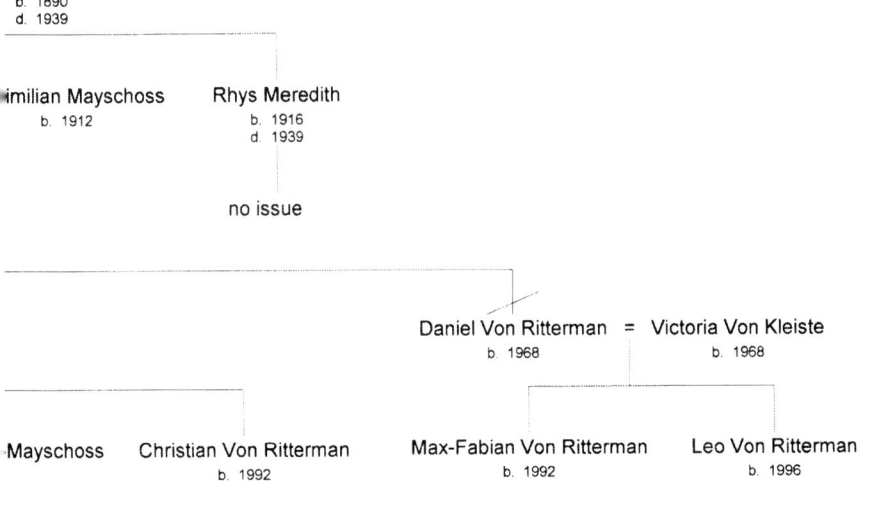

beth Perraut
b. 1890
d. 1939

imilian Mayschoss
b. 1912

Rhys Meredith
b. 1916
d. 1939

no issue

Daniel Von Ritterman = Victoria Von Kleiste
b. 1968   b. 1968

Mayschoss   Christian Von Ritterman   Max-Fabian Von Ritterman   Leo Von Ritterman
b. 1992   b. 1992   b. 1996

Chapter One
Paris, June 1940

M iss Rhiannon?' The teenage maid timidly addressed the attractive young red-head sitting at the desk, head bent over her work.

'Yes, Marie? What is it now?' Irritated by yet another unwelcome interruption, Rhiannon frowned and carried on writing without looking up.

'Can't my grandmother or Aunt Agnes see to the matter? I'm rather busy.'

The maid glanced nervously at the tall German officer in a grey uniform, standing quietly by the study door, and stammered, 'Please Miss, I don't think . . .'

Detecting a note of rising panic in Marie's voice, Rhiannon finally looked up. 'You don't think what? Oh!' She stared at the young fair-haired German in stunned surprise, then dismissed the mouse-like maid with a nod. 'Thank you, Marie, you may go.'

'Yes, Miss Rhiannon.' Glad to leave her employer to deal with the situation, the girl scurried out of the room.

Wondering what could be the matter, Rhiannon met his steely gaze steadily before politely asking in her fluent, idiomatic German, 'May I help you?'

The captain, highly impressed, studied the stunningly beautiful girl for a moment, before replying smoothly, 'I believe Thérèse Perraut, your grandmother, received an official visit two days ago from my commanding officer, informing her that I was to be billeted here.'

The girl's green eyes flashed in the evening light. 'Did she indeed? Well, she didn't tell me. She's not at all well.' Slipping from behind the desk, a large black German shepherd dog at her heels, she added, 'It would have been nice to have been informed, but since I only returned from visiting Great Aunt Alicia yesterday I'll put it down to Grandmother's absent-mindedness.'

The stranger could see now that Rhiannon was very tall for a woman, with a slim hourglass figure. She was clad in an elegantly cut, emerald green silk dress, her long reddish-gold hair clipped back neatly with a heavy antique clip, her discreet make-up and stylishly expensive jewellery presenting a sharp contrast with the two hostile older women who had passed him silently in the hall.

'Do you smoke?' Her strangely cat-like eyes regarded the handsome blue-eyed officer with slight concern.

'No, I don't.'

'Good.' Offering her hand in a friendly gesture, she added pleasantly, 'I'm Rhiannon Meredith, by the way. And you are?'

Shaking hands with this frank and good-natured girl, whose open and gracious manner promised nothing but friendship and trust, the already smitten young man regarded her intently, and replied politely, 'Captain Maximilian Mayschoss. I'm delighted to make your acquaintance, Miss Meredith.'

Rhiannon smiled sweetly. 'I'm very pleased to meet you too, Captain. Perhaps you'd like to wait in the sitting room while I prepare your room? You may bring up your luggage when I'm finished. Would you like some tea while you're waiting?'

'Yes, very much so. Thank you.'

As Captain Mayschoss followed the slender young woman into the hall, the massive wolf-like dog stood facing him, its brown eyes never leaving his for a second.

'Come away, Tiger.' Sharply calling the hostile animal to her side in English, Rhiannon commented nonchalantly, 'You needn't worry about the dog, Captain; he's always on guard, like the rest of his breed. My late father obtained him from Germany, because he wanted something that would match up to the German army rescue dogs we took back to England with us from Ypres in 1918. The sitting room's through there.'

The well-built young man settled comfortably in an armchair, intrigued by his exquisite and self-assured hostess, her comments about the dog having already given him some vital clues about her family background. Noticing a large photograph of Miss Meredith, taken in that very room with what seemed to be her (elegantly dressed) family, he went over and examined it closely. His practised eye quickly took in the tall and distinguished, greying older man and attractive, tall and slim blonde woman in her forties at his side. Standing close to her, a beaming and well-built giant of a young man with Rhiannon's colouring towered above them, his arm lovingly round Miss Meredith as he held her closely and possessively, the girl's head resting trustingly on his broad shoulder. The inscription on the back of the photograph led the interested captain to discover its date, July 1938 – and the names: Sebastian, Elisabeth, Rhys and Rhiannon. They were indeed her parents and brother. Knowing that Rhiannon's father was dead, and that she owned the house he was billeted in, Captain Mayschoss felt it was logical to assume that her mother and brother were also dead, probably in some sort of accident, allowing for their obvious youth and good health. He was still studying the photograph when Rhiannon brought in some exquisitely presented refreshments, the fiercely protective Tiger at her side.

'I assume this is your family, Miss Meredith?'

'That's right, Captain.' Glancing at the image, a distant expression on her face, she placed the tray on the gold and onyx table. 'They were all killed in a car crash near York in January 1939, just six months after that picture was taken.'

'I'm very sorry.' Replacing the photograph on the sideboard, he glanced sympathetically at her.

'These things happen. That's why I sold Meredith House, our family home, and came to live here in Maison Meredith – which Father bought from my grandmother in 1919. My grandfather, Doctor Claude Perraut, was rather extravagant, and when he died he left her with huge debts and no means of paying them. When she was declared bankrupt she and my aunt were effectively made homeless, but my father allowed them to stay on, as housekeepers.'

The young officer looked impressed. 'That was very generous of him.'

Rhiannon smiled. 'Not really. He never really liked my mother's family, and referred to my grandmother and aunt as the two old witches. My mother persuaded him not to throw them out. It wasn't his generosity.'

'I see.' The amused officer suppressed a smile. 'Where did you learn your excellent German, Miss Meredith?'

'We had a German housekeeper and governess at Meredith House. Magda was the widow of an English officer friend of my father's. He made my father promise to look after her should he not survive the war, and he was killed in action in 1918. So when my parents brought me and Rhys, my twin brother, back to England as toddlers at the end of the war they employed her. Anti-German feeling in Britain was virulent then, which meant she preferred to leave the shopping to our maids, and only went out with us for protection. Poor Magda died of cancer in 1938.'

Fully understanding his hostess's lack of hostility towards him, the intrigued Captain Mayschoss asked curiously, 'She didn't have any children of her own, then?'

'No. Rhys and I were the family she never had. Since you're so interested, I'll bring you some of our family albums to look at while I'm busy.'

'Thank you. I would like that very much.'

When she returned, Rhiannon handed him three heavy leather volumes, then left the captain to leaf through her family history. Studying the period 1914–18, it became clear that Rhiannon and her twin had been born in war-torn Ypres on 5 August 1916, while their army nurse mother was working alongside her young surgeon husband in the primitive military hospitals there. Photographs of Magda showed a plump, motherly woman, with her fair hair in a bun; other pictures depicted her employers in their uniforms at Scarborough Hospital, and later ones portrayed Rhys as a trainee doctor. Flicking though another album, the young German found photos that charted Rhiannon and Rhys from childhood to adulthood, with their university degree awards occupying a prominent place. The rest of the pictures reinforced the image of a devoted and tightly knit family, with German shepherd dogs present on many occasions. Judging by the last album family holidays had been spent all over Europe, especially in Germany, Austria, Ireland, Wales and Scotland, and also Italy and France.

Already strongly attracted to Rhiannon Meredith, Max closed the last book thoughtfully. Her striking good looks, charismatic personality and impeccable family background made her an ideal potential wife, and mother to the large family that he hoped one day to raise.

When Rhiannon called down that she was ready, the young man took up his suitcases and she showed him the room. 'Before you unpack, Captain, I'd better tell you about meal times and our living arrangements here. My grandmother and aunt relax in the parlour while I occupy the sitting room, to avoid arguments: my French relatives and I don't exactly get on well together. Marie and Aunt Agnes do all the housework and laundry, and I help with the shopping. We all do our own washing up and cooking. My meal times are 7.15am for breakfast and 6pm for dinner, while my relations eat at 6.30am and 7.30pm. I eat simple German and English dishes, with the occasional Italian meal, while my grandmother and aunt prefer traditional French cuisine – so if you want anything complicated or fancy you can either go out or eat with them.'

Replying that her own meals would be fine, and that the proposed arrangements suited him perfectly, the captain watched Rhiannon slip gracefully out of the room and breathed in her perfume, his mind now firmly made up that, unlike his fellow officers, he would not be needing to explore Paris nightlife for pleasant female company.

A short while later, his unpacking finished, Captain Mayschoss joined Rhiannon for supper. Afterwards, installing himself in a comfortable armchair, he listened appreciatively to a Bach concerto playing softly in the background as his gaze rested peacefully on the regal red-head sitting by the fireplace, as she worked away steadily at a pile of papers, a contented Tiger stretched out at her feet. Getting up to change the record, Rhiannon explained that there was an extensive library of her books in the study next door, which he was welcome to borrow whenever he wished. 'They're in English, French and German, and cover everything from history to the classics. Some are books dating back to my university days, but there are some lighter works as well.'

Thanking her, the impressed German began to wonder how he could keep this exceptionally well-educated and pro-German upper-class girl a secret from his fellow officers, and from Colonel von Kleiste himself; the latter was likely to insist that Miss Meredith was invited to the grand reception to be held later that month. How could he keep this treasure under wraps until he had secured her as his wife, or at least made her his own?

Offering to show him round the house just before midnight, Rhiannon let Tiger out into the garden, and on her return took him on a whistle-stop tour. 'The study's through here. That's exclusively my domain, as my grandmother and aunt don't care much for reading. Are you a bookworm yourself, Captain?'

'I most certainly am. Like you, my tastes are very wide-ranging, though I might not be comfortable with the more difficult English and French works.'

He followed his chatty hostess into the hall, then into the dining room – its elegant décor dominated by a massive marble fireplace, fine paintings and a magnificent oak table. The young officer paused admiringly. 'I presume the art is your late father's choice?'

'Yes. So is the furniture here, and in the study and sitting room. My mother chose the decoration upstairs, all except my grandmother and aunt's rooms, and the parlour, which are still in traditional French style. If you care to accompany me to the first floor, I'll show you the bedrooms and bathrooms. As you'll see, my father had a passion for gold-plated taps, Roman busts and statuettes, not to mention luxury in general. The smaller bathroom's still elegant, but not nearly as impressive. You may of course use either, and there's also a downstairs lavatory near the vestibule. The attic on the second floor's used for storage, and the only room that's out of bounds downstairs is the parlour – unless, of course, you happen to like the idea of my relatives' company.'

'Not especially, no.' The young man cast a glance at the wickedly grinning girl beside him. 'And thank you, by the way, for the carafe of water on my bedside cabinet. It'll be greatly appreciated.'

'Oh, it's a pleasure. Bring it down each morning and I'll refill it. So! Is there anything else you'd like to know, or see, before I turn in for the night?'

'Nothing that I can think of.'

'Excellent! Then in that case I'll say goodnight.'

Bidding his sociable new acquaintance a polite goodnight in turn, the deeply thoughtful captain watched the willowy girl and her dog vanish into the room next door, then retired to his own chamber. He was more than impressed with this direct and gracious Anglo-French woman, and had no intention of giving up this unexpected prize to anyone.

Chapter Two

Good morning, Captain. Did you sleep well?' Rhiannon glanced up briefly from cutting the bread as he entered the large sky-blue and cream kitchen. 'There's some sliced ham and cheese on the table. Do pour yourself some coffee while you're waiting. Would you like any fruit juice or stewed apple?'

'Both would be appreciated, thank you, Miss Meredith.'

Leaving his empty carafe on the windowsill, the young man sat down to a hearty breakfast and observed the busy girl. She had changed her green silk dress for a similar one in yellow, her luxuriant hair hanging loosely around her shoulders. Sensing the stranger's keen interest in his owner, Tiger watched him intently, the dog's intelligent eyes following his every move.

'Do you always study people so closely, Captain, or have I suddenly grown another head? I don't get in the least bit nervous when people stare at me, so you needn't think your steely stare unnerved me when you arrived last evening. Would you like any more coffee?'

'Yes, please. What's your profession, Miss Meredith?'

'I'm a teacher at a private girls' school in Montmartre. Luckily I can take Tiger to work with me – something that wouldn't be allowed in a state school. Which branch of the German army are you with?'

'At present I'm working at the espionage and counter-espionage headquarters, which perhaps explains why I look at people so attentively.'

'So I can imagine!'

Chatting away with the amused red-head, the captain passed a pleasant half-hour at the kitchen table, before suddenly realising that he was late for work and making a hasty but polite exit.

Maison Meredith was situated in the Rue Madeleine, a quiet, middle-class suburb of Paris, and by the time Captain Mayschoss reached German Army Headquarters the sun was beating down relentlessly. Signs had been erected in German throughout the city, directing military personnel to all key locations, and certain buildings were reserved for the use of Germans only. Co-existing uneasily with the occupying army, the nervous Parisians noted, however, that the troops had been on their best behaviour since the signing of the Franco-German Armistice on 22 June 1940, treating women with great respect and paying scrupulously for everything they purchased. Posters all over the occupied city proclaimed that the French could trust the German soldiers, an illustration of a child being used to emphasise the point. Less well received were the ration books and coupons that had been issued for just about everything from food to cloth, the confiscation of all wirelesses, and the strict curfew at 8pm: French civilians had plenty to complain about, and resistance groups had sprung up all over France. Jews and known Communists were lying very low indeed.

Colonel von Kleiste looked up disapprovingly as his junior officer entered the bureau. 'You're rather late, to say the least. Don't let it happen again. How does your accommodation suit you?'

'Very well indeed, thank you, Colonel.'

'And have you made the acquaintance of Miss Meredith yet? I understand she was due to return the day before your arrival.'

'I have.'

'And what's she like?'

Replying that she was very uncivil, hostile, plain and dowdy, the cunning captain added that there was absolutely no point in inviting her to the grand reception, since she would certainly refuse to come.

'What a pity! Still, I can't say that I'm so very surprised.'

Dismissing his junior officer, the tall older man frowned, then picked up a file and began to study it intently.

Returning to his luxurious billet that evening, the hungry captain was immediately attracted by the irresistible smell of dinner drifting through the hall. He went into the kitchen to find Rhiannon preparing a lamb and vegetable stew. 'Good evening, Miss Meredith. That smells absolutely delicious.'

'Good evening, Captain. The tea's still hot if you want some.'

'Thank you.' Pouring himself a cup, the relaxed young army officer sat at the table and watched his hostess lazily, while Tiger wolfed down his own meal – before turning his greedy attention to the casserole itself.

'Oh no, don't you dare, Tiger!' Rhiannon added some seasoning and looked down threateningly at the dog. 'Don't you dare touch this!' Then, adopting a more polite and formal manner, she switched from English to

German. 'Captain, perhaps you'd like to go through into the dining room while I serve out the stew. There's fruit and cream to follow if you want it.'

'That'll be excellent. Thank you.' Correctly anticipating a superb meal, Captain Mayschoss sat down at the table, his eye caught by a magnificent oil painting of moonlit Scarborough harbour, hanging above the white marble fireplace. After pouring two glasses of wine, he tucked into his repast contentedly, asking for a second helping immediately after he had finished the first, then polishing off his dessert with equal enthusiasm. 'I really enjoyed that.'

'Good.' Silently amused at how much he was like her late father and brother when it came to food, Rhiannon suggested that he should move into the sitting room while she cleared the table and brought in tea and biscuits.

An hour or so later Madame Perraut, in need of some black wool from the sitting room sideboard, knocked cautiously at the door. On entering, she glared ferociously at the enemy German officer, who was absorbed in a book.

'I only came in for some wool, Rhiannon.' The elderly Frenchwoman found the desired article and regarded her granddaughter sternly, finding the enemy's close presence to her quite appalling.

'Oh, I see.' The girl looked up from her marking for a second, then resumed her work. Casting a look of pure hatred at the officer, the black-robed and white-haired woman left the room, her frail form a sharp contrast to the slim but strong figure of her relation. 'If looks could kill!' Rhiannon shook her head ruefully. Finishing her work with a grateful sigh, the young woman glanced curiously at the good-looking Abwehr officer. 'Do you speak any other languages, Captain?'

'Yes, I do. I learned English and French at school, then continued my studies at the officers' training academy, where we were encouraged to develop our general education.'

Rhiannon nodded. 'Well, you'll have plenty of opportunities to practise your French now, at any rate. If you come across anything in the course of your reading that you don't understand, do feel free to ask.'

'Thank you. I will.'

Aware of the strong rapport that already existed between them, and was increasing by the day, Captain Mayschoss smiled smugly to himself, quite sure that he could easily secure this exquisite and rather vulnerable Anglo-French girl for himself. Meanwhile, Rhiannon, still desperately lonely after the tragic deaths of her parents and brother, was likewise conscious of the growing intimacy between the captain and herself, coming to enjoy his company more and more. She was even daring to hope that, unlike the various boyfriends and lovers she had had in the past, and discarded as unsuitable husband material, he might just be 'The One' at long last.

Five days later Rhiannon reached the end of a long-drawn-out lesson, during which she had tried but miserably failed to teach her pupils the finer points of French grammar, dismissed the bored youngsters with profound relief, then headed for her favourite restaurant for lunch. Swinging along the Montmartre streets, with Tiger padding obediently at her side and aware of the interested glances from passing German soldiers, Rhiannon made her way to the Lion d'Or, knowing that she and her dog made a strikingly unusual pair. Pets, especially large and hungry ones, were being abandoned in droves by French families who were finding it hard to get by on barely adequate rations.

Arriving at the almost full restaurant, Rhiannon noticed one remaining table for two which had a free place, and politely asked the aristocratic-looking army officer if she could join him. It wasn't long before he and the lively red-head were engaged in conversation, the stunned officer soon discovering that he was talking to the 'very uncivil, hostile, plain and dowdy' Miss Meredith. Introducing himself as Captain Mayschoss's commanding officer, he silently vowed to give the captain a lecture he would not forget. Finding out all about the fascinating girl and her family with his well-chosen questions, Colonel Konrad von Kleiste discovered to his absolute fury that she did not even know about the grand reception at the Town Hall the next day.

'I see . . . Might I look forward to the pleasure of your company with Captain Mayschoss, were he to bring you an invitation this evening?'

'But of course, Colonel, if he asks me.'

'Oh, you may rest assured he will.'

Rhiannon nodded with a puzzled air, then asked her new acquaintance to tell her about the young man's life and family. 'He's found out everything about me, but I know nothing about him except his name, rank and department. He always dodges my questions. Is he always this secretive, Colonel?'

'Unfortunately, yes.' The inwardly furious officer frowned. 'But given the circumstances you've got every right to know a bit more about him.'

Finding out that Captain Mayschoss was twenty-seven years old, unmarried and a Roman Catholic, from Kassel near Hanover, Rhiannon smiled. She asked what his father did for a living.

'He's production manager at a large agricultural business.'

'And does the captain have any brothers or sisters?'

'Yes. One married, but childless, older sister.'

'Indeed. Thank you, Colonel. I rather doubt I'd have dragged all that out of him. Although we chat a great deal in the evening, he seems to prefer asking questions to answering them.'

'That sounds about right.'

After chatting with Rhiannon for another hour, the charmed Colonel von Kleiste returned to Abwehr Headquarters to give his captain a piece of his mind. He called the young reprobate into his office, and glared at him disapprovingly. 'Well, Captain, I met the delightful Miss Meredith by chance this lunchtime at the Lion d'Or, and I can only guess at your reasons for giving me a totally false description of her, and not even mentioning our prestigious social event to her. What do you have to say for yourself? I'd have thought that this educated, beautiful and charming young lady would have made you an excellent partner at the reception. Her family background's impeccable and decidedly upper-class, and her parents' war record is admirable. Your appalling conduct towards this lovely girl is disgusting and ill-mannered. And your lies to me about her – well, there's no possible excuse. What do you have you to say in your defence?'

Realising far too late that it would have been wiser to have told his commanding officer the truth, Captain Mayschoss replied, 'I'm very sorry indeed to have offended you. I can only assure you that nothing like this will ever happen again.'

'It had better not, Captain.' A slightly mollified von Kleiste nodded coldly. 'An invitation has already been typed for you to give to her, and I expect to see you both at the reception tomorrow. Miss Meredith has given me her word that she'll attend if you invite her as your escort. Is that understood?'

'Yes, Colonel.' Relieved, Maximilian Mayschoss looked impassively at the sternly frowning older man, not even bothering to justify himself.

'Good. Now go.' Icily dismissing the young German, von Kleiste shook his head, wondering uneasily what his unresponsive junior officer was planning next.

Duly receiving the invitation after dinner, Rhiannon slipped it behind the carriage clock, and decided it might be wiser not to ask for the reasons behind its late arrival. 'Thank you so much for inviting me. Would you like tea or coffee, Captain?'

'Tea, please.' He paused, then commented unexpectedly, 'Perhaps, as long as you don't mind, we could drop our titles now that we're not strangers any more – in private at least.'

'By all means. But if the colonel hadn't told me about your background, you'd still be a stranger to me. Do you prefer to be called Max or Maximilian?'

'Max is preferable by far. Among my family and friends only my detested sister uses my full name.'

Rhiannon laughed, then went to make the tea, leaving a relaxed young man to reflect on how well his courtship of this tolerant Anglo-French girl was going.

Later, as they sat chatting cosily, the captain quietly asked how her family had been killed.

Rhiannon regarded the photograph on the sideboard wistfully. 'Oh, quite horribly, I'm afraid. My father was a very safe and careful driver. Unlike my madcap brother he never took risks. On the day of their accident road conditions were treacherous, with icy patches everywhere. Tiger and I were at home as I had influenza, and my family had gone to visit friends in Leeds. On their way home a drunken driver slammed into the side of our Mercedes, according to an eye-witness, and my father lost control and swerved across the road. The car then plunged down a steep hillside and landed at the bottom of a ravine, and exploded. They were all killed instantly. I don't talk about it much: it's still far too painful, as you can imagine.'

Max nodded.

'My brother used to take his Jaguar sports car for many a spin, his chief passion being racing it along Yorkshire's quiet country roads, with me as his foolhardy companion. I was the only one brave or crazy enough to take part in his wild adventures. My twin, unlike any of my boyfriends, was also my cherished soulmate, and I his.'

'Well, he's not your only soulmate now, Rhiannon.' Max pulled her close, and kissed her passionately on the mouth, his hands caressing her glossy waist-length hair. 'I've wanted to do that ever since we first met.'

'I know . . .' She looked up at him quizzically. 'Did Colonel von Kleiste give you a stiff lecture on etiquette, Max?'

The young man smiled. 'Rather! And right now he'd probably give me one on morality as well.'

Rhiannon shook her head at him in mock-disapproval. 'Given the lies you've probably told him about me, that doesn't surprise me at all. Rhys was a very convincing liar too, when it suited him, but he seldom fooled my mother; Father, however, was often led up the garden path. On the few occasions that he got angry with my brother, Rhys was very penitent, as my father resembling a charging bull when he was really enraged.' Resting her head against her attentive companion's broad shoulder, Rhiannon added, 'An officer nearly lost his life in 1915 because he showed too much interest in my mother while she was serving as an army nurse. Father, intensely jealous and pushed to the limit by this man's obvious passion, gave him a vicious beating and had to be forcibly restrained by his colleagues.'

'And then what happened?'

Relaxing against the velvet cushions, Rhiannon still clasped tightly in his arms, a fascinated Max listened to the rest of the story. 'Oh, Mother went weeping to Father's CO and got him off the hook. And after that my father's rival was transferred to another unit. How she did it is a mystery, but since she loved her husband dearly she'd have done absolutely anything to save him, even sleep with his CO if necessary. She had the courage to face the horrors of the Great War, so saving my father in that way wouldn't have worried her.'

'Quite!' The young German raised his eyebrows. 'Your mother wasn't a particularly pious Catholic, then.'

'She felt she had to save her husband – that's all. In general, though, I think it's fair to say that the Merediths are liberal Catholics, not fanatical like the Perrauts.'

'So I've noticed.' Max smiled. 'And neither are my parents, thank goodness. Devout, yes, but they're nowhere near as strict as your grandmother and aunt.'

Outside it was growing dark. The heavy black-out curtains were already drawn, and a small bronze lamp cast strange shadows round the room.

'Do you want any supper, Max? I'm not hungry, but . . .' The red-head glanced up at her silent companion.

'No, Rhiannon, but I do want you.' Gently pushing the yielding girl down, he kissed her lingeringly, sensing her willing response to his advances. Slipping her arms round his neck, she murmured something indistinct as his body made contact with hers. Slowly unzipping her silk dress, Max felt her grip tighten as he gently undid her bra and began to caress her quivering body. Overcome with passion, Rhiannon began to undress him in turn, clinging wildly to him as they made passionate love, desire flooding through them both and shutting out the outside world.

'Oh, Rhiannon!' Burying his face in her long fragrant locks, Max kissed her neck sensuously; then heard her low cry as time stopped for them both, and a white-hot heat seared through his body. Lying on the floor nearby, Tiger listened to the impassioned murmurs and grunted, then drifted into a deep sleep.

Chapter Three

Woken up early the next morning by loud birdsong outside the window and bright sunlight streaming into the room, Max was immediately aware of an indignant Tiger sitting alert by the bed, brown eyes fixed possessively on the girl who was sleeping peacefully at the young officer's side. Outside on the landing Thérèse and Agnes Perraut could be heard talking, their heavy footsteps fading as they went down to the kitchen. Drawing Rhiannon gently into his arms, Max lay still with her warm and naked body close to him.

As she finally emerged from her slumbers she stretched luxuriously and yawned, then, noticing the large black dog staring devotedly up at her, grinned mischievously. 'You're very lucky that Tiger stayed on the floor last night. Since he was five months old he's always slept on my bed. Now that he seems to have accepted your presence, there's only my formidable great-aunt for you to face when she eventually decides to swoop down for a visit.'

Max regarded his companion lazily. 'Tell me about her.'

'Well, there's a lot to say. Are you sure?'

The captain nodded, happy for an excuse to stay in bed.

'Great-Aunt Alicia married a French lawyer called Henri Reynard. She lost all four of her sons in the Great War, two others having died in early infancy, and now she's caring for her husband, who's dying of cancer. After my parents returned to England in 1918 they always spent Christmas and New Year with the Reynards, alternately at Meredith House and at the Reynards' home in Chartres, and visited them several times a year. As a child my father thought the world of his aunt, and he was the only one in his family to acknowledge her existence after her disgrace – which I'll tell you about in a minute. When he was at boarding school, Father found out her address, by bribing a servant of his grandparents, and secretly wrote her long letters. Later on, after he'd started university, he began to visit her and her family in France – unbeknown to his family. And in late 1913, on his invitation, she, Henri and their sons attended his wedding – much to the disgust of the rest of the family, who pointedly snubbed them all. Later on, when Rhys and I arrived, we quickly became my aunt's substitute grandchildren, and she and my uncle were absolutely devastated by the deaths of my parents and brother.'

Max stirred. 'What about that scandal?'

'Well, it's going back a few years. When my great-aunt was eighteen, and very beautiful, her family promised her hand in marriage to a wealthy but middle-aged lord, Anthony St Clair. She much preferred the younger, dashing and ambitious Henri Reynard, whom she had met while on holiday in France, and promptly eloped with him, much to her wealthy and upper-class parents' disgust and anger. They disowned and disinherited her – not that she cared. She and Henri made a fortune together, and even now, after fifty-four years of marriage, they're still utterly devoted to each other and deeply in love.'

'She's obviously a woman of great intelligence and strength of character. Just like her lovely great-niece.' Max rolled over and kissed Rhiannon's bare shoulder. Responding immediately, the red-head murmured as he took possession of her again, while Tiger slumped down on the floor with a resigned grunt.

Later that morning, after a full English breakfast, Max changed into his magnificent dress uniform and set off for his exclusive officers' club, while Rhiannon did the washing up before taking Tiger for a long walk. On her return she drifted upstairs to choose a suitable outfit for the grand reception. Settling on a lacy sea-green creation, with matching jet jewellery, fine dark-coloured stockings and stylish but comfortable high-heeled shoes in black suede, she carefully crimped her heavy locks and made herself up, adding a dab of her favourite perfume. She finally glanced in the mirror, and was off, after shutting an unimpressed Tiger in her bedroom: Madame Perraut and her daughter both disliked dogs intensely. Passing her disapproving older relatives as she left, Rhiannon gave them a vague smile and set off to meet her lover, arriving just as the Town Hall clock struck twelve. 'There you are Max. I'm bang on time, just as I promised. Pretty good for someone who's half-French.'

'But you also have an English father. In all my dealings with the French none of them has yet managed to arrive on time, unlike the British, with whom we're sadly at war but are like us Germans in so many ways – punctuality especially. And now we'd better go in, before my commanding officer thinks we've failed to turn up and decides to court-martial me.'

'Oh very funny. Still, if you hadn't told him such terrible lies about me . . .' Rhiannon laughed, unaware, as was her amused companion, of the person standing silently nearby and watching the young couple intently as they joked together. Their use of familiar forms of address and their relaxed body language told him all he needed to know about their close relationship.

'Good afternoon, Miss Meredith. You were saying . . . ?'

'Oh, hello, Colonel.' The shocked girl stared in horror, then, quickly recovering her composure, grinned. 'You know the old adage about not overhearing good things about oneself . . .'

'Quite. Perhaps it's a pity that I didn't wait a little longer to hear Captain Mayschoss's reply. Captain, you and Miss Meredith appear to be getting along remarkably well together. Shall we go in now, before I decide to court-martial the pair of you for gross disrespect?'

'Yes, Colonel.' Max regarded the older officer impassively, and followed the secretly amused Baron von Kleiste into the Town Hall, heads turning as Rhiannon glided by. The baron suddenly realised why his shrewd subordinate had not wanted to invite his stunningly beautiful landlady. He frowned, then stiffened as his arch-enemy approached.

'Ah, Colonel. Perhaps you would be so good as to introduce me to this charming young lady. And likewise to the captain here.'

Konrad von Kleiste, ever mindful that the grey-uniformed man standing in front of him was a fellow baron and also a dangerously powerful high-ranking Gestapo officer, reluctantly did as he was asked. The fascinated Kurt von Rittermann was quite unable to take his eyes off the vision of loveliness. Bowing a little too long over Rhiannon's hand for an intensely jealous Max's liking, he proceeded to find out as much as possible about her, the uncomfortable girl starting to feel like a trapped butterfly as she answered his many questions.

Deciding to fight back, the fed-up red-head commented dryly, 'Perhaps I should write an autobiography for you, Colonel, so you can add it to your files. My family's history would make fascinating reading, especially the bit about my beautiful Welsh namesake who was burned at the stake along with her faithful black dog for sorcery in the sixteenth century. She cursed the English judge who convicted her – and he duly choked to death. My late twin brother always joked that I'm her demonic reincarnation – as I was born exactly four centuries after my ancestor, in a field-hospital on the Western Front during a heavy German bombardment, while she died during a violent thunderstorm. My parents were so convinced that this was the case that they named me after her – Rhiannon Morgana Meredith.'

'Indeed! In that case I'd better watch my step in case you put an evil spell on me, Miss Meredith.' Von Rittermann laughed, his normally cruel grey eyes glinting with unaccustomed merriment. 'We certainly have a natural comedienne here, Colonel von Kleiste, not to mention a fascinating and charming young lady.'

'Absolutely.' Von Kleiste regarded the beautiful red-head and the tall, fair-haired man, then added frostily, 'Miss Meredith is here as Captain Mayschoss's escort, so if you would kindly excuse us, Colonel . . .'

'But of course – now that I've had the pleasure of meeting her. It's been an honour to make your acquaintance, Miss Meredith. Until we meet again.'

'Goodbye, Colonel.' Rhiannon inclined her head graciously, suddenly conscious of the utterly fascinated attention of some nearby German officers, wondering why all of a sudden she had two men interested in her. As for a silently fuming Max, by now he had resolved to marry her as soon as possible, even if it meant clashing with the deputy head of the Paris Gestapo, and the inevitable risks that this would involve. He had met her first, and would not willingly back down and lose her, colonel or no colonel.

The rest of the afternoon passed without incident for the young couple, the excellent buffet occupying their interest for the next hour or so. By the end of the reception Max and Rhiannon had chatted to many of his fellow officers, and some of the well-heeled French guests. The Gestapo colonel observed the vivacious red-head from a distance all the while, soon realising that, judging by his possessive manner, Captain Maximilian Mayschoss had already claimed her as his own. And since he was billeted with her, and was much closer to her in age than he was, he obviously enjoyed clear advantages over his older rival. Even so, the colonel silently vowed to do all in his power to win her over. He grimaced: the tragic loss of his fiancée, and a failed marriage soon afterwards, made him all the more determined to succeed, and to provide a male heir for his vast fortune. Von Rittermann realised he had found a suitable future baroness: all that remained was to convince her of the fact as soon as possible, then snatch her away from this petty-bourgeois adventurer of a captain.

Chapter Four

Rising early for Sunday Mass as usual, two months later, Madame Perraut and her daughter regarded the closed door of Rhiannon's room disapprovingly, knowing perfectly well that it was unoccupied – a fact soon confirmed by the sound of Tiger's whine coming from the hated German's bedroom and Rhiannon's laughter ringing out seconds later. Shaking their heads disgustedly, the morally outraged Frenchwomen went downstairs, feeling as if the devil himself had taken residence. Meanwhile the contented lovers were discussing their own plans for the day, a culture-loving Max intending to visit some of Paris's finest sights while Rhiannon visited her indomitable great-aunt.

Finally descending to the kitchen at nine o'clock, the red-head let Tiger out into the garden, then began to prepare the lavish English breakfast that the young couple enjoyed on Sundays – a family tradition long established by Rhiannon's father and one that the appreciative German officer was not slow to adopt. Breakfast over, Max set off to the Sacré Coeur, while Rhiannon quickly cleared the dishes, then left with Tiger for the railway station.

The train to Chartres was packed. Finding all the compartments full, apart from one occupied entirely by Germans, Rhiannon shrugged and went in, immediately conscious of their interested and sly glances: some of the officers recognised her, and were well aware of her close links with Captain Mayschoss as well as Colonels von Kleiste and von Rittermann; not to mention the fact that she now worked at Army Headquarters. That she was the captain's lover was beyond all doubt, the couple's attempt at formal behaviour towards each other fooling no-one.

Sensing the Germans' keen interest in her, Rhiannon read serenely until the train arrived at Chartres. Putting away her novel, she smiled graciously before composedly departing.

'How was your journey?' Alicia greeted her great-niece affectionately, and ushered her into the airy and elegantly furnished house. Snowy, the old lady's fussy bichon frise, jumped up delightedly at the much larger German shepherd, his tail wagging furiously. 'I thought we'd have our lunch in the garden while Henri rests indoors. The weather's so glorious today.'

'That sounds wonderful, Aunt. Oh, by the way . . .' Rhiannon paused. 'I'm two months pregnant with Max's child. He's promised to marry me as soon as permission's granted for German officers to take Western European wives of Aryan stock. Colonel von Kleiste, his commanding officer, who's promised to be our baby's godfather, has also offered to be a witness at our wedding, and I hope you and a couple of Max's colleagues will be there too. Max's parents are as delighted as he is about the child, as his sister Maria's had a hysterectomy – leaving Max as the only one who can give Karl and Elsa grandchildren.

'Oh yes – since I last saw you I've resigned from my teaching job. Thanks to Max, I'm now working full-time at German Army Headquarters as a translator. Colonel Neumann, my new boss, lets Tiger accompany me to work, and has given me my own little office. After the child is born I'll work part-time, and though I know that I'll be ostracised by my friends and neighbours once my condition becomes apparent I don't intend to let it worry me. Just think, Aunt. Soon we'll have a new generation; the Meredith-Mayschosses. Max has agreed to add Meredith to our children's surname, so they can inherit the Meredith-Reynard fortunes. I'll have a new family to love and care for.'

'Good Lord! Captain Mayschoss certainly doesn't believe in beating about the bush, does he? And do you really feel that you know him well enough, after only two months, to want to marry him?'

'Oh yes, Aunt. Max is everything I wanted in a husband. The only real problem is Kurt von Rittermann, whom I told you about in my last letter.'

'You did indeed, and the less you see of him the better. And now, my love, I think it's high time I met your husband-to-be, and Colonel von Kleiste if your lover can arrange it. How does next weekend sound? If I arrive on Saturday, can you meet me at the Gare du Nord at eleven o'clock?'

'Oh, that'll be absolutely fine. But who's going to look after Uncle Henri?'

'Jeanne, my maid. Incidentally, how's your grandmother?'

'Very frail, I'm afraid. Her heart's failing rapidly now. The doctor has given her about two months to live, and she spends most of her time resting. Aunt Agnes, who's caring for her, has decided to enter a convent after her mother's death. I know that poor Uncle Henri is failing fast, so perhaps after . . .'

'So perhaps after his death I'll sell my house and come to live with you?' The old lady nodded reassuringly at her hopeful great-niece. 'But of course I will, my dear. You'll be all I have left soon. Now then – as we've decided on our plans for the future, how about going into the garden for lunch?'

'Definitely. I'm so hungry.

Alicia hesitated. 'You were going to give Max your father's and Rhys's clothes and other possessions.'

'I have – all but Father's gold watch and silver-plated shaving kit, and a few bits and pieces I want to keep in their memory. The watch is for Max's twenty-eighth birthday in November, three days after your seventy-third, and the shaving kit's for his Christmas present. I didn't tell you: for my birthday Max gave me a large bottle of my favourite perfume and a book of Goethe's poems. He can be quite romantic when he chooses to be.'

'So I've noticed, judging by all these plans only two months after his arrival.'

Of medium height, slim, and always very elegantly dressed, Alicia had been considered a beauty in her heyday, with classical good looks, clear blue eyes and golden blonde hair. Still a very handsome woman, her gracious manners and devastating charm hid her intensely ruthless streak and hard-as-nails character. Utterly devoted to her great-niece, to whom she had left her considerable fortune in her will, the venerable old lady regarded her younger relative fondly. 'Ah well, no doubt everything will slot into place eventually. And now I suggest we spend the rest of the day with Henri. He's always greatly enjoyed your company, and it'll do him the world of good to have a visitor.'

Arriving back in Paris on the last train that evening, Rhiannon and Tiger headed speedily home, the eight o'clock curfew uncomfortably near. Passing Gestapo Headquarters on the way, the red-head looked curiously at the black staff car waiting outside, then, recognising Colonel von Rittermann coming out of the main entrance, wondered what to do.

'Ah, good evening, Miss Meredith. And where have you been today?'

'Oh, just visiting my great-aunt in Chartres, to tell her that Max and I . . .' Rhiannon hesitated, then added quickly, 'Oh dear – is that the time? I'd better get home before the curfew.'

'Never mind that. I'll make sure you get back safely. You were saying?'

'Well . . . that Max and I are to become parents in March, and intend to get married as soon as official permission is granted.'

'I see.' The stony-faced Gestapo chief's silver-grey eyes narrowed to furious slits, as he contemplated the prospect of losing this lovely girl as his baroness. 'Please accept my congratulations, Miss Meredith – the captain is a very lucky man.'

'Thank you, Colonel . . .' Rhiannon frowned uneasily at the undisguised anger and resentment in his voice. 'You did say that you'd see me safely home. Or have you changed your mind now that I've offended you with my news?'

'Not at all – a promise is a promise.' The baron regarded the red-head seriously, knowing that she was employed at Army Headquarters at Konrad von Kleiste's instigation. 'But first, perhaps you would like to come in for a drink?'

'All right . . . but I'd appreciate it if I could telephone Max and my great-aunt, to say that I'll be late, as they'll be terribly worried if I'm not back by eight o'clock.'

'But of course. I quite understand.'

Showing his unexpected but welcome guest up to his office, the Gestapo officer waited while she rang home; then, pouring himself a brandy and Rhiannon a glass of red wine, waved her over to the plush settee in the corner. 'I have, as you can see, everything needed for total comfort here: a drinks cabinet, a dining table for when I wish to catch up with extra work and lack the time to go out for lunch, and a comfortable place to enjoy a nap. I've even got a small library over there – and a gramophone, so I can enjoy my favourite music when the mood takes me.' Then, lighting a cigarette, a relaxed Kurt von Rittermann chatted for a good hour, before finally taking Rhiannon home in a chauffeur-driven car.

Rhiannon explained her predicament to a concerned Max later that evening, as they relaxed after dinner. 'I didn't dare refuse his invitation, and by the time we'd got talking there simply wasn't enough time to get home before the curfew. Had I risked it I might have ended up being arrested.'

'Never mind. At least you made it back safely – even if the old wolf did succeed in enticing you to his lair.' The young man frowned, and suggesting that the next time she visited her great-aunt she should come home a bit sooner.

'Next time I'll take an earlier train,' Rhiannon promised, 'even if it means cutting my visit short.'

'Good. I don't remotely trust Colonel von Rittermann to behave himself with my future wife, even if she's pregnant. Anyway, we'd better get an early night: you're back at work tomorrow. Speaking of which, how do you enjoy working for Colonel Neumann?'

'Oh, a great deal more than trying to teach those empty-headed girls. The colonel's very friendly, like all the men working there, but the women just stare at me as if I'd landed from Mars. Not that I'm particularly keen on them either.'

'Or any other female, apart from Alicia and your late mother and governess,' Max laughed.

'It's not my fault if I prefer male company. Women just talk about babies, fashion and domestic matters; I prefer to discuss more academic subjects.'

'Which is precisely why I find you such good company, Rhiannon; as does Colonel von Rittermann, unfortunately.' The young officer slipped his arm round her, and concluded ruefully, 'It's a real pity that he can't find a mistress of his own social standing, as my commanding officer has. If he did he might leave you alone. Still, perhaps he'll meet some aristocratic French woman. Then we'd all be happy.'

A few days later, while at work, a surprised Rhiannon was informed by her head of department that Colonel von Rittermann required her services urgently and that a staff car was waiting to take her to Gestapo Headquarters immediately.

Quickly collecting her papers together, Rhiannon grabbed her handbag and briefcase. After leashing an enthusiastic Tiger, she headed towards the main entrance, where a lovingly polished Mercedes awaited her,

'Good morning, Colonel von Rittermann. Colonel Neumann said that you wanted to see me.'

'I do indeed, Miss Meredith. Briefly, the situation is this: I have in my cells an Englishman whose strange accent neither I, nor anyone else here, can understand. He doesn't understand German, or for that matter very much French. To complicate matters, he appears to be illiterate. Your task is to communicate with him, find out whatever you can, then persuade him to talk. And should I need to apply any physical persuasion I'll still need your help.'

'In other words I'll have to be present while you torture him?'

'You will indeed – unless you can spare him that by winning his co-operation first.'

'I can but try, I suppose.'

Leaving an indignant Tiger in the office as instructed, Rhiannon reluctantly followed Kurt von Rittermann down to the cells, her heart sinking.

The door clicked open. Rhiannon looked uneasily at the short and unkempt man who was standing with his back to her, and spoke as calmly as she could. 'Hello. I've been sent to talk to you since no-one else here can understand your English. Which part of Britain do you come from?'

For a moment the prisoner stood stock still, then spun round and stared at her in stunned amazement. Quietly repeating her question, Rhiannon explained the situation to him, adding nervously, 'God knows, I don't want to have to watch you being tortured, but that's what will happen to you if you refuse to co-operate.'

'All right. I come from Barnsley, in South Yorkshire. I'm on a special mission in Paris, and I was nabbed yesterday by the bloody Boche. I tried to take my poison capsule to avoid torture, but a damned Jerry stopped me. So here I am, waiting for that bastard Colonel von Rittermann to rip my bloody guts out.'

'Not if I can help it.' Doing her best to understand his thick accent, Rhiannon talked with the man for what seemed like hours, eventually discovering that he had come to Paris with another Englishman, who spoke French fluently, as an explosives expert.

Receiving this information with obvious satisfaction, the high-ranking Gestapo officer nodded in a pleased manner. 'Excellent work, Miss Meredith. And tomorrow you can try to find out exactly who he was meeting, or has already met, and their whereabouts. And now, as it's almost midday, I suggest that we take lunch in my office.'

'As you wish, Colonel.'

Rhiannon accompanied him to where the waiting Tiger sat bolt upright, his mournful brown eyes fixed on the closed door. 'Poor old lad! Can my dog have some water, along with some toast and meat, please?'

'But of course he may.' The grey-uniformed baron smiled good-humouredly at the beautiful red-head and her canine companion. 'And what would you like to eat?'

Requesting a cheese salad and baked potato, with fruit and cream to follow, together with sparkling mineral water and a pot of tea, Rhiannon added, 'My mother was positively huge when she was carrying me and Rhys. I've got no wish to put any more weight on than is strictly necessary, and that means eating sensibly.'

'As you will.' Colonel von Rittermann shrugged and ordered their meals, before pouring two glasses of white wine from one of the bottles in his silver-plated ice bucket.

Returning the next day to carry out the colonel's orders, Rhiannon, against all her expectations, found that her compatriot was ready to talk further; von Rittermann had given her a sickeningly detailed account of what awaited any Resistance member or enemy secret agent who refused to co-operate, and this had convinced the Englishman that he should tell her all he knew. 'And now what will happen to me? Will I be sent to a prison camp? Or shot?'

'I'm really sorry, but the latter is most likely.' Rhiannon shivered, adding that she would put in a good word for him with the colonel.

'Oh well, if they shoot me, they shoot me.' The prisoner glanced at her. 'Anyway, it's been nice knowing you. Does your charming colonel usually execute his unfortunate guests?'

'Yes. Always. His philosophy is that dead men don't tell tales.'

'Charming indeed. Well, if you survive this war I'd be grateful if you'd pass on the news of my death to my wife and family back in Barnsley, along with a message to them. I'm not able to write down their address for you, but if you'll make a note of it . . .'

'I'll certainly do that for you.' Rhiannon tearfully took the details, then hugged him impulsively, unable to hold back her sobs. 'I'm so sorry, but he never spares anyone who might be a threat to him later. Even my fiancé, who's a captain in the German army, is extremely wary in his dealings with him, and doesn't dare challenge him openly.'

'A wise man indeed. Never mind, I know you'll do your best to help me.' The Englishman shrugged resignedly, and held out his hand in a gesture of final farewell. 'War is war, I suppose. Goodbye, and thank you for trying to help.'

Sadly shaking hands, Rhiannon blinked back her tears, then dejectedly departed. She was not in the least surprised when Kurt von Rittermann refused even to consider sparing the enemy agent's life.

The young mother-to-be drank her coffee in depressed silence, her first experience of Gestapo brutality leaving her completely shell-shocked. Gradually hardening herself, as the ruthless colonel called on her services more and more as the months passed, she soon learned to block out any emotions, knowing that this was the only way in which she could keep hold of her sanity. This was a bitter lesson that Kurt von Rittermann had learned during his cruel, lonely and sadistically disciplined childhood.

.

Chapter Five

Hello, Aunt. Do let me carry your case. Good heavens! What have you got in it? Bricks?'

'Not exactly, my love. Simply a couple of books I thought you might enjoy, along with the things I need for the weekend.'

Carrying the heavy suitcase Rhiannon smiled affectionately at the dignified old lady. 'More like a dozen, I think. Oh hello, Snowy. I haven't greeted you yet, have I?' Stroking the sweet natured little dog, she smiled at her elderly relative and introduced her to the large black standard poodle standing quietly by Tiger. 'And this is Bess, whom I found abandoned and starving when I was out with Tiger soon after I last visited you. She was wandering the streets of Paris accompanied by, of all things, an elderly Siamese cat. Both animals are now established members of my household, and Tiger, as you can well imagine, is absolutely delighted to have a lady friend at long last.'

Stopping at a café on the way back to the Rue Madeleine, Rhiannon and her great-aunt enjoyed a long chat about their plans, the three dogs lying obediently at their feet near a bowl of water.

'And while you're working,' said Alicia, 'I'll be more than willing to care for the new addition to our family – but I'm not sure about both these dogs. Does Colonel Neumann allow you to take them both to work with you?'

'He does – as long as they stay in my office. Then at lunchtime we all go out for a good walk in the park and enjoy a meal at the Café Bleu.

Tiger and Bess usually have some toast and whatever they can scrounge from me.'

'That sounds ideal for all of you.'

Later that afternoon, meeting Captain Maximilian Mayschoss for the first time, Alicia was immediately impressed with his steady gaze and self-assured manner; that and his obvious affection for her great-niece, who likewise seemed deeply attached to this tall and good-looking young army officer. Quite unable to find fault with his ready answers and excellent manners, the old lady decided that he would be an ideal husband for her beloved Rhiannon. 'Well, Captain, I hope that you'll be very happy together. Since I have every intention of moving in with my great-niece once I have lost Henri and the Perrauts are gone, I obviously wish to remain on good terms with you, for all our sakes. This being the case, I'll make the parlour my private domain, leaving you both to enjoy your privacy in the sitting room.

'As you're well aware, once Rhiannon's condition becomes apparent and especially once the baby is born, she'll need all the support we can give her. Just as I did all those years ago, she's transgressed society's moral conventions – and will henceforth be ostracised.'

'Something which I deeply regret, but sadly cannot do anything about, Madame.' Max frowned. 'But once the war is over we'll return to Germany with our family. In the meantime I'll naturally give Rhiannon as much support and protection as I possibly can, as will my commanding officer.'

'Of that I have no doubt, Captain.' Alicia smiled approvingly, then went to help her young relative prepare dinner – barely acknowledging the silent and stiffly resentful Agnes as she passed on her way to her dying mother's room.

Shown in by an awe-struck Marie later that evening, a charmed Colonel von Kleiste was promptly introduced to the august matriarch. The pair immediately hit it off, much to Max and Rhiannon's relief. Deeply impressed by this cultured and upper-class Englishwoman, with a tolerant broadmindedness that matched his own, Konrad von Kleiste chatted in a relaxed manner to her over dinner.

'And now that you've tried our popular British lamb with mint sauce, boiled potatoes and assorted vegetables, we'll be having apple pie and cream, then coffee and biscuits in the sitting room.' Rhiannon grinned wickedly at the mature aristocrat. 'Another well-loved British regional dish eaten in coastal areas especially, is fish, chips and mushy peas – but perhaps not one that you might appreciate, Colonel. Max likes it enormously – either that or he's being very polite.'

The young man shook his head emphatically. 'On the contrary. I'd tell you immediately if I didn't like it, or any other of your meals. But as it happens I enjoy fish and chips greatly, along with all the other dishes you serve. The only things I really detest are snails, frogs' legs and rare meat, along with cheap table wine and many of the French cheeses, which to me at least smell revoltingly like sweaty feet.'

'Quite, Captain.' Konrad von Kleiste regarded his unusually animated junior officer with an amused expression.

The rest of the evening passed quickly for a rather merry Konrad von Kleiste. For Alicia it was both a pleasant revelation and a painful surprise, Rhiannon's husband-to-be reminding her so much of Benedicte, her beloved eldest son who had been killed in action during the Great War aged only twenty-six. Always her favourite child, his ready wit and joy of living had lit up her life until that terrible day when the dreaded telegram had arrived; her three other sons subsequently joining the list of fatalities in turn.

'Would you like some more coffee, Colonel? Captain, how about you? Rhiannon?' Pushing the distant but hauntingly sad memories to the back of her mind, Alicia poured out three more cups, all the while observing the devoted young couple sitting together on the settee, Tiger and Bess lying contentedly at their feet. Equally observant of his talkative and sociable junior officer, and the deeply attentive red-head by his side, the shrewd baron smiled mysteriously to himself, very pleased with the way events were turning out.

Returning to his luxury living quarters by chauffeur-driven staff car shortly after midnight, the sleepy colonel immediately retired to bed with his mistress – feeling rather tired but in a very good humour, having enjoyed a truly splendid evening.

For Alicia, likewise, the evening had been a great success. Her mind was now laid completely at rest regarding her future great-nephew-in-law, and the rest of her stay was a much-appreciated break from caring for Henri.

'So, what do you think of my august relative now that you've finally made her acquaintance?' Setting off for work on Monday, the morning of her great-aunt's departure, Rhiannon looked enquiringly at Max.

'Well, to put it in a nutshell, she's everything your grandmother and aunt are not. I like her very much indeed. After the birth she's going to be an absolute Godsend to you, especially if we end up with twin sons – something which seems to run in your family, from what you've said. In the meantime I'll just have to put up with your French relatives, and wait while events take their natural course. And, of course, hope that official permission comes through for our marriage in the next six months.'

Chapter Six

The autumn leaves were beginning to fall when Germany launched Operation Sea Lion. The invasion of Britain was a primary objective of Adolf Hitler's plans – but it petered out with inglorious defeat at the hands of the RAF that September.

Finally losing her husband the next month, a devastated but also deeply relieved Alicia sat on the front row in the bitterly cold church with her great-niece, Max and Colonel von Kleiste, the two army officers tactfully sporting plain clothes for the occasion, and listened reflectively to the priest's moving words at Henri's well-attended Requiem Mass.

'I'm so sorry, Aunt, but it had to happen sooner or later.' Rhiannon squeezed her revered relative's hand comfortingly as the coffin was lowered into the ground an hour later. 'Do you still want me and Max to visit you while you're grieving, or . . . ?'

'Good Lord, yes. I most certainly do, my love.' The elderly lady regarded the red-head and the sympathetic Germans with a grateful smile. 'And thank you so much for coming, all of you. You and the captain are naturally most welcome to stay for refreshments, Colonel, if you're able to spare the time.'

'But of course, Madame, we'll be honoured to. My chauffeur's under orders to wait until our return, and we can easily stay for as long as you wish. And should you or Miss Meredith need anything in the future, all you have to do is to pass your request to the captain here.'

'Thank you, Colonel, you're most kind.' Alicia inclined her head graciously, well aware that her great-niece had acquired a very influential and powerful friend.

Two months later a by now obviously pregnant Rhiannon and her loyal great-aunt attended their second funeral, the seventy-year-old Madame Perraut passing away in early December. Studiously ignoring the scornful and deeply disapproving looks cast her way by the deceased's family, friends and neighbours at the burial, the red-head shivered in the icy wind while a heart-broken Agnes sobbed desolately beside her. Rhiannon reluctantly hosted the wake, suddenly very grateful indeed for Alicia's moral support. Max had wisely vanished to his club, well aware that his presence would cause his future wife even more embarrassment.

Later in the month the mourning Agnes entered a convent, and the still-grieving elderly Englishwoman moved in, having already found a buyer for her house and most of its contents. 'So, now that I'm settled in Agnes's old bedroom, and Jeanne is sharing Marie's, we have two spare rooms – one of which will be needed as a nursery. And now I suggest that we start a big clear-out of the Perrauts' possessions, then box everything up and see what our maids would like to keep before donating the rest to the poor.'

'Of course, Aunt, but I'm going to keep all my grandmother's and aunt's private papers and photographs.' Grinning at her lover as he beat a hasty retreat to the peace and quiet of the study, Rhiannon began to help her august relative, while their four animals looked on, their noses twitching as they investigated the boxes piled up in the hall.

Coming home from work on a bitterly cold day a week before Christmas, Max and Rhiannon watched the Parisians rush by, their sole objective to return to whatever food and warmth awaited them. Suddenly they saw a hysterical and ragged little girl racing blindly towards them, pursued at a distance by an angry and cursing man who, from his lurching gait, certainly appeared to be more than a little drunk.

'Good heavens, what have we got here?' Rhiannon took the full force of the child as she cannoned violently into them, then clung on to her for dear life. She looked disgustedly at the dirty and foul-smelling drunkard now only a few feet away from them.

'Come here, you little bitch. I'll teach you to run away, you . . .' Abruptly backing off in terror as the two fiercely protective dogs began to snarl viciously at him, and the enemy officer drew his gun, the swarthy and thick-set man stared bewilderedly at the visibly contemptuous German and the pregnant woman, and stammered lamely, 'My four-year-old daughter, Marie-Claude . . . She's run away from home yet again and . . . well, she's a real bad 'un – nothing but trouble.'

Rhiannon's eyes blazed furiously. 'On the contrary. It would appear that it's you who are the bad one. And judging from her filthy and neglected state you and your wife aren't fit to have a child. How many more have you got, pray?'

The thick-set and unkempt man scowled bad-temperedly at her. 'Nine, and Marie-Claude here is the most disobedient of the bloody lot. Nothing but trouble . . .'

'That's good, because in that case you won't mind if I have her instead.' Getting out her purse and throwing a handful of coins at his feet, Rhiannon glared ferociously as he greedily snatched up the francs. 'Henceforth she's mine, and you've renounced all further rights to her. What is your and your wife's name, and when is Marie-Claude's birthday?'

'Jacques . . . Jean-Pierre and Gisèle Jacques . . . and the brat was born in November or December, I think.'

'Are you Jewish? Show me your identity card to prove that you're who you say you are.'

The Frenchman shook his head emphatically, and showed the document to her. 'No, we're not. Lapsed Catholics. Not been to church for years.'

Rhiannon nodded coldly and watched him shuffle away, his precious money clutched tightly in his hand. Turning to a silent Max, she said, 'I fully intend to keep her – there's simply no way I could have returned the poor mite to that brute.'

'So I've already noticed, my love. Just as long as this is the last of your waif and strays.'

Assuring him that it most certainly was, Rhiannon explained to the trembling child that she would never see her parents again, and that she now had a caring new home where she would never be beaten and would be both well fed and well loved.

'Never beaten?' The little girl stared up disbelievingly at her rescuer.

'Never beaten, and that's a promise. Is that why you ran away? Because your father used to beat you?'

'Yes, and . . . he . . .'

Tramping home through the heavy snow, the appalled young couple learned all about the girl's life of hell with her birth family: their damp and rat-infested slum, her father's drunken rages, and his violence towards his wife and children; not to mention the obvious references to sexual abuse that the father regularly inflicted on his daughters, right down to little Marie-Claude herself . . . and finally they heard all about Ralph, her 'real daddy', whose surname she did not know.

A few hours later, while relaxing in the sitting room with Rhiannon and Max after dinner, Alicia intently studied a cleaned-up Marie-Claude, head shaved to rid her of an infestation of nits, thinking, as were Rhiannon and Max, that she had not inherited her clear silver-grey eyes, crooked little fingers and fine aristocratic features from her father. 'Ah well, she looks a little more presentable now, I suppose, especially since you've dressed her in one of your blouses and cardigans and burned those old rags she came in. I presume she'll be sleeping in your old room from now on?'

Rhiannon smiled. 'Of course . . . and the next things we need to do are organise a visit to the doctor and dentist for her, have some new clothes made to measure, and feed her up. Marie-Claude is now to be known as Cassandra Elisabeth Meredith-Mayschoss, and will be christened with my own child next year. I'll be her godmother and Max has agreed to be her godfather. Once she's properly settled in I'll start with her education, or re-education – but we have to do something about her uncouth table manners and total lack of social graces right away.'

'I'll certainly help with that, along with her English, French and the three Rs.'

'And dear Rhiannon's roped me in to help teach Cassie German and all there is to know about Teutonic culture, so there you are.' Max shook his head ironically at his fiancée. 'Furthermore, I'm to be addressed as Uncle Max, while you and Rhiannon are her aunts. Perhaps, on reflection, every Meredith female should come with a warning: "Beware of the bossy organiser."'

'Oh, very funny, Max.' Rhiannon laughed and hugged the warm four-year-old to her. 'Little Cassie doesn't think I'm bossy. Do you, Cassie?'

'No, Aunt Rhiannon.'

Not understanding why the two other adults were laughing, the confused child, her new name still a puzzle to her, stared at them, bewildered.

'Poor Cassie. In time you'll become accustomed to us and our ways. In the meantime you're quite safe and need fear nothing. And this teddy bear is a little gift from me to welcome you to our home. My father gave me Casimir on my fourth birthday, and I know that he'd be very happy for you to have it now.'

'Oh! No-one ever gave me anything nice before.'

The overwhelmed child touched the much-loved old Steiff bear reverently. Then, clutching the toy to her, she suddenly burst into tears and buried her face in Rhiannon's lap, her thin and badly bruised body racked with violent sobs.

'Ah well, no doubt we'll succeed in rearing this pitiful waif somehow.' A moved Alicia looked steadily at Max, smiling grimly. 'And it'll be far better for us to try to forget the nine unfortunate siblings she's left behind.'

Chapter Seven

Early the next morning Alicia quickly washed and dressed, then went to check on Cassandra. She found the disorientated little girl sitting bolt upright in bed, her treasured bear clutched in her arms. Washing and dressing the child firmly but kindly, the old lady regarded Cassie's makeshift outfit with a frown. 'We really must get you some proper clothes made, young lady; there's absolutely no question of you going out like that. In the meantime I'll just have to find you something more suitable of mine to wear, and also get you a toothbrush. Were you the youngest in your family?'

'No, but I was the last girl.'

'Ah! Don't you mean you were the youngest daughter, Cassie?'

Nodding, the shaven-headed mite obediently followed Alicia into the latter's bedroom, and was promptly attired in an old vest and cut down dress, the clothes hanging loosely on the skinny little girl.

'Never mind. They'll have to do for the moment, I'm afraid.'

Alicia led her hungry charge down to breakfast. 'There you are.' Placing a bowl of porridge in front of Cassie, the indomitable matriarch produced a large plate of sliced bread, meat and cheese, along with some butter and a dish of fruit, then poured out tea for herself, Max and Rhiannon, and a generous glass of milk for the still hungry child. 'Here you are, little one – and have some crusty bread and ham and cheese and stewed apple to fill you up. Now, what do you say?'

'Thank you, Aunt Alicia.' The little French girl looked timidly at her before staring at Rhiannon's exquisite gold necklace in awed admiration, unable to tear her gaze away.

'If you like jewellery that much I could always give you one of my old unwanted ones.' Promising to let the delighted child choose something from her trinket boxes later that evening, the good-natured red-head smiled, then left with Max to get ready for work.

'Dear me, what a lucky girl you are, Cassie.' Alicia sipped her second cup of tea and poured the beaming four-year-old a glass of fruit juice. 'And once I've washed up you can help me put up some decorations. Father Christmas will be paying us a visit on Christmas Eve, then the next day we'll be attending Mass.'

'Father Christmas? Who's he?' The little girl looked at her with a puzzled expression.

'Well . . .' Explaining all the English Christmas traditions to a fascinated Cassie, the old lady added, 'But he only leaves presents for children who are good and none for the naughty ones.'

'Oh, but I'm good.' The child glanced uncertainly at her guardian. 'Aren't I, Aunt?'

'You are indeed, my lamb.'

Hugging the suddenly wistful child to her, Alicia blinked away a tear, her heart full.

And now for Cassie a new and dreamlike world began to unfold. The sort of life she had always dreamed of and so longed for, without beatings, pain and cold. There were no rats or cockroaches in her new home, no rows, no vile smells or dirty disorder. The sheer space of the house left her amazed that so few people were in it, and only the dogs' barking disturbed the peace from time to time. Rhiannon was everything her wretchedly miserable and work-worn mother was not, and Alicia's kindness and patience seemed endless.

Max was something of an enigma to the little French girl. A man who did not shout at other people, or swear, or beat up his family. A fresh-smelling and dapper young man who bathed daily, changed his clothes regularly, shaved; calm, steady, and cultured, but with an air of quiet but strong masculine dominance. He was clearly no push-over. And he treated her with the utmost kindness, never seeking to touch her physically and extended to her the same respect that he showed to his girlfriend and the old lady, Rhiannon's great-aunt. How different he was from her own father – or at least the man she had thought was her father until she had heard her parents rowing over a man called Ralph who had once been a regular customer of her mother. Ralph, it seemed, had paid her mother generously just to spend time with her, and judging from what she had heard was very wealthy (a lawyer, no less) and very posh.

During the conversation that she had overheard, her father had exclaimed that she was not his daughter at all. This got the child longing for her rich and upper-class father, and as soon as the chance presented itself she took to her heels and ran away into the grimy streets of Paris, vainly seeking this man called Ralph, but never finding him or even knowing where to look. Instead she had found her aunts Rhiannon and Alicia, and the incredibly kind Captain Mayschoss. While the memory of the man Ralph remained, he began to assume less importance and interest for her.

Other aspects of her new life amazed her. The wonderful hot fires in the luxurious and airy rooms, Rhiannon's exquisite collection of fine Dresden china, the three dogs and the strange-looking cat, who were treated with the same love and care that was given to her. And being the only child in the house was the strangest thing of all. Used to sharing a tiny slum with nine siblings, the peace of being alone in her large and beautiful apple-green and cream bedroom, with Casimir, her teddy bear, beside her and Casilda the cat curled up on the bed, delighted her. Sometimes she had to pinch herself to convince herself that it was real, and she woke up each new morning, especially after a recurring nightmare about her French stepfather, to find the same dreamlike life with a sense of great joy.

Six days later the delighted child finally received her new garments. Her elderly foster aunt lost no time in discarding the makeshift outfits and dressing the excited youngster in a blue embroidered dress, matching cardigan, long white socks and shiny black leather shoes. 'There you are, Cassie. Now look at yourself in the mirror and see how pretty you are.'

'Oh! Is that really me, Aunt Alicia?' The little French girl stared bewilderedly at the stranger reflected back at her, then added sadly, 'But I can't be pretty, not without my hair. Aunt Rhiannon has beautiful hair, all long and thick.'

'So will you, my love, once it grows back. In the meantime you can wear a smart new beret or woolly hat when you go out with us, and no-one will know you're bald. And now we're going downstairs to show Uncle Max and Aunt Rhiannon your fine new clothes.'

'Yes, Aunt Alicia.' The child took a curious last look at her reflection and followed the stately old lady obediently to the kitchen.

'Well, just look at you, Cassie. What an elegant young lady you are now. Isn't she lovely, Max?'

'She is indeed.' Glancing up from his task, he smiled warmly at the radiant little girl, then put down the carving knife. 'How would you like to accompany me on some of my days out in Paris next year, Cassie? We'll go to all manner of interesting places. You could see where I work and also meet my superior officer, who will, I'm sure, be very pleased to make your acquaintance.'

'Oh yes, Uncle Max. Is he kind like you?'

'But of course he is. Not all men are cruel, Cassie. I'm sure you'll like my fellow officers. They'll all be nice to you.'

'Oh! When can I come?' The bright-eyed child beamed up at her foster-uncle.

'How does next week sound? Yes? Good. Did you hear that, Rhiannon? Cassie will be coming along on some of my field trips, given the colonel's permission of course.'

'By all means, Max, if that's what you both want.' Rhiannon nodded amiably, then commented that the meal was ready to be served.

'Good Lord. Your husband-to-be certainly doesn't believe in beating about the bush, does he?' Alicia shook her head at her great-niece. 'Still, it can't help but bond him to Cassie, so why not?'

Rising bright and early the next day, an overjoyed Cassandra gleefully unwrapped her first ever Christmas presents, exclaiming in delight at the fashion dolls, picture books and warm fur-lined boots. Then, slipping on her fleecy dressing gown and slippers and grabbing her beloved bear, she padded off to thank her foster-family, beginning with her Aunt Alicia before knocking at the young couple's door.

'Good morning, Cassie. Did you like your presents?' Yawning sleepily, Rhiannon raised herself on an elbow and smiled good-naturedly at the tiny figure looking up adoringly at her.

'Oh yes, Aunt, especially the books. Can I come into bed with you, please?'

'I suppose so, yes. But take off your slippers first.'

Scrambling up determinedly, Cassie snuggled up contently against her new parents, and asked curiously, 'When will I have another brother or sister?'

'In March. Then you can help me and Aunt Alicia care for him or her. Today, though, after a quick breakfast, we'll all be attending Mass at Notre Dame Cathedral, and then going for lunch at a restaurant. After that your uncle intends to visit his club, while the rest of us return home and take the dogs out for a long walk in the park.'

'And then what?'

'Dinner of course, and then we'll relax over coffee and biscuits.'

Max laughed and stretched luxuriously. 'But soon we'll all have to get up for Mass, so don't get too comfortable, young lady.'

Later that morning the child listened in reverent silence as the priest led the Christmas service, her enraptured eyes taking in the magnificent interior of the building and its glorious multi-coloured windows, her attention especially caught by the rose window as the winter sun made it glow vividly.

'And now what are you doing? And why isn't Uncle Max in uniform?' Cassie stared up puzzled as the three adults crossed themselves at the altar, Rhiannon and Alicia lighting candles.

'Well, we light candles because it's a way of saying a prayer for someone we love who's died. As for Uncle Max, he simply decided not to wear his uniform today, that's all.'

'And what did you do at the altar?'

'We were showing reverence for Our Lord. I'll explain, and then you can go up and cross yourself as we did.'

'Oh yes, Aunt.' Listening intently to the young woman's simple explanation, the four-year-old nodded earnestly, and then, did as she was bid, her face aglow with happiness.

Proudly telling his commanding officer all about Cassie's remarkable transformation a few days later, Max added, 'Her table manners are good now, and she says please and thank you without having to be told. We've also started to educate her: German and English, as well as reading, writing and simple arithmetic, are our priorities. She's still suffering from terrible nightmares, and often creeps into our or Alicia's bed for reassurance, but fortunately not without knocking at the door first. With any luck this will improve as she becomes more self-confident. Oh, by the way, she really wants to come along with me on one of my espionage trips. If you agree, I'd like to use her to help me blend in with the crowd.'

'By all means, Captain. Bring the child in to see me tomorrow. In the meantime, it's only fair to warn you that her family background is, to put it mildly, rather doubtful. Jean-Pierre, her registered father, is a convicted thief and house-breaker, and her mother's a prostitute. Her real father must be one of her mother's punters – and perhaps he really is a lawyer named Ralph. Her older brothers are petty crooks, and her elder sisters all work in their mother's profession. Perhaps it would be wise to pass all this on to Miss Meredith and her great-aunt, along with the child's date of birth. According to official records it's 8 December 1936 – and her second name's Elisabeth.'

'Of course, Colonel, but I doubt this'll make any difference to them. They're both very fond of her already. She's a very appealing and sweet-natured child, and she's quick to learn too.'

'Well, in that case I can only wish you the best of luck in raising her.'

Dismissing his junior officer with a nod, Konrad von Kleiste smiled mysteriously to himself, then began to make notes in the little girl's file, very satisfied with the way events were turning out.

What an event Cassie's meeting with von Kleiste turned out to be. Trotting nervously through Abwehr Headquarters, clutching Casimir to her, her hand gripping Max's for moral support, Cassie was aware of the amused and incredulous glances of Max's fellow officers. A child at Headquarters! Whatever was Captain Mayschoss thinking of? At first she looked shyly away, then decided to try smiling and using some of her limited German – Good Morning, Good Day, Good Evening, Please and Thank You.

And it worked. The sheer number of Germans who smiled back and courteously returned her greetings made her dizzy with success, which helped her cope with her interview with Baron von Kleiste.

The colonel found the girl quite delightful, but couldn't help wondering about her von Rittermann-like silver-grey eyes and crooked little fingers. Addressing her fluently in her own native tongue, albeit with a heavy Bavarian accent, he asked many questions and talked to her for what seemed like ages. More than a little shy of this dignified and aristocratic older officer at first, Cassie soon found the bravery to answer with confidence, finding him to be both kind and charming – just like Uncle Max. It was hardly surprising that the colonel approved of Max's plan for Cassie to accompany him on his observational trips around Paris – to her great delight and Max's satisfaction.

Cassie soon became a familiar and much-loved sight at Abwehr Headquarters, trotting contentedly around with her Uncle Max, her cheerful smile and merry laughter lighting up the severe military atmosphere with the refreshing innocence and joy that only a truly happy child can radiate.

One rainy Saturday afternoon in late January, while Max was out at his club, Kurt von Rittermann suddenly decided to pay Rhiannon an unannounced visit, for reasons unknown to all but himself. Hearing the bell ring, Cassie shooed the three barking dogs away from the door, opened it . . . and stared up in utter astonishment at the tall, sinister-looking and grey-uniformed German officer, who was carrying a large bag, which turned out to contain hard to obtain items such as soft soap, silk stockings, shampoo, perfume, make-up, washing powder, tea and coffee.

'Hello. May I help you?' The sweet little French girl and the cruel-featured North German looked at each for a moment in stunned silence, then, when Rhiannon asked who was at the door, Cassie snapped out of her trance and, despite her instant dislike of the man, politely asked his name. Von Rittermann for his part considered her distinctive silver-grey eyes and crooked little fingers – traits of his family. Having heard from Rhiannon about Cassie's history, he wondered if his cousin Ralph, recently killed in a booby-trapped military train, had sired an illegitimate child. By his own admittance he had been fond of frequenting prostitutes. The

German sighed. There was no need to mention this to anyone: the child was safe and happy with Rhiannon now, and as Ralph was dead there was no way of confirming his suspicions. But just suppose this child was indeed Ralph's daughter . . .

'Colonel Kurt von Rittermann. I've come to see your Aunt Rhiannon.'

Inviting him in, the child watched as her aunt regarded the unexpected and rather unwelcome visitor with disbelief. Then, remembering her manners, Rhiannon called for some refreshments and ushered him into the elegantly furnished sitting room.

'Thank you for your present. And what brings you here?'

'Oh, no particular reason, Rhiannon. I just fancied paying you a visit in your own home.'

The baron's observant eye took in the room's contents in seconds. Like its owner, the decoration was elegant yet also refreshingly original. An impressive bronze Chinese dragon adorned a lovingly polished antique oak table, while a stack of records stood by an open gramophone and some delicate Dresden china figurines were attractively displayed in a spacious display cabinet.

Cassie peeped curiously round the door. 'Your refreshments are coming soon, Aunt. Can I borrow some of your bears and play at schools, please?' She skipped in and took several of her favourite animals from a cabinet before disappearing again; not, however, without darting a hostile glance at the sinister-looking stranger.

When the tea tray was brought in by Jeanne, Rhiannon explained that Alicia was out visiting friends and Max was at his club. 'Would you like tea or coffee, Colonel?'

Graciously serving her guest as he watched her composedly from Max's favourite armchair, Rhiannon chatted away amiably. Kurt von Rittermann's sudden desperate need for pleasant female company had been admirably met.

After a long and enjoyable conversation the baron rose, and asked if he could see the rest of the house.

'But of course you may.'

Hoping that Max would stay away just a little longer, so as to avoid any unpleasantness, Rhiannon took him round her house, followed closely by the three protective and guard-conscious dogs.

Finally the nobleman reluctantly departed. Heavily pregnant as she was by another man, he would still have willingly accepted Rhiannon into his life as his wife and mother of his future offspring. Even allowing for the fact that Cassandra clearly disliked him, as would Rhiannon's great-aunt in all probability, he still wanted her to be his. Perhaps he would win her over before it was too late.

And for the next eighteen months von Rittermann visited weekly, laden with a huge array of black market goodies for his cherished Rhiannon – silk stockings, designer clothing, exquisite jewellery and expensive toiletries. He even brought new shoes and beautiful clothes for Rhiannon's foster daughter, despite knowing that she hated the sight of him. Despite her antipathy, these were accepted more than willingly by the child – and gradually she began to accept his presence with better grace.

Rhiannon was deeply concerned; Max was furiously resentful. These incredible presents from the deputy head of the Paris Gestapo and his regular visits provided a rich source of gossip for their neighbours, not to mention on the German army grapevine. A perplexed Konrad von Kleiste, hearing about the situation from the unhappy young couple, could only shake his head grimly and advise them not to cross the dangerously powerful and viciously ruthless von Rittermann, and graciously accept his overtures of friendship. No-one in their right mind ever challenged the Gestapo baron, and those who did paid for it with their lives.

Inevitably these weekly visits to Maison Meredith meant that von Rittermann often met the hostile and formidable Alicia. She treated the Gestapo officer with impeccable courtesy and respect, but also managed to make it abundantly clear that she regarded his visits as highly unwelcome. Max very wisely stayed away when the baron came to call, following a deeply concerned Konrad von Kleiste's prudent advice.

A few months later Max finally received the news he had been waiting for so impatiently. Adolf Hitler had decided that from 11 March 1941 German officers would be permitted to take foreign European wives of Aryan stock. He promptly submitting Rhiannon's family documents, which proved her pure non-Jewish bloodline for four generations on both sides, while his fiancée successfully underwent an official health check and a detailed inquiry into her family's medical history. Only healthy and disease-free women were allowed to marry German officers – thus ensuring genetically sound children for the Third Reich.

They married in a Chartres register office on 20 March, with Alicia, Konrad von Kleiste and some of Max's colleagues as witnesses, a wide-eyed Cassie dressed all in white, which contrasted with Rhiannon's luxurious dark brown fur coat, looking curiously on. After the brief ceremony the wedding party proceeded to church, Max's family priest having come all the way from Kassel to conduct the ceremony at the young officer's request.

'Congratulations to you both, and may you have a very happy and fruitful marriage.' Quite aware that the heavily pregnant bride was only a week or so from giving birth anyway, the priest smiled, then blessed the young couple – while back in Germany an ecstatic Karl and Elsa celebrated the marriage as well as their beloved son's promotion to the rank of major with a bottle of the best quality French champagne, which had arrived with one of the monthly food parcels that Max sent from Paris.

Reflecting bitterly on the marriage, while the wedding party enjoyed a lavish reception, a brooding Kurt von Rittermann scowled and muttered. 'So I've finally lost her as my baroness, at least while the major's alive . . .'

Then, consoling himself with the thought that he could at least see Rhiannon regularly, the deeply disappointed officer turned his sadistic attention to the latest detainee who was waiting fearfully in the cells below.

Chapter Eight

I'm ready, Aunt Rhiannon.'

Excited by the idea of visiting Versailles with Uncle Max, Cassie danced joyfully into the sitting room one dull morning in late March, her teddy bear trailing behind her. The healthy and energetic four-year-old, her head now covered in short, glossy chestnut curls, had been accompanying the young major on his espionage assignments since early January 1941. As expected, she had proved to be the perfect cover for the Abwehr officer as he prowled round Paris in the guise of a prosperous French businessman, Sebastian and Rhys's exclusive and expensive wardrobes being ideal attire for these plain-clothes missions.

'Well, enjoy yourself, Cassie, and stay with your uncle at all times. We don't want to lose you.' Busily occupied with the compilation of a new family album, the mother-to-be smiled, then gave the lively child a big hug. 'Off you go, and behave yourself.'

'Of course I will, Aunt.'

The small red-coated figure skipped out to where Max stood waiting at the front door, and slipped her gloved hand into his. 'Here I am, Uncle – bang on time.'

'An expression learned from your Aunt Rhiannon, I think.' The amused German laughed, then, aware of the sudden silence as he and Cassie walked down the tree-lined road, their gossiping neighbours staring after them in hostile suspicion, looked down gently at the puzzled child. 'One day you'll come to understand why they hate us so much, but for the moment you'll just have to accept it. But rest assured that it's not you who's hated, but me and your aunts.'

'Yes, Uncle Max. Will Aunt Alicia be having a German lesson with Aunt Rhiannon while we're at Versailles?'

'I should think so, yes. Once your baby brother or sister's born that's the language he or she will be learning, along with English – so your Aunt Alicia wants to learn German too.'

'Is that why the neighbours don't like us? Because you and Aunt Rhiannon speak German and English, not French like them?'

'Well, yes, in a manner of speaking . . .'

Max nodded thoughtfully at the sharp-witted youngster, suddenly conscious that he and Colonel von Kleiste would have to be very careful what they said in front of Cassie, especially once her understanding and mastery of German, still very limited but improving rapidly, became more fluent.

Arriving at their destination an hour or so later, the pair headed towards the statue-bedecked gardens. Max soon located his target: a group of scruffily dressed men who hardly bothered to glance at the elegant Frenchman and his happily chattering little girl who passed. He followed their muttered conversation from a nearby bench as best he could, and picked up several pieces of useful information while responding fluently to Cassie's contented chatter.

After the unsuspecting French Resistance members had finally departed a smugly smiling Max took his enthusiastic charge round the château itself, the little girl staring in ecstatic wonder at the gilded luxury around her.

'Oh, Uncle Max! That was a golden bed. And look at all these mirrors and the painted ceiling.'

'This room's called the Hall of Mirrors, Cassie.'

'And who's the beautiful lady in the picture over there?'

'That's Queen Marie-Antoinette, who was guillotined during the French Revolution – along with her husband and many members of their family.'

'Oh. What does French Rev . . . and guillotined mean?'

Explaining as best he could to the deeply attentive child, Max took her round the rest of the palace; the enthralled Cassie asking question after question.

Afterwards, suddenly feeling hungry, Max and Cassie sought out the nearest café and ordered a simple lunch of ham and cheese crêpes and crusty bread, Cassie much preferring the idea of her milky coffee to the young officer's strong beer.

'Look, Uncle Max. We saw that man in the garden with all those other men. Doesn't he look sleepy? And . . . oh! He's just dropped something out of his pocket.'

Max quietly instructing his observant companion to retrieve the scrap of paper the moment the hapless Frenchman left the premises. As they left the café he scanned the scribbled note with a satisfied expression, then transferred it to a secure inside pocket and immediately departed for Army Headquarters, all the while heaping lavish praise on the delighted little girl who trotted obediently at his side, her hand firmly in his.

'Did you enjoy your day out, Cassandra? '

The child gave a dazzling smile as she entered the spacious office. 'Oh yes, thank you, Colonel. I was really clever today. I found an important bit of paper for Uncle Max.'

'Did you indeed, young lady? Ah, thank you, Major . . .'

The baron studied the note for a moment, then looked up in stunned amazement at the composed young man and his innocent companion. 'Incredible. How any member of the Resistance could be so stupid and careless as to carry such vital information on his person defies belief. Names, addresses, times of meetings – even details of the next targets – it's all there. I'll hear how your surveillance mission went later on, Major, but first I want you to arrange all necessary ambushes, surveillance teams and, in the case of the names I've underlined, immediate arrests.'

'Yes, Colonel.' Max hurried out of the office, leaving his puzzled charge staring after him.

'We heard a lot of things in the park today. A nasty-looking man called Raoul kept talking about killing someone called Alain on Sunday, and . . .' Blurting out everything that her sharp ears had picked up, Cassie added, 'Raoul said that Alain isn't to be trusted and has to die.'

Konrad von Kleiste nodded seriously. 'I see . . . well, thank you very much for your information, Cassandra. And what else did you hear?'

Returning a short while later, Max was immediately instructed to warn an Abwehr mole operating in a Resistance group under the name Alain that he had been rumbled, and was to pull out at once. Having heard the major's account of the rendezvous he had observed, the two officers discussed a new plan of action.

'You can leave our little protégé in my secretary's office, where Miss Werner can keep an eye on her and show her the new toys I've provided.' The colonel smiled indulgently at the incurably inquisitive four-year-old. 'After all, clever little girls like you deserve the best, don't they, Cassandra?'

A few days later, on the evening of 28 March, Rhiannon finally gave birth to non-identical twins, the elder boy green-eyed like his mother, the younger taking after his blue-eyed father. 'Well, Max, there you are – the Meredith curse has struck again. Twins – and, as is usual in our family, boys. I'm going to call them Rhys Alexander and Sebastian Siegfried. If we ever have a daughter she'll be Amber Rhiannon.'

'By all means, my love, but let's be content with our two wonderful sons for now.'

Thanking the German army doctor and nurse for their expert care, the proud father held his healthy new-born babies in his arms before reluctantly allowing a solicitous Alicia and Cassie their turn. 'So, are you satisfied with little Rhys and Sebastian?'

Rhiannon looked enquiringly up at her husband. 'Obviously. And not just with them either.'

Max gave his exhausted but happy wife a warm hug. 'And now we must let you rest, or the good doctor and midwife will be lecturing me on my lack of consideration.'

The rest of the year passed in a whirl of activity for the growing Meredith-Mayschoss family. A double pram and many other necessary items were provided by a benevolent Konrad von Kleiste, who, true to his word, duly became the twins' godfather at the private christening service held six weeks later. Max and Rhiannon likewise became godparents to their beloved Cassie, whom they had now legally adopted thanks to von Kleiste's influential help. A record of the happy event was preserved for the family photograph album, along with some pictures taken especially for the proud grandparents back in Germany.

As unimpressed with the proceedings as Max's deeply jealous and resentful sister and brother-in law, Maria and Franz, Kurt von Rittermann welcomed the young mother's return to work in October with a sense of deep relief. The depressing result of his medical check-up in September finally launched him on a final desperate gamble to secure the son and heir who would one day succeed him as Baron von Rittermann, and inherit his vast estate. The daringly unorthodox course of action that he planned was to change the lives and destiny of himself, Max, Rhiannon, even Konrad von Kleiste and his family, in a way that none of them could have anticipated.

Cassandra was to play an important part in Kurt von Rittermann's plans. In May, for reasons so far known only to himself, he had suddenly drawn up a new will, naming Cassie as his new heir, having lost Ralph in January. His next two choices were Rhys Meredith-Mayschoss and Sebastian, with Cassie's eldest son one day to inherit the title of Baron von Rittermann if he left no sons or daughters. Cassie had greatly impressed von Rittermann during his weekly visits to Maison Meredith as an intelligent little girl of real promise. Under her adoptive family's wise guidance and education she would surely flourish. His hated family back in North Germany was thus doomed to receive not a penny of his fortune, and none of his estate.

The baron determined not to tell Cassandra's adoptive family or anyone save his lawyers and commanding officer about this emergency last will and testament. A copy of the will was safely stored at Von Rittermann House, and the original was left with his lawyers. The baron had second and third copies in his apartment and office, just in case. All he could do now was sit back and wait for his beloved Rhiannon's return to work in October.

Chapter Nine

A light rain was falling as Rhiannon slipped into Gestapo Headquarters one mild day in early October after six months of maternity leave – during which, however, Kurt von Rittermann had regularly called on her services, much to a deeply jealous Max's intense fury. The young woman quickly towelled herself and her two damp dogs before entering the baron's plush office.

'Good morning, Colonel.'

'Good morning, Rhiannon, my dear. Welcome back. I'd appreciate it if you could translate these documents into German for me – preferably by midday.'

'Of course, Colonel . . .'

Noting his unaccustomed use of her Christian name and an endearment with some surprise, the puzzled red-head nodded – and set to work with a will.

Returning from the cells just before midday, the German aristocrat filed away the completed translations and ordered lunch, before pouring two glasses of wine and settling down with his treasured companion on the settee. 'So! Now that's all finished there's something important I wish to discuss with you, Rhiannon . . . well, three things actually. Firstly, although I know you're only supposed to be working part-time, I'll still require your services. As your head of department, Colonel Neumann will, naturally, expect you to put in the hours agreed in your contract, but as you employ two servants and also have your great-aunt to care for the children, it shouldn't be impossible for you to come in five mornings a week, and put in whatever time is required at Army Headquarters during the afternoon. Should you need any more help with Cassandra and the twins you could always employ a live-in nanny from Germany – something I'd definitely recommend rather than a French girl.

'And now, to other matters. My family – and yours. Five months ago, while I was looking through some of the more interesting books from Ralph's apartment, I found a draft of a love letter to a certain Gisèle Jacques. In it he begs her to leave and divorce her husband, dump her nine children, come to live with him along with little Marie-Claude, give up prostitution for good and marry him. It's interesting that, despite Gisèle's protestations to the contrary, Ralph believed that the child was his daughter. The letter also makes it clear that he sent Gisele ever since Marie-Claude's birth in December 1936 – and extra food every week since July 1940 as well. Monthly letters seem to have been their only form of contact after the child was born, because my cousin bewails the fact that Gisèle falsely registered Marie-Claude as her husband's, and refused point blank to let Ralph see them, despite his many desperate requests. Ralph writes that he wants to see for himself if the child has the von Rittermann silver-grey eyes and crooked little fingers – and that Gisèle's steadfast denials don't convince him.

'Now Ralph never discussed his private life with me, and I never discussed mine with him, but he did admit his fondness for the type of women that I'd avoid like the plague. So purely out of curiosity I had Madame Jacques brought to Headquarters for routine questioning, to see if I could get any information about her and Ralph – and I have to admit that she wasn't at all what I'd expected. On the contrary, she was very cultured and well spoken, and of obvious middle-class origins – not to mention quite good-looking: she must have been a real beauty in her youth.'

Rhiannon gazed at the baron, stunned, and begged him to continue.

'Well, naturally taking great care not to identify myself in case she recognised me as a relative of Ralph, I asked a few routine questions, then, without mentioning any names, told her exactly what had happened the evening her daughter ran away from home, and what had happened to her since. Her reaction on discovering that her drunken husband had sold Marie-Claude for a handful of francs to a German army officer and his French girlfriend was one of utter fury, then many tears. A few questions later, and I'd found out that Gisèle had conceived and given birth to Marie-Claude while her husband was in prison, and that the child was that of Ralph von Rittermann . . . though she never told him as much.

'From what Gisèle said she loved my cousin deeply, but was torn between being with him and staying to care for her other nine children. She didn't dare tell Ralph that he was the father, because she knew very well that he'd have been round immediately to see his daughter. Knowing that her husband could be violent, she dreaded any encounter between the two men.

'On being informed that Marie-Claude had been legally adopted by the wealthy couple who'd rescued her, the husband being by lucky chance a close relative of Ralph von Rittermann (a lie, I know), Gisèle nodded and began to sob again, especially when I told her that no further contact would be allowed with her daughter - although progress reports would be sent every month if she wished to receive them. Finally, when I said that Ralph had died, and explained how and when, she broke down completely. I did what I could under the circumstances: I had a strong coffee brought in, and left her for a good fifteen minutes to mull things over and calm down. When I went back I promised, on behalf of Ralph's benevolent relative and his wife, to reinstate the weekly provisions that Ralph had sent until his death, as well as pay her rent. I've kept this promise. When I sent her home with a large bag of food and other essentials, she begged me to pass on her dear love to Marie-Claude and her thanks to the wonderfully kind and generous couple who'd adopted her. From now on, Rhiannon, I'll provide for my cousin's daughter, as he'd have expected me to do. Do please pass all this on to your husband, your great-aunt, Colonel Konrad von Kleiste and, of course, little Cassandra herself.'

Von Rittermann paused, and regarded the nonplussed Rhiannon intently. 'This leads me to the third thing I have to tell you. Recently I've been diagnosed with cancer of the prostate gland, which means my need for a son and heir is all the more pressing. Please don't be shocked by what I have to say. If you're willing to bear me a child, which I'll acknowledge as my natural son in my will, and legally adopt so as to ensure his rights of inheritance, I'll accord you and your family complete protection in return. Your being Catholic and I Protestant is of no importance, and I have no objections whatsoever to him being raised in your religion. All I demand is that at eighteen my son adopts my name and assumes his rightful title of Baron von Rittermann; then at twenty-one he'll come into his full inheritance. I will, of course, leave you a generous slice of my fortune, along with whatever's needed to run my estate at Celle and maintain my son until he reaches his majority. A good education for him is a priority, of course. But if he dies before his twenty-first birthday then my title will revert to the next in line for a while – an ailing man of eighty-five, who has two unmarried daughters way past childbearing age. The von Rittermann estate and three-quarters of my fortune will pass to Cassandra and the rest to your two sons in trust, and they'll come into their inheritance aged twenty-one.

'Should Cassandra not reach her twenty-first birthday, then Rhys will inherit all her share under the same legal requisites, and his younger brother Sebastian a quarter of the estate. Should Rhys die before he's twenty-one, then Sebastian will inherit everything in trust. In the event of any normal and healthy child being born to you after my death but obviously sired by me, then he or she must take precedence over Cassandra and her adopted brothers.

'The part of my fortune that I've left to you will remain yours whatever happens to my son or his half-brothers and Cassandra. After my death you and your family will be able to move into my mansion and will enjoy full control over the estate, and you, your husband and great-aunt will be responsible for its management until my son and heir reaches maturity. For the moment, however, Von Rittermann House is being used as an army base and hospital with my full permission, but when you and your family move in an entire wing will be put at your disposal.

'So, will you bear me a son, Rhiannon? I know already that the Meredith family has a marked tendency to produce sons. That being the case, the chances of us having a boy should be excellent.'

'But, Colonel . . .' She stared in utter bewilderment, not knowing how to reply.

'And please call me Kurt. I have a Christian name like everyone else, and would prefer you to use it.' Gripping her hand, he added bitterly, 'I'd have made you my baroness and had legitimate children by you, but the rapacious Major Mayschoss had the great good fortune to meet and marry you first. If this is the only way that I can have you, and secure my son and heir, than so be it. For the second time, Rhiannon, will you do it?'

Well aware that her safety and that of her family would be threatened if she refused to co-operate, Rhiannon realised she had no choice, She agonised for a moment. 'Well . . . yes, but on three conditions. Firstly, should I bear you a daughter you must promise not to go back on your word regarding the protection of me and my family. Secondly, that protection must come into force from today. And thirdly, Colonel von Kleiste and his immediate family must be covered by it, much as you dislike him. Not only is he a very good friend to me and my family, but he's also the godfather of my twin sons, and would, I'm sure, be quite willing to be godfather to your son also – something which would benefit the boy immensely, as it would provide him with an excellent role model. My husband's a very educated and cultured man, but neither he nor I could provide a young aristocrat with the necessary social connections and graces that Baron von Kleiste will be able to.'

'Of course. In the meantime, to ensure that my family don't get their greedy hands on anything, I'm going to make a will drawn up under the terms that I've laid out. This will obviously be replaced as soon as we have a child.

'From today you're my mistress, which means I can relegate my contemptible mouse of a secretary to employee. Dinner won't be ready for a good half-hour, so there's no risk of us being disturbed.' Matching his actions to his words, von Rittermann immediately locked the office door, undressed his shocked and apprehensive companion, then removed his own clothes before pushing Rhiannon unceremoniously on to the settee. She submitted with a sense of shocked surprise as he peremptorily possessed her, his love-making more brutal than seductive. The baron kissed her hungrily on the lips, his hands caressing her curvaceous form. 'Dear God, Rhiannon. I've wanted you for so long. What a magnificent baroness you'd have made.'

'Well, I still don't intend to divorce Max.' The spirited young woman frowned. 'But I'll give you a child, I hope a son, and I'll raise him in your ancestral home. All I hope is that Max doesn't leave me for acceding to your . . . request.'

'If he does, and I'm still alive, you can all come and live with me instead.' The besotted officer held the slender naked girl possessively, his silver-grey eyes suddenly intense. 'But since he'll be well aware of that, I rather doubt that he'll ever grant me such great satisfaction. In the meantime, if anything should happen to your husband in the course of his duties I fully intend to marry you – even if I have to take your three other children and dragon of a great-aunt on board as well. As for Colonel von Kleiste, well!' Kurt von Rittermann shrugged, then, glancing at his watch, suggested that they should get dressed before the serving staff brought in their meal.

Max and Alicia showed not the least surprise on hearing about Cassie's true parentage, while Konrad von Kleiste merely smiled wryly as Rhiannon recounted what von Rittermann had told her. The older colonel was, none the less, very quick to congratulate his Gestapo counterpart on 'the welcome new addition to the von Rittermann family' in a voice heavy with irony . . . which left von Rittermann not in the least amused.

Cassie was delighted to have such a father, and pored rapturously over the photograph of Ralph that his cousin gave her. She now had a fine and aristocratic German father: her daddy Ralph had not been a figment of her imagination after all. But it came as a shock to the child to discover that she and the colonel were related, since she did not like him at all.

October and November 1941 passed uneventfully for Rhiannon and her family – but December proved otherwise. On finding out that Konrad von Kleiste, his mistress and Heinz, the live-in nanny Christa's soldier boyfriend, were all going to spend Christmas Day and New Year's Eve at Maison Meredith, a jealous and indignant Kurt immediately invited himself along and told Rhiannon to prepare a place for him at her table on both occasions. Rhiannon nodded uneasily – then told him that she might be a month pregnant with his baby. She realised it might not be best to tell her husband about either her pregnancy or her relationship with Kurt and their agreement if the baron was to be attending their family celebrations.

Predictably enough, Max objected violently to Kurt von Rittermann's presence at his table, but was soon persuaded to swallow his pride by a convincing and authoritative Konrad von Kleiste: it would be unwise indeed not to let sleeping dogs lie (especially vicious and dangerous ones like the Gestapo deputy chief). By mid-December Rhiannon was quite sure she was with child – much to her lover's ecstatic delight – but decided to keep her pregnancy secret, as planned.

Christmas Day went off well enough – considering the fact that Max and Kurt utterly hated each other and coldly ignored each other, apart from a brief nod of formal acknowledgement when Kurt arrived for pre-dinner drinks. Rhiannon, elegantly attired in a low-necked gold silk evening dress and jade jewellery, her luxuriant reddish-gold hair falling down her back in a mass of glossy ringlets, a wide-awake Rhys in her arms, simply gave the two love rivals an embarrassed smile, then promptly vanished into the sitting room with Cassie – who was very proud of her new midnight-blue embroidered satin dress . . . courtesy of Kurt von Rittermann.

New Year's Eve was tolerable too, Max and Kurt carefully avoiding each other. Konrad von Kleiste, Rhiannon and Alicia looked on with infinite relief.

But try as she might, Rhiannon could not put off telling her great-aunt and husband about her pregnancy for ever, and early in January they listened in grim silence as she explained everything, begging Max not to leave her and not to put their lives at risk by seeking revenge on Baron von Rittermann. She had no wish to lose any more family members to tragedy and misfortune, while von Rittermann was terminally ill and would not survive the war . . . perhaps, if Max could only have a little more patience . . .

Seething with anger, her husband nodded reluctantly, his blue eyes cold with fury. Alicia could only smile sadly and advise the pair to stand firmly together – wise advice that Konrad von Kleiste repeated on being told of the situation.

Well aware of the position his unhappy wife found herself in, Max managed to reassure her of his enduring love and utter loyalty – and

Rhiannon's worries largely eased once she knew her cherished Max would not leave her.

Chapter Ten

Just imagine, Aunt, the French Jews have to wear bright yellow stars in public now.'

Coming home with Max and Cassie from Abwehr Headquarters one evening in late May 1942, a six months pregnant Rhiannon shook her head incredulously at Alicia and Christa. 'They look so self-conscious as they pass by, poor things, and the French look at them with such contempt. I know the neighbours are hostile because of my marriage to a German officer, but at least I'm not shunned by strangers when I'm out and about on my own, without Max. But to have to wear a star announcing your Jewishness to the world, especially at the moment . . . well, that's so unfortunate for them.'

'Oh, it's a lot more than that, my love,' replied her great-aunt. 'All we can do is wait and see what happens next. But fortunately we're not Jewish, so it's no concern of ours. After all, the French don't need any lessons in anti-Semitism from the Germans – as the Dreyfus Affair proved.'

'Oh, absolutely,' said Max. 'And the brutality of the French militia sometimes even outdoes the German Secret Police. As for all their talk of democracy, the French government can be ruthless enough when it suits them, I assure you. So! Up you come, Sebastian. Have you and Rhys been good little boys for Christa today?'

'Yes, Daddy.' Replying in chorus, the boisterous toddlers were swept up lovingly into their parents' arms; the red-headed and green-eyed Rhys looking conspiratorially at his blond and blue-eyed twin before smiling sweetly at their nanny, whose sometimes wilfully disobedient charges never played up when their parents or great-great-aunt were around.

Assuring her employers that the twins had indeed behaved very well, the plump and dark-haired German girl followed the family into the dining room, and listened reverently as Major Mayschoss said Grace – both Max and Rhiannon believing in a disciplined and Christian upbringing for their children. Tucking into her beef and dumplings enthusiastically, Christa smiled dreamily to herself, absorbed in thoughts of her boyfriend Heinz, a good-looking young German soldier, and the approaching weekend.

Wrapping Paris in a haze of humid heat, August brought news of the Siege of Stalingrad, and also a devastating phone call from Germany in which Max was informed by his shattered father that Elsa had just been diagnosed with breast cancer – and was desperate to see her little grandsons before it was too late. Could Max and Rhiannon get some time off over Christmas and the New Year, and stay at Kassel for a week or so?

For a moment the young officer stood deep in thought. 'I don't see why not. Rhiannon's baby is due later this month, but she should be well enough to travel in December. With any luck my commanding officer will allow me time off.'

'God bless you, son.' Karl smiled through his tears, and passed the receiver to Elsa, who was waiting eagerly for the chance to speak to her adored son.

'How are the children and Rhiannon? Will her great-aunt and Christa be coming with you?'

Asking Max a string of questions, Elsa finally learned that only he, his wife and their children would be coming – assuming that leave was granted by Colonel von Kleiste.

'Oh, I do so hope that he does.' The matronly housewife looked wistfully at Karl, then asked to have a chat with Rhiannon, feeling sure that this young red-head whom she knew only from telephone conversations and from photographs would prove to be charming, and everything she had ever wanted in a daughter-in-law.

Shortly thereafter, Max phoned his mother to let her know that Rhiannon had given birth to a third son, and also that leave had been granted for the family trip at Christmas. 'We'll be staying for ten days, with two days allowed for travel each way, and we'll arrive on the 23rd. Alexander Kurt, as my wife's named our new arrival, is very robust and healthy, just as the twins were.'

'Oh, Max, how wonderful. Please pass on our warmest congratulations to dear Rhiannon. And do send us some photographs of Alexander as soon as possible.'

'But of course, Mother.'

Having brought his long chat with his mother to a close, Max asked Alicia to inform the Gestapo deputy chief that he was now the father of a healthy baby boy.

The old lady nodded cynically. 'Well, the sooner he knows the better, I suppose. He'll definitely come to see his son and heir tomorrow evening, so make sure you're civil, Max. Just so long as he doesn't expect Rhiannon to give him another son next year. Four children are quite enough, especially during a war.'

Far-sighted and shrewd, Max was only too aware that Germany was heading for defeat at the hands of the Allies, if Hitler remained in control – especially because Germany and Italy had rashly declared war on America the previous year. The inevitable solution was an army plot to remove Hitler before it was too late. Should this succeed, Germany might yet win the war or at least negotiate an honourable peace – but if it failed, the inevitable mass arrests and executions in its aftermath would bring nothing but disaster for both the army and possibly Konrad von Kleiste – and therefore Max himself. And who better to protect them both in such a dangerous situation than Colonel von Rittermann himself . . .

Laden with just about everything the baby could need during its first month of life, the Gestapo deputy duly arrived the next day. To rub the salt further into Max's wound, the proud father proceeded to visit the house every evening for the next twelve days, until Rhiannon was well enough to take the baby to his apartment. Other visitors to congratulate Rhiannon were Oberführer Windler, Head of the Paris Gestapo, and Colonels von Kleiste and Neumann – all three men obviously more than a little sweet on the charismatic red-head, a fact that was observed by Kurt with a sardonic smile and by Max with a strange mixture of pride and jealousy.

'Here he is, Kurt.' Taken to his sumptuous flat by staff car, a triumphant Rhiannon entered von Rittermann's sitting room with Alexander in her arms. 'My husband won't ever care for little Alex as much as he does for Cassie and his own sons, but he's promised to accept him as a member of our family. But your son's bound to sense Max's indifference to him. All I can do is tell Alex the truth as soon as he's old enough to understand, and then I hope that he and his stepfather can learn to live together in peace. But even if Max and Alex do take a dislike to each other, Max isn't a cruel or vindictive man. He'll treat the child with fairness and respect, and with kindness.'

'Which is precisely why your husband will make such a good father-figure for Alexander.' Taking the baby in his arms, Kurt gazed down devotedly at the son he had thought he would never have, and touched the tiny hands with a sense of wonder. 'He's got the von Rittermann grey eyes and crooked little fingers – both sure signs that he's really my son. Alexander Kurt is a very fine baby indeed, and will, I'm sure, prove worthy of his illustrious aristocratic ancestors.' The proud father smiled down at his offspring. 'He's perfect, absolutely perfect. Let's celebrate this young gentleman's birth with the finest champagne.' Settling down on the settee, little Alexander cradled securely in his lap, the elated baron added, 'Now I've been finally granted a son I must see him every day, or at least during the week. I've already had a word with Colonel Neumann, who's agreed that you may take the baby to work with you at Army Headquarters when you return to work in January, and I insist that next month and until the end of your maternity leave you bring the child to my office every morning. For now I'll visit you twice weekly, and also send round the car every Saturday afternoon at 1.30pm to bring you to see me here. As for transport to and from work, my staff car's at your disposal.' Slipping his arm round Rhiannon, the new father continued, 'And last, but certainly not least, there's the important matter of my son's legal adoption. Tomorrow morning at nine my lawyer's bringing me the necessary paperwork for you, your great-aunt and your husband to sign, including an adoption consent form, and I'd appreciate it if you could all be here to conclude our agreement.'

Promising that they would be, Rhiannon nodded, then listened as the baron described how he intended to write a long letter and autobiography for his son, which she was to give him as soon as he was old enough to receive it. 'And after my death you may take away all my personal papers and diaries, as well as a dress and work uniform, along with any other of my possessions that you think will help keep my memory alive for Alexander. For now, though, this gift is for you – something you would have worn officially as my baroness.' Handing his stunned mistress an ornately carved box, the aristocrat watched as she took out the emerald set, the gleaming green stones glistening in the light.

'Oh, Kurt, they're beautiful.'

'Try them on and see how they suit your eyes.'

'But they must be priceless.' Rhiannon stared in the mirror and shook her head. 'I'll certainly not be wearing this, expect in the safest of circumstances. It must be worth a small fortune – and I'd never forgive myself if it was stolen. Thank you, Kurt, it's . . . magnificent.'

Five weeks later Alexander was christened in a private ceremony by a German priest. His godparents, Konrad von Kleiste and his wife Luise, regarded Kurt von Rittermann's presence without surprise, Max having already filled them in on the situation.

'Well, you have your son and heir now, even if you chose a somewhat unorthodox way of going about it.'

The army chief frowned at his fellow baron. 'Well, since I had no other options left, and Rhiannon is, of all the women I have ever met, the most suitable choice to raise my son, preserve his inheritance and manage my estate, what else could I do? You have both a legitimate son and grandson to inherit your title, Colonel, not to mention numerous other male von Kleiste relatives, so you can afford to be smug. But I appreciate your gracious good will in consenting to be Alexander's godparents, and I won't forget such generosity, I assure you.'

'One must fulfil one's duty towards a fellow aristocrat, Colonel.'

The Abwehr colonel nodded civilly, then politely departed with Luise to chat with the priest and Rhiannon's family, leaving the Gestapo officer to reflect on the significance of these words.

Three months later Alexander had grown into a lively and responsive child. Von Rittermann now possessed a large album crammed with pictures of his beloved only son. 'What's he trying to say, Rhiannon?' The enslaved father stared in fascination at the happily babbling little boy sat on his knee.

'Oh, that he loves you, I expect. And I faithfully promise to telephone you every day from Kassel, Kurt.'

'If you don't I'll phone you at your in-laws, so be warned.'

Still displeased at the thought of being deprived of his mistress and son for two whole weeks, the baron hugged the cooing infant. 'After all, it isn't only your mother-in-law who's dying . . .'

'I know.' The exasperated red-head glanced round her lover's finely furnished sitting room; von Rittermann now insisted that she and Alexander visited him on Saturday afternoons while Max was at his club. 'But the specialist's given you at least a year to live, and we'll only be away for a fortnight.'

'True, but I'll still miss you both terribly. Ah well, just so long as you don't make a habit of leaving me.'

'But of course I won't.' Rhiannon smiled reassuringly at the indignant aristocrat, and added, not without a touch of irony, that loyalty was her middle name.

Von Rittermann laughed, and kissed her lovingly.

Chapter Eleven

W e're setting off now. Goodbye, Aunt Alicia, goodbye, Christa.' Cassie waved excitedly as the train began to pull out of the station, then went to sit with Max, her eyes shining. 'I've never been out of France before, Uncle. Is Germany a big country?'

'It is indeed, young lady, and also a very beautiful one, as you'll see for yourself later on. Pass me a chicken and stuffing sandwich from the picnic bag, please, Rhiannon – I'm still quite hungry.'

'But you can't be – not after that huge breakfast you ate.' The young woman shook her head disbelievingly, then handed her husband his snack. 'There you are . . . but please try to save some for lunch. The rest of us would like some too.'

Rhys and Sebastian stared enviously at their father and tugged insistently at her coat. 'I want one please, Mummy.'

'And I do too.'

'Oh, all right then, boys, but when your lunch is gone it's gone. Cassie, do you want a sandwich as well, before our greedy menfolk eat them all up?'

'Yes please, Aunt.'

'There you are, children. Well, what do you say?'

'Thank you, Mummy.'

'Thank you, Aunt Rhiannon. Oh no, you mustn't give Tiger and Bess any, boys. The dogs have their own food, haven't they?'

'They most certainly have, Cassie. Good heavens, what am I to do with my gluttonous husband and sons?'

'Nothing – because there's absolutely nothing to be done, my love.' Max laughed uproariously, and smiled affectionately at the two angelic-looking toddlers munching contentedly. 'You know the old saying, "like father like son", or in this case "sons".'

Suddenly aware of a French ticket inspector glowering at them, Max glared arrogantly back before icily handing over their ticket.

'What a nasty man.' Rhys stared aggressively at the official's hastily retreating back, and growled, 'Shoot him, Daddy.'

'Yes, shoot him. Bang, bang!' Shouting the last two words at the top of his voice, the fair-haired Sebastian clenched his fists fiercely, his blue eyes flashing with impetuous rage.

'Well now, boys, if I were to shoot every Frenchman we happened to dislike, and who dislikes us, there'd be no Frenchmen left in France, I'm afraid.' Max regarded the furious child and his red-headed twin brother with a droll smile, proud of his sons' fine spirit. 'So, how about lunch now, Rhiannon? It's midday.'

'As you wish.' Carefully handing wide-awake baby Alexander to Cassie, the young mother began to distribute the remaining sandwiches among her hungry brood.

'Welcome home, son. I knew you wouldn't let us down.' Meeting the travel-worn family at Kassel railway station, Karl and a tearful Elsa warmly embraced Max, who towered over his grey-haired parents. 'How was your journey?'

'Oh, excellent . . . and this is Rhiannon.'

For a moment they stared up in awe-struck admiration at the flame-headed young Amazon.

'I'm delighted to make your acquaintance at last, Mr and Mrs Mayschoss. Max has told me all about you and your family, and I'm sure he's told you about mine.'

'He has indeed . . . welcome to Kassel, my dear. My wife has been looking forward so much to meeting you and her three little grandsons; as well as your adopted daughter, of course.'

'Oh, how wonderful it is to see you all. And thank you for my grandchildren, Rhiannon . . . they're so . . . well, wonderful.'

Bursting into happy tears again, Elsa hugged the two tired toddlers to her before exclaiming delightedly over the wide-eyed Alexander secure in his mother's arms. Then she turned to the little girl at Rhiannon's side. 'And this must be Cassandra. How do you like Germany, Cassie?'

'Oh, very much thank you, Mrs Mayschoss. We have three dogs and a Siamese cat, but Snowy and Casilda have stayed behind in Paris with Aunt Alicia and Christa. This is Tiger, and this is Bess, and we all love them very much, even Uncle Max, who didn't used to care for dogs and cats very much.'

'I see . . . Now that you've finally arrived let's head home, for coffee and cakes.' Completely taken aback by this very pretty, but rather forward and pert little girl, Elsa glanced at her secretly amused son.

'Oh, you needn't worry, Mother. Cassie's a very well-behaved and sweet-natured child, but she does have a lot to say for herself.'

'Quite.'

Karl glanced shrewdly at the lively youngster with the long glossy chestnut curls, aware, like his wife, of the terrible life that Cassie had led until only two years before. 'Well, off we go. I'll carry two cases and you can take the others, Max. You, Rhiannon and little Alexander can sleep in your old bedroom, the twins are in the guest room, and Cassie's sleeping in Maria's old room.'

For the enraptured Elsa the next few days passed in a whirl of busy excitement and intense happiness. Quite delighted by her charming and vivacious daughter-in-law, and utterly besotted by her grandsons, she soon forgot all about her illness. Only the thought of her daughter's arrival two days after Christmas causing her smile to slip a little: Maria had hated her good-looking and gifted younger brother since childhood, with Max returning her antipathy in full measure. And now that he and his stunningly beautiful Anglo-French wife were the proud parents of three fine sons, Maria and her henpecked husband would not be in a very good humour. Instinctively preferring their academic and quick-witted son to his morose and rather plain sister, the Mayschosses were well aware of Maria's bitter resentment, but had always found it hard to conceal their favouritism – which was now well nigh impossible to hide.

For Maria, alas, Max's wife and children made a less positive impression – the childless thirty-six-year-old hating the larger-than-life Rhiannon on sight two days later. Meanwhile, Franz gazed at her in adoring rapture, sending his furious wife into a fit of intense jealousy. Quite unable to tolerate either this or the sight of her parents cooing devotedly over her detested brother's petted and pampered little boys, the wretched Maria finally exploded in a violent rage as Elsa served the afternoon refreshments. 'Damn you, Maximilian – you and your high and mighty wife. And as for your spoilt brats, and saucy madam of an adopted daughter who can do wrong in our parents' eyes . . . I've had quite enough of you all, especially my disloyal husband – who's done nothing but stare at that red-headed temptress since we arrived.'

'Maria! How dare you talk about Rhiannon, little Cassie and our adorable grandchildren in that disrespectful manner. It's certainly not Max's or Rhiannon's fault that you have no children of your own, and such appalling behaviour's quite inexcusable, especially when your mother's so gravely ill.' Karl shook with fury. 'Either apologise, or don't show your face here again. I've put up with your moods and your temper for far too long, and I've had quite enough now. So, what's it to be, Maria?'

For a moment the lanky dark-haired woman stared indecisively at her father, before beginning to sob bitterly. 'You've always loved him more than you ever loved me; and now his precious wife has given you three grandchildren she's everything to you – everything I'm not, and never will be. All my life it's been Max this, Max that, and now it's Rhiannon this and Rhiannon that as well, along with you singing your praises of your grandsons all the time. Compared to my brother and sister-in-law I'll always be a failure to you, as will my husband – because he was rejected as unfit for service by the army.'

'We don't hold any of this against either of you, Maria. All I ask is that you apologise to your brother and his wife; then all will be forgiven and forgotten.'

'All right, I'm sorry. Please forgive me, Mother: I didn't mean to upset you.'

'No, of course you didn't, Maria.' Elsa, very pale, nodded grimly, then continued to serve the coffee, her hands shaking.

'Please let me do that for you, Mrs Mayschoss.' Quickly handing Alexander over to Cassie, Rhiannon took over from her grateful mother-in-law – prompting a wistful Elsa to comment sadly to her husband later that night, 'Oh, why couldn't we have had a daughter like Rhiannon, instead of Maria? Max's wife is an absolute angel, and everything I wanted in a daughter. Still, we've been blessed with a wonderful son who's given us three adorable grandsons – so God's been good to us, Karl.'

Chapter Twelve

The next morning Rhiannon took the four children and two dogs off to the park as usual, leaving Max to talk with his mother. Karl had left long ago for work, his position as manager of a large food production factory giving him an important role in the war effort – reflected in the spacious and well-appointed residence in which he and his wife lived.

Initially very shy towards the German children that her godmother encouraged her to mix with, Cassie now positively looked forward to visiting the park. She revelled in the companionship, as did the twins, whose equally lively and outgoing personalities likewise soon made them many friends.

'Oh, look, there are Petra and her brothers, Aunt Rhiannon. May I join them, please?' Cassie's silver-grey eyes sparkled.

'But of course. Off you go.' Rhiannon watched the impetuous six-year-old race delightedly off across the snowy park to see her friends, then slowly followed her with the three boys. Tiger and Bess ran freely around, their boisterous games of chase and fetch the ball causing more than a few families to usher their children away from the wildly energetic young dogs. 'Good morning, Mrs Jensen. I do hope that my wayward daughter isn't being a nuisance.'

'Not at all, Mrs Mayschoss. Ah, hello Rhys and Sebastian, and little Alexander of course. What curiously coloured eyes your youngest son has – almost silver, just like Cassandra's.'

'Well, Alex is a most unusual baby, in more ways than one.' Wondering what Petra's mother would say if she knew about the circumstances surrounding Alex's birth, and his ultimate inheritance, Rhiannon smiled and began to chat.

Meanwhile, back at the Mayschoss home Elsa listened to her son's account of busy family life back in Paris with keen interest, her careworn face lighting up with pride. 'Oh Max, you can't imagine how wonderful it is to see you all this Christmas. Rhiannon's a delightful girl, and your three children are absolute treasures. And little Cassie's a sweet child. Oh, by the way, Ilse enquired about you yesterday, but lost interest when I told her that you're a happily married man with four children.'

Max nodded – his indifferent expression summing up his cold attitude towards the many girlfriends he had gone out with for a short while and then abandoned. 'Quite, Mother. And now you've heard all my news, why not tell me yours?'

'Well . . .' Fired with a new zest for life, now that her beloved son was near her, Elsa began to talk animatedly, her eyes shining with happiness.

New Year's Eve arrived with another heavy snowfall, and temperatures plunged way below freezing as Elsa and Rhiannon prepared for the celebrations. Karl proudly took his son to visit his colleagues at work – and even the managing director welcomed the young army officer with a drink in his office.

When all preparations were finished and the menfolk were still absent, Rhiannon decided that it was time to telephone her possessive lover and slipped away from the kitchen to inform him of the day's events – assuring an anxious Kurt that little Alexander was fine, despite the freezing weather.

'It's very cold here in Paris, but not that cold. Providing you keep Alexander warmly wrapped up, he shouldn't suffer any ill-effects. And thank you for your last letter: it was most interesting - especially where you described Maria's outburst. When are you due back? I do miss you both terribly.'

'On the 4th, as you very well know. And you needn't try to make me feel guilty, because it simply won't work. Max needs to be with his dying mother, and the children and I needed a holiday, not to mention poor Christa who can't find looking after Rhys and Sebastian easy. Besides, she's madly in love with Heinz, and she's enjoying the chance to be with her fiancé over the festive season. He's a charming young man, though as he's a common soldier I don't suppose you'll be the least interested in him. Max and I invite him to Sunday dinner, and you should see his respectful manner. Colonel von Kleiste jokes about us running a home for unwanted waif and strays.'

'For once he might have a point. What is it about the English that they need to have homes for unwanted animals and leave fortunes to domestic pets?'

'Because that's how we are, Kurt, just as you Germans are as you are and the French have their strange quirks. My Irish grandmother never lost her aristocratic airs and graces, and our housekeeper Magda had some very odd ideas – and flew into a real rage if any of the maids failed to show her sufficient respect or to clean to her impossibly high standards. She even tried to turn the very spoilt little twins of her employers into good Germans, much to our tutors' disgust.'

'So I can imagine, my love.' Kurt von Rittermann howled with laughter, spilling his brandy on the hearth. 'Come back to Paris, Rhiannon. Life's very dull indeed without you.'

'I promise. But I'd better go now, as Max and his father have just returned home and it would be better if Karl and Elsa don't suspect that I've been calling my lover from their house.'

'All right, but I still expect to hear from you every day. Goodbye, Rhiannon . . . I love you.'

'And I love you too . . . Goodbye, Kurt, and look after yourself.'

For a moment the red-head stood in reflective silence, wondering if were indeed possible to love two men at the same time. Feeling a tug at her necklace from a tiny fist, she smiled affectionately at the grey-eyed baby. 'Little Alex . . . my little Alex. How I love you. You're so like your father, yet I hope you won't resemble him completely, for all our sakes.'

For Elsa the remaining hours with her son and his family positively sped by, the dying woman trying her hardest not to think of their imminent return to Paris. But the dreaded day finally arrived, and a sobbing Elsa hugged her adored son and his family at Kassel railway station.

'God bless you, son. It was good of you to visit us.' Karl embraced Max with tears in his eyes. 'Have a safe journey back, and don't fail to telephone us the moment you arrive home.'

'Oh, we'll phone, don't worry. We're going to be collected at the station by staff car and chauffeured to our door, so that part of the journey will be without problems.'

'Oh good. Just like we are when we go to work in the mornings, and Colonel von . . .' Abruptly silenced by a discreet nudge from Rhiannon, Cassie was unceremoniously pushed into the carriage. She waited until the two waving figures on the platform had vanished from sight before asking in a puzzled voice, 'What did I say wrong?'

'Well, for one thing my parents know nothing about Colonel von Rittermann, and that's how it should be; at least for the present.'

'Oh! But Colonel von Rittermann *does* send his car to take you to work every morning, and they know that Aunt Rhiannon works for him.'

'So they do, Cassie, but that's all. And your uncle and I prefer it if that's all they know for now. Now settle down, children: we've got a long and tiring journey ahead of us. I'm going to have a snooze, so unless it's a dire emergency please don't disturb me, any of you.'

Chapter Thirteen

We're back, Kurt. And now you know that I'm a high and mighty red-headed temptress, with three spoilt brats of sons and a saucy madam of an adopted daughter – not to mention being guilty of having a husband whose birth pushed his resentful sister into second place. Not that I feel remotely like a *femme fatale*: all I want to do after a hard day's work is to relax with my family or bury myself in a good book – which is now a rare luxury, I'm afraid. Even Max has been given heavier responsibilities and more work by his commanding officer, but because he's set his sights on promotion to the rank of lieutenant-colonel he's got no intention to complain about it.'

'Obviously not, seeing as he's Konrad von Kleiste's star junior officer. I realised that the major was determined to advance himself, both in rank and socially, the moment I first met him in June 1940 – and his marriage to you was clearly an essential part of both.' Stubbing out his cigarette, the German aristocrat greeted his mistress with a loving kiss and settled his happily crowing baby son on his knee. 'Thank you for the long letters you've been sending me, and your telephone calls. Alexander's certainly grown since I last saw him: the sooner I arrange another sitting with the photographer the better.'

'With both dogs included in some of the pictures as usual. What work do you have for me today, Kurt?'

'Only a couple of translations for the French militia – something that shouldn't take up much of your time. In the meantime I'll take a look at these files and nurse my son.'

An hour or so later, after a passionate session with her lover, Rhiannon finally found out more about his family background. 'My own history isn't anywhere near as colourful as yours, I'm afraid. I come from a long line of North German aristocrats, and my parents were very distant and formal towards my sister, my elder brother and me: we didn't see much of them. When Ernst died unexpectedly of scarlet fever, aged ten, I was the only surviving male heir and suddenly became very important to my parents. I was assigned my own tutor, who was harsh even by the standards of the day. Then two years later I was diagnosed with tuberculosis, and spent twelve months at a clinic in the mountains before going to grammar school. At eighteen I began my military service, but was invalidated out on account of my damaged lungs, so I decided to study economics and political history at Hamburg University. Then I joined the civil service. Finally, when I was thirty, after many unsuccessful relationships, I became engaged to Alice von Wilder – the sister of a fellow aristocrat and friend. We were very much in love, Alice and I, but I lost her when she was killed in a riding accident just before our marriage: she was thrown from her mount and trampled to death. That same year, 1924, my parents died – leaving me with a title, huge fortune and estate, but no beloved Alice to share it with. She was two months pregnant at the time of her death, something which haunted me until Alexander was born. Three years later I married Olga von Adler, a marriage I immediately regretted the moment we left church. Our quarrels seemed to go on from morning till night. Olga hated fulfilling her wifely duties, so as you can imagine our marriage was soon over. Then in 1930 I became a member of the National Socialist Party, and four years later I joined the Gestapo.

'When I first set eyes on you, thirteen years later, I was instantly smitten. If it hadn't been for Colonel von Kleiste's strong support for his favourite junior officer I'd certainly have detached you from the major by threats or force. And when you informed me that you were carrying the major's child I had to back off, but I never gave up hope. You know the rest.

'So that's my life, Rhiannon . . . not a very happy or fulfilled one, but much happier since you consented to be mine and gave me a child. Alexander's the final blessing, a son I can love as my son. I know that after my death his mother will love him as mine never loved me, and will safeguard his inheritance.'

'Oh!' Rhiannon sat in stunned silence for a moment, not knowing what to say. At last she was a little closer to understanding the baron's often cold and cruel character, even if his explanation didn't justify his sadism to prisoners in his charge. 'What were you planning to do to poor Max? Have him packed off to the Eastern Front?'

'It was something that I pushed for. That or Africa. But his commanding officer refused to part with him.'

Five weeks after this illuminating conversation, Rhiannon found her lover engrossed in a top secret military report concerning the Siege of Stalingrad. 'What does it say, Kurt? Or aren't you allowed to tell me?'

'Apparently 400,000 Germans and 750,000 Russians were killed during the fighting, and the Red Army claims to have captured 91,000 of our men. This all happened on 31 January 1943, and it confirms for me that we can't defeat the Russians or the Russian winter when our army's only got summer clothing and equipment. Russia's a huge country: it'll swallow us up. Even the great Napoleon was defeated there. This terrible waste of German lives is so unnecessary.'

'So we all know what's happening, but prefer not to think about it.'

Von Rittermann shook his head grimly.

'And another thing, Kurt . . . where have all the Jews vanished to? One moment they were walking the streets wearing bright yellow stars, and now they've disappeared as if they never existed.'

'Oh, that. They've been sent to work camps, to labour for the greater good of the Third Reich. I rather doubt they'll suffer long. So! That's quite enough of current affairs for today. Tell me what you'd like for lunch, and I'll order it.'

Not long after this, as Rhiannon slipped into Gestapo Headquarters one freezing late January morning, a wide-awake Alex in her arms and her two large dogs padding obediently at her side, she noticed Oberführer Ulrich Windler, head of the Paris Gestapo, and Kurt deep in conversation – but not so deep that she was able to slip by unnoticed, Windler himself being more than a little attracted by her.

'Ah, good morning, Mrs Mayschoss. And how are our fine young friend and his beautiful mother today?'

Replying that they were both in excellent health, as was the rest of her family, Rhiannon regarded the two high-ranking officers composedly, studiously ignoring sly glances from passing Gestapo personnel. She and Max were used to this by now. Used to the rumours that had been circulating for a while about her adulterous relationship with Kurt, and the inevitable suspicions from Abwehr Headquarters that she was a spy for the Gestapo: the army hated and distrusted the Gestapo, and Rhiannon had a foot in both camps. Whose side was she really on? Her betrayal of her own country, as well as that of her husband, was now being frequently discussed. Not to mention the speculation regarding the paternity of her youngest son, thanks to the undisguised love and pride that von Rittermann showed for her, as well as the distinctive silver-grey eyes and crooked little fingers which the baron and young Alexander shared. Max's male colleagues treated him with the utmost respect to his face, but with a curious mixture of envy and sympathy behind his back – the former because of his wife's apparent shameless adultery, the latter because an appreciative Konrad von Kleiste had marked him out for further promotion and was known to consider him his most gifted subordinate. Rhiannon was treated with a barely veiled contempt and distrust by army personnel, especially her husband's fellow officers. All that Rhiannon and Max could do was stand back to back with their heads held high, facing the storm with a united strength – just as her parents had faced the horrors of the Great War together.

Jerking back to the present, her parents' resolute faces suddenly in her mind, Rhiannon smiled politely at the officers and readjusted an uncomfortable Alex. 'Hush, little man, we all know you're still there.'

'He's certainly a fine-looking infant, and the very picture of a healthy and racially pure Aryan child, Mrs Mayschoss. Colonel von Rittermann tells me that your French mother was blonde and blue eyed, and that your father was green-eyed and red-headed, the result of having an Irish mother.'

'That's right, Oberführer. Rhys is as red-headed as I am but Sebastian takes after my husband, with his blue eyes and fair hair. Alex, happily for him, has also been spared the fiery colouring and definitely takes after his father in looks, not to mention character. Not that I or my children are really pure anything, given our mixed-race heritage. My great-aunt is completely English, though. Given that I'm of English, French and Irish descent, and my sons have German blood, I'm not sure how we stand in the light of the Führer's policy to promote a pure German and Nordic Aryan race . . . as mere mongrels, perhaps?'

The two men laughed. 'Not really, Mrs Mayschoss; let us say pure Aryans of many different strains instead.'

Ulrich Windler regarded his deputy amusedly. 'She's a refreshing change, completely different from the dour females we usually employ.'

A proud Kurt von Rittermann acknowledged the compliment with a smug smile, his pride in his exquisite mistress and baby son immeasurable. 'And Mrs Mayschoss is also an excellent member of staff. Perhaps now you can see why I treasure her services so much, Oberführer. And now, if you'd kindly excuse us, there's a great deal of work awaiting us.'

'But of course, Colonel.'

Windler, fully aware that Rhiannon was Kurt's mistress and little Alexander was his son, watched reflectively as the trio departed. Von Rittermann certainly believed in making hay while the sun still shone for him.

By the beginning of June the baron had managed to get his unimpressed mistress pregnant again. Now promoted to the rank of lieutenant-colonel, Max was far too occupied with his career and family life to raise any serious objections on learning that the child was again not his, leaving a nonplussed Rhiannon to cope with the burden of yet another baby. In the back of her mind was the worry that their much-loved nurse Christa might also become pregnant and leave: she and Heinz had recently married. Although Heinz still lived in barracks, he managed to see his new wife several times a week.

'But you may not get a son this time, Kurt. Don't raise your hopes too high.'

Replying that he didn't mind either way, the baron shrugged and smiled – the idea of a daughter rather appealing to him.

And so the industrious twenty-six-year-old began her third pregnancy. Max's parents delightedly sent their warm congratulations, while Maria and Franz could only resign themselves to another wave of 'Max and Rhiannon this, Max and Rhiannon that' whenever they saw Karl and Elsa. Meanwhile, Konrad von Kleiste and his wife offered to stand as godparents again, without asking who the father was.

Deciding that a daughter would at least be different, Rhiannon chose the name Amber Rhiannon.

'And if it's a boy?' The contented German looked enquiringly at his mistress.

'Oh, I really don't know; perhaps Kurt Siegfried. How does that appeal to you?'

'As it happens, very much indeed . . . as does Amber Rhiannon. What does your husband think of it?'

'Well, he likes it. My in-laws think it's a bit strange, but it appeals to me and that's what counts.'

Christmas 1943 and New Year came and went. Konrad von Kleiste and his mistress, Heinz Kruger and Kurt von Rittermann passed both celebrations at Maison Meredith, just as they had in 1941. A very proud Kurt's obvious devotion to Alex left no-one in any doubt that Rhiannon's youngest son was indeed his child. As the baron sat contentedly on the settee, lovingly playing and talking with his son, a very observant Max looked on with an air of cold indifference. Alexander was now a lively sixteen-month-old toddler, already walking on unsteady feet and learning to put simple sentences together.

Finally making her appearance on 30 March 1944, the silver-grey-eyed tot with crooked little fingers and downy red hair was welcomed into the world on a bitterly cold morning by a German army doctor and nurse, and immediately became heiress to a generous part of her delighted father's fortune – and the inheritor of the entire von Rittermann estate if her brother died before the age of twenty-one or without a male child.

As he had after Alexander's birth, the proud von Rittermann

immediately rushed round to see his new baby, laden down with goodies, and visited every day for the next week, until Rhiannon was strong enough to visit his apartment. Neumann, von Kleiste and Windler, all bearing gifts, likewise visited to congratulate Rhiannon.

'And please don't expect any more children, Kurt. You have two, Max has two and there's a fifth to consider in Cassie. That's quite enough for me.'

'And for me, my love.' The proud new father held his week-old daughter delightedly, forgetting the illness that was now weakening him. 'She's beautiful, Rhiannon. That's right, Alexander, come and look at your baby sister. Isn't she lovely?'

'Yes, Father. Am . . . Am . . .'

'Amber! Say Amber, Alex!' Rhiannon hugged the fair-haired little boy to her. 'Amber! Amber, Mummy!'

His father beamed approvingly. 'Very good, Alexander. And now we're indeed a family. We must call upon the photographer's services yet again to record this happy event.'

Just as enthusiastic in their acceptance of their half-sister, Rhys and Sebastian beamed happily at her as she lay in her mother's arms. 'Why can't she speak, Mummy?'

'Because she hasn't learned how to yet, Rhys.'

'And why has Amber got grey eyes like Alex?'

'Well, there are only so many colours eyes can be, Sebastian.'

'And when is she to be christened, Aunt Rhiannon?' Cassie held out her arms and took the infant carefully.

'Soon, in about seven weeks' time. And what do you think of your great-great-niece, Aunt Alicia?'

'She's delightful, Rhiannon – but I hope you're not planning on any more. Five's enough for anyone.'

Waiting until the four older children were in bed and Christa was out, Alicia asked her great-niece how often the proud father would see his children, now that Rhiannon was taking six months off work.

'Well, during the week Kurt will send the car round at half past one, and we'll all see him at his apartment five days a week. Now that he's not so strong he's had to retire, and his deputy's officially replaced him – so he'll always be there. We'll see him on Saturdays as well, while Max is at his club.'

'I see.' Alicia nodded, silently wondering what Sebastian and Elisabeth Meredith would have made of this unorthodox arrangement. 'Ah well, at least Max seems to have taken to the child. He even held her, minutes after her birth.'

'He's always wanted a daughter, and she's at least half mine . . .'

Rhiannon smiled mysteriously at the puzzled old lady. 'Why worry anyway? When Kurt's dead Max will love Amber. You and I will love Alex, and we all love the twins and Cassie. Everyone's going to feel loved by someone.'

'Quite, my love.' Shaking her head at her infuriating relative, Alicia sighed. 'Good Lord, what a strange set-up we have. Still, we'll not lack for anything in the end, so it could be worse.'

Almost three months later, in May, Elsa died. A devastated Max had received a week's leave before her death to see her for the last time. Welcoming his son home, a heart-broken Karl took him up to where his dying wife lay, her pain-racked eyes lighting up as Max entered the bedroom.

'Max, you've finally come. Are Rhiannon and the children with you?'

'No, Mother. There just wasn't time to bring everyone, but my wife and Alicia send their dearest love. I promised you I'd be here when you really needed me, and here I am.'

'So you are. God bless you.' Elsa smiled though her tears. 'God couldn't have sent me a better son.'

'Nor me a better mother.'

As a deeply moved Karl looked on, Max kept a devoted vigil until her death a few days later. The family priest noted the absence of Maria and Franz with a disapproving frown.

'Well, Father, Maria's had a nervous breakdown, and her husband's health is none too good, so . . .'

'Quite, but when your mother is dying, surely . . .'

Far tougher than Elsa physically, Kurt von Rittermann hung desperately on to life as his illness ravaged him: regular visits from his mistress and two children drove him to fight death till the bitter end. But fate had another nasty shock in store for the Mayschoss family, as a stunned Rhiannon was soon to discover.

Chapter Fourteen

On the morning of 7 June 1944, a date Rhiannon would never forget, she answered the phone – then froze, as Konrad von Kleiste's voice informed her that Max had been badly injured in an explosion. Leading an investigation into the activities of the increasingly bold French Resistance, he had been lured to a booby-trapped warehouse. Max had miraculously survived the blast; most of his colleagues had not. He had immediately been taken to the military hospital, one leg shattered from the knee down.

'When can I visit him, Colonel?'

'Tomorrow, once he's comfortable. I'll telephone in the morning and let you know.'

'Thank you, Colonel.'

Rhiannon sighed heavily and turned to a grim Alicia. 'My poor Max. But at least he's still alive, Aunt. It could have been a lot worse.'

Explaining to Christa and the silent children that Max had had a serious accident, Rhiannon asked the lively twins to make sure they behaved themselves for her and Christa.

'Yes, Mummy. Is Daddy going to be all right?' The anxious three-year-olds looked worriedly at their mother.

'God willing. And before you ask, Cassie, no, you can't come with me to visit Uncle Max tomorrow. Maybe the day after with your brothers, if you're all very quiet and good.'

'And Amber too, Mummy.' Already deeply devoted to his baby sister, the toddler tugged insistently at Rhiannon's dress.

'By all means, Alex. Thank goodness we have you, Christa. I rather doubt we'd manage without you now.'

'Thank you, Mrs Mayschoss.' The German girl glowed under her employer's praise.

Reporting back to the deeply concerned von Rittermann the next day, Rhiannon shook her head sadly. 'Poor Max was heavily drugged, but he seemed to be aware of me. Should the leg refuse to heal it'll have to be amputated, but they expect him to pull through. He's strong and fit.'

'That's excellent news indeed. You and your great-aunt will need him to keep your three boys on the straight and narrow as they grow up. Sons need a father, and your husband will be an ideal father figure for Alexander and Amber once I'm gone. And now let me give you a word of warning, Rhiannon.' Von Rittermann hugged his children to him. 'As soon as Lieutenant-Colonel Mayschoss is fit to travel you and your family must leave France for my estate in Germany. It's only a matter of time before the Allied Forces reach Paris: they landed in Normandy a couple of days ago. Brussels will be the next to fall, and from then on Germany will be trying to keep the Allies out of the Fatherland. You and your great-aunt won't be shown much mercy by the celebrating French once the Allies get here, so you must start your preparations immediately. In all likelihood I'll be dead by then . . . I've also decided that you'd be wise not to go back to work at either Gestapo or Army Headquarters once your maternity leave ends. Your name's been removed from all relevant documents, and your personal files have been destroyed.'

Rhiannon squeezed his hand reassuringly. 'We've already made plans to travel to Celle, so you needn't worry. Have you written your letters to our son and daughter yet?'

'Yes, I have, and I've put together a family biography and a family tree. Tell the children about their true parentage as soon as you feel they're old enough to know, then read them my letters and documents. Here . . . take them and keep them safe.'

'Thank you. Kurt . . . I think I should come to live with you, together with Alex and Amber, until Max is out of hospital. Max is in no state to mind, and as long as I spend a few hours each day with my other children neither will anyone else. I can easily bring a couple of large suitcases with the things we need. Tiger and Bess must come with us as well, I'm afraid.'

Kurt von Rittermann's heart bounded with sheer joy and gratitude. 'What an excellent idea.' He smiled, and kissed his mistress lingeringly on the mouth. 'Just tell me when you need transport and I'll arrange everything with my chauffeur.'

Visiting Max the next day with her brood, Rhiannon found him wide awake and cheerful.

'These are for you, Uncle Max.' Cassie handed him a beautifully designed 'get well soon' card, along with a basket of fruit and a box of his favourite Belgian chocolates. 'I made the card myself, and we've all signed it – even little Amber, but she did need my help.'

Touched by his family's obvious devotion, the young officer smiled affectionately. 'Thank you, sweetheart. I can see that I'm going to be thoroughly spoiled. Perhaps you could bring a newspaper and some books tomorrow, Rhiannon, so I can keep my brain active: now that the painkillers are working I can concentrate on something other than my leg. The doctor's told me that with any luck I'll be out of here in eight to ten weeks. Have you begun to prepare for our departure yet?'

'I've made lists of what we'll be taking with us, or sending on. I've also found a buyer for Maison Meredith, but only at a heavy financial loss.'

'Never mind; we can afford it. And how's our friend?'

'Oh, not too bad. Battling his illness with his usual fierce determination.'

'Are you coming in to see me tomorrow, or is Alicia?'

'I am, of course. You'll have family visits every day, as well as visitors from Abwehr Headquarters, of that you may rest assured.'

By the fourth week it was clear that, semi-crippled as Max's leg would remain, the threat of amputation was over.

'Thank goodness for that.' Rhiannon hugged him impulsively. 'Your father's going to be all right, children.'

'When are you coming home, Daddy?' Rhys looked wistfully at his father.

'As soon as the doctor says I can, but we'll not be staying in Paris. We're going to Celle in Germany, where we'll be living in a magnificent old house, just like a castle. Sebastian, Cassie, Alex, come closer and look at this photograph. This is where we'll be living from the middle of August.'

'Oh, Daddy, it's so big. Will we be able to play in the park?'

'You will indeed, Sebastian. And we can all explore the forest for wild animals and go riding, not to mention travelling to church in a fine old carriage. We're going to be very comfortable indeed.'

Almost six weeks later, on 20 July, the army bomb plot failed to kill Adolf Hitler – the Führer merely being left in a state of shock. Immediately issuing whole lists of high-ranking army officers to be arrested, tortured and executed, the enraged leader left the Gestapo in complete authority over the army, and everything Max had feared would happen came to pass. For himself there was no danger, since Windler, Head of the Paris Gestapo, at his former deputy's special request, had promptly crossed

Max's name off the list of officers to be arrested. Also at von Rittermann's request, he had tried to prevent Colonel von Kleiste's removal to Berlin for questioning, but could not – although he managed to obtain a promise that the colonel would be released within a week.

Duly released as promised, a battered and bruised Konrad von Kleiste, his body aching from the intense torture he had suffered, was met by his wife and daughter, then taken home to recover in the peace of his beloved mansion at Bamberg, in his native Bavaria. Knowing full well who was behind his miraculous escape, the grateful colonel instructed his wife Luise to send an invitation to the Mayschoss family to spend two weeks with them that September, taking care to sign it himself: 'With many thanks for all you have done for me, Rhiannon. Your devoted friend, Konrad.'

For Kurt von Rittermann, time finally ran out on 2 August 1944 as he lay in his apartment, surrounded by his devoted family. Assured by Rhiannon that all preparations had been completed for her family's departure, and that Max was to be discharged from hospital within a week, the ghostly invalid smiled weakly. 'Good. The sooner you leave Paris the better. Although I don't want you and our children to attend my funeral, it would give me great happiness to think that you'll visit my grave at Celle every week. My spirit will faithfully watch over you all in my ancestral home; I don't intend to leave you in death. And now, before I slip away, come and sit by me, Rhiannon, and bring my children so I can be with you all to the end.'

'Come here, Alex. Your father wants to see you. He's going to heaven very soon.' Placing the tearful little boy close by Kurt's side, and holding Amber near to him, Rhiannon took her lover's wasted hand and held it firmly. 'Everything I've promised you I'll do will be done. And as long as I, my husband and my great-aunt live, Alex's and Amber's inheritance will be safeguarded and your estate managed with as much skill as we can muster. I'll see that both our children are protected and loved, and that their lives are much happier than yours was. I love you deeply, Kurt. God bless you, and may the Lord have mercy on your soul. Say goodbye to your father, Alex. This is probably the last time you and Amber will see him in this life.'

'Goodbye, Daddy. I love you so very much.' The heartbroken Alex clung to his father convulsively, his baby sister joining in with his sobs.

Feeling himself drifting away, the dying man gazed at his grieving family, his silver-grey eyes intense. 'And I love you all deeply too, my beloved boy . . . I always have and I always will.'

With that he was gone.

Rhiannon kept a vigil by her lover's side through the night, not leaving him until the next morning. Before departing, she cut three locks of greying hair from his head, packed up two of his spare uniforms, some of his favourite books and records, and all his more personal possessions in a couple of suitcases, not forgetting their framed family portraits. The methodical red-head collected all her luggage together, informed the valet and live-in nurse that the colonel was no more, and rang the chauffeur to ask to be taken home, also reminding him that he was to take her and her family to the military hospital at nine on the morning of the 11th, then to the railway station. 'And having done all that you may expect a very generous tip indeed.'

'Yes, Mrs Mayschoss, and thank you.' Taking the proffered high value banknote with alacrity, the driver hastened to carry out her orders, quite sure that the next tip would be well worth waiting for.

Chapter Fifteen

Take a last look at Maison Meredith before we leave it for ever.' Standing with the now-pregnant Christa, Rhiannon and the five children, their luggage at their feet, Alicia squeezed her pensive great-niece's hand sympathetically. 'We've all been very happy here, I know, but the good times in Paris are over and our future lies in Germany. Even poor Christa has to leave her beloved husband behind, something which grieves her very much, I know.'

The young red-head nodded sadly, still haunted by Kurt's death only three days before. As the large black Mercedes-Benz belonging to his successor and a second car generously provided by Ulrich Windler drove up to the house, she said gratefully, 'Still, at least we don't have to run the gauntlet of our neighbours on foot. I rather doubt we'd have managed to get past.'

After their drivers had stowed all the cases safely away, Rhiannon climbed into the first car, observing their neighbours' hate-filled faces and not remotely surprised by the vicious insults hurled in her wake. 'Whore, indeed! I'm a respectable married woman.'

The old lady laughed. 'Oh, I wouldn't take any notice, my love. You should have heard the dreadful names my parents called me when I refused to marry Lord St Clair and eloped instead. You're certainly not the first Meredith female who's flouted society's moral conventions, and you'll certainly not be the last.'

'There's Max.' Approaching the military hospital, they halted to collect the young man. Helped in by two nurses, he quipped humorously, 'Very impressive, Rhiannon. It's not often that a crippled army officer is ferried about in style by the Gestapo.'

Wedged between Alicia and Christa, Cassie stroked the two big dogs and relaxed against the soft leather upholstery. 'It's really luxurious in here. Wouldn't it be nice to travel back to Germany like this?'

Max shook with laughter. 'It would indeed, young lady, but I'm afraid you'll have to settle for a first class railway carriage like the rest of us. We won't be coming back to Paris for a long time now, so take a good last look.'

Reaching the station, the chauffeurs left the family and their luggage at the main entrance.

'Now all we need is a porter.' Carrying Amber in her arms, with Alex and the ever faithful Tiger and Bess in attendance, Rhiannon went to find one, while Alicia quietly asked Max if he knew that his name had been erased from the list of officers to be arrested, thanks to von Rittermann.

The Abwehr officer nodded. 'I hated the idea of Rhiannon sleeping with him and bearing him a son, but had she refused, my commanding officer and I would be dead now. I can't believe how lucky we are. Even my accident's turned out to be a blessing in disguise, as it's given us the excuse to leave Paris before the axe falls.'

Alicia smiled brightly. 'Ah, here's Rhiannon at last with a porter. Now all we need to do is get on that train.'

Chapter Sixteen

Celle, 17 August 1944

Dear Konrad,

I have so much to tell you that I scarcely know where to begin; but first I must thank you again for your kind invitation to stay with you for a fortnight. We will of course be delighted to accept, and Max is furthermore determined that his being on crutches will not prevent us from coming by train. Incidentally, he's proving to be surprisingly agile on them, and manoeuvres his way round Von Rittermann House and the estate with considerable ease.

Our journey to Celle was not without problems, and was also rather sad; even our four elder children commented on the many bombed-out buildings we passed. We also got caught in a very heavy air-raid while we were staying overnight at Lieges, but simply made our way down to the underground shelter with everyone else. Fortunately Max had the authority to insist that our dogs remain with us, because there was no way Great Aunt Alicia and I would have left our beloved pets behind. During the bombing raid the children and animals were very frightened, but we all huddled together in the dark and prayed as the bombs rained down overhead. We made it back to our hotel afterwards, and found to our relief that it was still standing and completely undamaged, unlike many other buildings around it. And then we reached our final destination after many other adventures, which we'll describe when we see you. The children were very well behaved throughout the journey, and seem to have grown up overnight. All the heavier and bulkier items that I sent on ahead arrived safely, and in good condition too, which was indeed a relief.

And now for our family news, which has surprised and delighted us. Firstly Karl, Max's father, has remarried, much to our great astonishment. His new wife, who was a good friend of his late wife, is called Anna Mayrhoffen. She's fifty-two years old, and lost her first husband and two unmarried sons at the Siege of Stalingrad in January 1943. As if that wasn't enough, Max's sister Maria had her home reduced to rubble during a raid on Düsseldorf, so she and her husband are now living with her father and stepmother at Kassel, as are two orphaned great-nephews and a great-niece of Karl's – so Maria and Franz have now got three children of ten, eight and six to care for. My father-in-law has a very large garden which he's turned over to fruit and vegetables – something to be grateful for as food shortages worsen and official rations become ever more meagre. Fortunately for us, Von Rittermann house has its own large farm, so even though the estate is heavily populated at the moment we're not going to starve, thank goodness.

I must tell you about our baronial estate. It consists of a private wood, a forest and a spacious park, not to mention a charming Italian garden, a small lake, folly and summer-house. There's a large stable block, many large barns, some paddocks, pastures, an orchard, four large and modern laundry blocks and the farm that I've already mentioned. As for the house itself, well, the most one can say is that it's absolutely huge. It's an army base and a hospital now, but part of one wing has been reserved for us. Stripped of all its fine furniture and artefacts the mansion looks quite bare, but it's a magnificent sight even so. Obviously Kurt had all the expensive furnishings stored away for safe-keeping, but our suite of ten interconnecting rooms in the military wing has been refurnished just as they would have been when Kurt and his family lived there, and our six bedrooms are all en suite. The remaining four rooms have, at our request, been converted into a dining room, sitting room, library-cum-study and family kitchen, so we can all live in some degree of comfort and privacy, with a sense of not being under each other's feet all the time. All the paintings, books and other possessions that we sent on from Paris have been installed now.

The house consists of two separate wings, each with a large kitchen, dining room, two drawing rooms and many bedrooms. There are also a library, banqueting hall, study, music room, school room and private chapel, and in the west wing there's a truly breathtaking long gallery, where all the von Rittermann portraits are hung. This is being used as a hospital ward, like most of the other rooms, while the library, school room and study are being used as offices by the army. The grounds are crawling with military personnel, as is the house itself – but we have our own little haven so we don't mind at all. All our meals, laundry and cleaning are done by the military domestic staff, so life is quite relaxing and carefree. The children absolutely adore exploring the spacious grounds, with the three little boys racing around like lunatics, then coming in for their meals exhausted but very happy.

We travel to church in the impressive, if

somewhat old-fashioned landau, complete with army driver. I've also discovered a quaint little dogcart in the stables which will be ideal for me to take Cassie to school and go shopping, and will permit my husband to explore the estate without tiring him too much. We're riding as well. Cassie is learning, and the three boys will soon. They and little Amber really love coming up in the saddle with me and my great-aunt and trotting round the grounds – Alex already assuming a most proud and dignified air as he travels on horse-back or by carriage. Max has nicknamed him 'the little baron' and calls Amber his 'little princess'. That Max loves Amber as his own daughter is beyond doubt, with Cassie and the twins likewise very dear to him. He only has a difficult relationship with Alex, who prefers to be with me, Aunt Alicia and Christa – but curiously not Cassie, who's excellent, however, with the other three children. Alex adores his baby sister, but avoids his two boisterous half-brothers like the plague. As you can see, we have rather a complicated family set-up here.

Fortunately Alex has his own bedroom, as do the twins, so we manage to keep them separate for at least part of the day. Max tends to take refuge in the study when the children become too much for him and he craves some peace and quiet. But we're all deeply grateful that we have a secure roof over our heads.

Max has already been promised a good position in the administration department here, once he's fit to work again. He's very pleased, as you can well imagine.

Personally I'm just glad still to have my cherished Max, and to be alive myself. Our family's safe and wants for nothing, thanks to Kurt, while you've survived and been released from Gestapo custody, Konrad, so I'm content. It's rather nice too that Maria has three young children to care for, while Karl has his family around him and has found a new wife. So, war

or no war, we can all find some joy in our lives
if we look hard enough.
Looking forward to seeing you both soon,
Your ever devoted Rhiannon

Seven days later, luxuriously installed on a chaise longue with her five
children, a glass of wine in her hand and the two dogs lying at her feet,
Rhiannon, elegantly attired in a black and green taffeta dress, sat talking
cheerfully with Baron von Kleiste and his wife. Nearby, Max, Alicia and
Christa chatted with some of the colonel's relatives, his mansion packed
out with family members who had been bombed out of their homes and
forced to seek shelter with Konrad and Luise. One of these was his only
grandson, Otto von Kleiste, at present observing the pretty little girl with
the glossy chestnut curls with great interest. He already knew that
Cassandra's adoptive mother had saved his grandfather's life through her
direct influence with von Rittermann. Fully aware of the youngster's
attention, the girl in the red velvet dress and white shoes smiled sweetly
back, rather taken with the good-looking fair-haired boy sitting with his
mother and two sisters.

'Dinner is served, Baron.'

Bowing deferentially, the butler departed, and the guests filed into the
white and gold dining room. Konrad led Rhiannon into dinner, while
Max, walking skilfully with the aid of crutches, accompanied the lady of
the house. Behind them came Alicia and Christa with the children, a six-
month-old Amber gazing around in wide-eyed fascination from her great-
great-aunt's arms.

'I want to stay with you, Mummy.' Somehow managing to position
himself next to his beloved mother at the table, Alex glanced uneasily at
Max, then beamed at Rhiannon, his silver-grey eyes triumphant.

'That's not fair. He always gets to sit next to Mummy.' Rhys scowled
at his proudly disdainful half-brother.

Sebastian added resentfully, 'And he always tries to push us out.'

'That's quite enough, all of you. Now eat your dinner and
behave.' Max glowered at the squabbling boys, his stern expression
quelling any further argument. An amused von Kleiste nodded
approvingly at his wife, both aware of how strikingly the late Kurt von
Rittermann's son resembled him, both in looks and character. Amber,
though, appeared to take more after her mother, her fiery red locks
and exuberant personality clearly marking her out as Rhiannon's
daughter. Only the child's tell-tale silver-grey eyes and crooked little
fingers hinted at her true paternity – something which troubled her
besotted stepfather not at all, such was his devotion to this charming
and vivacious little girl.

Far too interested in each other to take any notice of this squabble, Otto and Cassie chatted animatedly. 'So what's it like at Celle, Cassandra? What's it like living in a hospital?'

'Oh, it's not just a hospital. We've got our own rooms, and besides, it's rather nice chatting to the patients. Aunt Rhiannon takes us round the wards every week to cheer everyone up the inmates, and they all like to see us.'

Otto nodded. 'How do you fancy a walk in the park after coffee?'

'Oh, very much. As long as I'm allowed, of course.' The seven-year-old smiled delightedly, then started on her dessert of stewed apple and cream, her polished table manners and lady-like deportment a far cry from her rough demeanour just four years before.

It was a shock for Otto to hear about Cassie's parentage, and her upbringing in a filthy Parisian slum. She had decided that he should know the truth about her, even if she risked losing him as a friend. Having explained to the stunned young aristocrat that his grandparents knew all about her past, Cassie continued, 'I'll understand if you feel I'm not good enough to talk to now, or have as a friend, but at least you know now. Will you still speak to me, Otto?'

For a moment the confused youngster stared ahead, before deciding that since his grandparents had accepted her socially it would be quite all right for him to do so. He nodded. 'Of course I will, Cassandra. Of course we can be friends. What happened to you isn't your fault.'

Cassie smiled wistfully, a hopeful look in her troubled eyes. 'Do you really mean that? You're not just being polite? Aunt Rhiannon and Great-Aunt Alicia would be so upset if they knew I'd told you.'

'I do mean it, and I won't tell anyone.' Otto squeezed her small hand reassuringly, smiling warmly. 'Come on, I'll race you to the lake.'

'All right – but you're so much older and taller than me.'

Keeping up surprisingly well, the slightly built young girl finished just seconds behind Otto, her curls in a state of tangled disorder. 'Oh dear, what a mess I must look now.'

'Not at all. I think you're even prettier.' Otto regarded his delightful companion seriously, then added jokingly, 'We'd better not fall in the water, though, or we'll both look like drowned rats, and we'd get into terrible trouble. What do you want to do now? Go to the stables?'

'Oh, yes please. I love horses. I'm learning to ride.' Cassie beamed at her new friend, and followed him contentedly.

Chapter Seventeen

Three days into their stay Rhiannon, getting ready for bed, grinned wickedly at her husband. 'Well, what does it feel like mixing with the aristocracy?'

'It's certainly not an experience I'll forget in a hurry.' Max stretched luxuriously in the four-poster bed and yawned. 'You, Alicia and Christa are really lapping it up, aren't you? And Cassandra appears to have found an ardent admirer in Otto von Kleiste.'

'And why not, pray?' The glamorous red-head bounced into bed beside him. 'Cassie's a delightful young lady. As Alexander and Amber will have to learn how to mix with the nobility, we will too.'

'Yes, your ladyship.' Pulling his strong-willed wife close, the amused Max regarded her affectionately.

'You're a witch, Rhiannon . . . a beautiful and captivating witch.'

'Then just be careful that I don't turn you into a frog.'

Her husband kissed her lingeringly and looked down at her maliciously smiling upturned face. 'God knows, Colonel von Rittermann certainly met his match in you. As have I, perhaps, but I love you more than any woman I've ever known. Maybe that's why I care for Amber so deeply – because she reminds me so much of you.'

By the end of the first week Rhiannon and her family had become firm friends with their hosts' daughter Sophia and daughter-in-law Katharine, as well as numerous other von Kleiste relations. Konrad's son and son-in-law, Peter von Kleiste and Klaus von Reinholdt, were both high-ranking officers in the army abroad. Sophia was the proud mother of two daughters, three-year-old Hanna and Charlotte, just a year old; while her sister-in-law had three children: Otto was twelve and a half, Emma seven and Adelaide five. Rhiannon and her family were regarded with great interest by the von Kleiste clan, it being common knowledge among them that Alexander and Amber were the late Baron von Rittermann's children.

Always seeking to further her family's interests, Luise smiled shrewdly at her thoughtful husband. 'They're a very well-bred family, you know. Wealthy, educated . . . well worth taking into account once our four granddaughters attain marriageable age. Perhaps we'll secure young Alexander as a husband for Hanna or Charlotte. At the moment Hanna seems to prefer Rhys, and he her. And Amber would make a suitable match for one of our younger relatives – especially once she takes her father's surname at eighteen, and become an official part of the German nobility.'

Meanwhile, Otto and Cassie had become totally inseparable, much to their families' great amusement – no-one for the moment suspecting that their innocent friendship was to develop into something far deeper and more intense as the next few years passed and the Mayschoss and von Kleiste families began to visit each other several times a year.

Finally managing, at the end of the second week, to join Rhiannon on one of her walks in the grounds without Max, Luise or the children present, Colonel von Kleiste chatted comfortably with his good friend and discussed old times in Paris. Rhiannon commented regretfully, 'Kurt did his very best to try to prevent your arrest, but he lacked sufficient authority to succeed. Even so, he managed to secure your release after a week. Having witnessed just how brutal the Gestapo can be, I know you'll have suffered terribly in Berlin.'

'Well, let's just say that had he not managed to get me out of custody when he did, I wouldn't have survived much more.' The grey-haired nobleman looked grimly at his saviour, and frowned. 'God bless you, Rhiannon, for getting your lover to agree to me and my family being included in your protection deal. As a high-ranking officer and member of the aristocracy I honestly never thought that I'd need such protection, but I was wrong.' He gripped her hand and kissed it passionately. 'Words can't express my gratitude, but you may rest assured that I'll never forget your kindness as long as I live.'

'Some good's obviously come from me breaking my marriage vows. I'm very glad, Konrad.' She smiled pensively. 'Max was kept informed of everything throughout my relationship with Kurt, but he was still intensely jealous – even though he knew it was all for his and our family's protection, not to mention yours too. As you're both well aware I'm quite unable to tell a convincing lie, or deceive anyone, so honesty's always been my policy, however difficult or unpleasant it may be. Having said that, I'll certainly not be telling the truth if Germany lose the war and I'm questioned about my role in Kurt's official duties. Even I can keep quiet sometimes. I certainly don't want to be arrested as an enemy collaborator.'

'Should that occur, you may count on my unconditional public support and whatever aid I can give you.' The baron nodded seriously at his companion.

Returning home a day or two later, the Mayschoss family observed the failing German war effort with foreboding, the adults taking great care not to show their worries in front of the children.

Cassie, however, had worries of her own. Her first day at school was suddenly upon her, and Rhiannon could only give a second-hand description of how it might feel – as her father, Sebastian, after suffering a wretchedly lonely and unhappy time at boarding school, arranged for Rhys and Rhiannon to be educated at home by the finest private tutors. Only then had he sent the twins to study at York University – although he still insisted that they lived at home. It was during those long years that his two cherished children, having returned to their father's native North Yorkshire as toddlers in 1918, first fell under the influence of Magda Brading, the fifty-two-year-old widow of Sebastian's best friend and confidant.

From the first time she had set eyes on the affectionate and sunny red-headed twins, the besotted and maternal Magda had instinctively taken the place of their often absent mother, Elisabeth. Sebastian, seeing just how attached his children were to his super-efficient housekeeper and how much she loved them, had appointed her as their governess. Between their lessons the inquisitive twins accompanied the bustling older woman as she went about her domestic duties. Had she been of a more maternal nature herself, their mother would undoubtedly have objected to being ousted from her role, but she much preferred to pursue her career in nursing: the idea of staying at home as a meek wife and devoted mother did not appeal to her in the least – something her husband accepted with a shrug and others found quite appalling. Never having felt comfortable with her own children while they were young, Elisabeth only really learned to relate to them, or understand them, as they passed from childhood to young adulthood.

The inevitable result of this family arrangement was that Rhys and his sister grew up with a fiercely pro-German attitude in a country that bitterly hated the Germans after the Great War, and came to love Germany and German culture as if it was their own. Many a passer-by, recognising the Merediths' German housekeeper out for a stroll on Scarborough's beaches with the twins and the family's dogs would cast a look of hatred at the foreigner, only to be told by an enraged Rhys and Rhiannon to take their narrow-minded and typically English foreign prejudice elsewhere and to leave their beloved Magda alone. Sebastian meanwhile, something of an lover of Germany himself, with a great many good friends in that country, merely smiled when his children's unpatriotic stance was criticised, and stated firmly that Magda had every right to be left in peace by the good folk of North Yorkshire – and to be treated with respect. Elisabeth was delighted to have found a pearl of a housekeeper and such a trustworthy governess, so she preferred not to interest herself in the matter. All this, related by a decidedly naïve Rhiannon to a thoughtful Max, von Kleiste and von Rittermann, was then used quite cynically in their exploitation of her: Magda's earlier influence made it unbelievably easy to woo Rhiannon over to their side.

In the end it was Max who talked a panic-stricken Cassie out of her understandable fear of starting school, and being away from her family. He told her that she would be introduced to her teacher, and then, in the company of her godparents, would be given a guided tour of the school by the headmaster. There was no need to be afraid; nothing to fear at all. She would certainly make some wonderful new friends, and could even invite them home for tea if she liked. And, unlike Rhiannon's unfortunate father, she would never be sent away to boarding school, but would be able to return home every day. All this succeeded in reducing poor Cassie's terror.

When her first day at school arrived, Cassie was relatively calm. She nervously sat down at her allotted desk for a short and friendly introduction by her teacher. Even the other children, she found, were not the fearsome ogres she had imagined them to be: they were just children like herself. Some were friendly at playtime, which helped her to relax. They seemed very surprised to hear that she and her family lived at Von Rittermann House, and – as time passed – were delighted to accept her invitations to tea. For the apprehensive Cassie, life began to blossom. Her new-found friends were dazzled by her magnificent residence, but were still more than happy to invite her back to their decidedly less impressive homes. Soon Cassie came to love beautiful old Celle and its friendly townsfolk.

As the long dark war dragged on, Germany's problems continued to worsen. The population started to feel the very real effects of starvation, bitter cold and homelessness, and the largest cities were systematically bombed until only blackened and morale-destroying ruins remained.

By winter 1944 the Allies were advancing through the Ardennes, which became a confused battlefield. Launching a new attack, the Germans were on a temporary roll, and the army tenaciously resisted the

Allied drive into the Fatherland – exhorted by an increasingly unstable Adolf Hitler to fight to the bitter end. But March 1945 saw the Americans at the Rhine, and at the end of April Berlin was being threatened by the Russians. The bombing of Germany had intensified, and shortages of everything from food to fuel had reached crisis point. Finally occupying a ruined Berlin, where the defeated Führer committed suicide, the victorious Soviet army continued its relentless drive through Germany, panicking civilians fleeing in its path. A grim Max predicted that it would not be long before the struggling German army would be forced into surrendering – a prophecy soon fulfilled by the devastating news of surrender in early May.

Chapter Eighteen

In December 1945 a shattered Hanover lay in ruins, seventy per cent of the once prosperous city destroyed. Germany was under Allied rule, the Russians, Americans, French and British each having their own sectors of influence. Bamberg and Baron von Kleiste's estate were in the American zone, while Celle, in Northern Germany, lay under British rule. The dreadful secret of the Nazi death camps had been revealed to a shocked world, and a ruthless policy of de-Nazification within Germany and Austria was in full swing: all members of the SD, SS and Gestapo were hauled in for interrogation, and put on trial for war crimes.

People in rural areas still had food and homes, at least, but towns and cities throughout the former Third Reich were in varying states of destruction. Life was hard indeed, with the population living in a state of utter poverty and hunger in the ruins of their homes. Selling themselves for food, cigarettes and anything else they could cadge, the women and girls latched on to the Allied armies, and waited patiently outside their occupiers' billets for anything going begging. Winter, of course, brought even more suffering, with the Soviet army now wreaking a particularly vicious revenge; the French too had old scores to settle. The American and British zones were undoubtedly the best places to be – the Anglo Saxon races treating their beaten enemy far more fairly.

Deciding to see Hanover's state of destruction for themselves one bitterly cold day, a week before Christmas, a grim-faced Max and Rhiannon, their sleek black dogs at their side, surveyed the dismal ruins lining the route back to the now operational railway station with a sense of utter despair. Frowning at the sight of a burned-out church, Max said

101

sadly, 'We were warned about the vast scale of the destruction, but until you see it for yourself it's impossible to visualise it. It'll take years to rebuild our country, Rhiannon.'

'I know. But as none of us wanted this war, only Adolf Hitler and his cronies, we've no need to feel guilty. At least we've come through it safely.'

Max suddenly noticed a group of British Tommies ogling his lovely wife, and stiffened resentfully, recent memories of Kurt von Rittermann still fresh in his mind. Fiercely possessive, the deeply jealous young man steered his wife towards home, his blue eyes burning with an intense fury.

The Mayschoss household celebrated a quiet but still festive Christmas. On Christmas Eve Christa gave birth to a fine baby girl, whom she named Herta – wishing with all her heart that Heinz could have been there to see his beautiful daughter.

Karl and his family came to visit on the 28th. Stunned by the sheer size and magnificence of Max and Rhiannon's new home, he and his relatives could only speculate why von Rittermann had legally adopted Alexander and Amber, and bequeathed them everything. Max and Rhiannon said as little as possible about Rhiannon's relationship with the baron, and nothing at all about the two children's paternity.

'Ah well – it's certainly provided you all with a fine house.' An envious Franz looked at his in-laws with a puzzled expression – sensing, like Karl and Maria, that there was far more to the strange situation than met the eye.

Maria herself said nothing; her brother's good fortune made her hate him and his gracious wife all the more. True, he had suffered a crippling injury, and would always need the aid of a walking stick, but knowing Maximilian he would soon bounce back. In fact, if it were not for her own three adopted children . . . the dark-haired woman smiled fondly at the orphaned youngsters that she and Franz now regarded as their own, and coldly turned her back on her younger brother.

Rhiannon, who visited the magnificent von Rittermann mausoleum at Celle's cemetery every week with Amber and Alex, had begun to feel Kurt's vibrant and intense presence in the stately old mansion: she heard his voice softly calling her name and felt his gentle caresses, while the two fascinated children often smiled happily at a benevolent figure that whispered fondly to them, lovingly caressing their hair. The serious Alex and his vivacious but sensitive sister soon came to accept and welcome this familiar, friendly and comforting presence, Alex in particular immediately linking it with his beloved 'Daddy Kurt', who had been so very ill and had gone to heaven. A worried Rhiannon hoped that they were the only ones who were aware of the spirit, and soon realised that this was the case. Only the three dogs sometimes looked askance at this strange presence as it stood near to Rhiannon and her contented youngsters.

The old year passed. January 1946 was ushered in with a bitter spell of freezing wintry weather, and a growing sense of gnawing hunger, cold and despair for the destitute inhabitants of the ruined cities. Far more fortunate were the Mayschoss and von Kleiste families, who began to look forward to better times for their beloved Germany. The only clouds on their horizon were the fates of Peter von Kleiste, his brother-in-law Klaus, and Heinz. Peter and Klaus were incarcerated in an American POW camp, while Heinz was a British POW. Baron von Kleiste was able to send his relations regular parcels and letters, while Christa exchanged letters with her imprisoned love, the lonely soldier studying the pictures of his wife and child with a deep joy and hope. All, though, were well aware that it might be years before the families were reunited.

Chapter Nineteen

The next five years rolled swiftly by. Gradually the French, British and American occupied zones of the former Third Reich were steadily rebuilt, the Russian zone remaining in a state of poverty and relative devastation. All the while Rhiannon and Max watched their thriving brood grow – all of them active and intelligent. The five youngsters showed great promise in their studies, Alex in the sciences, the twins in mathematics and little Amber in languages and the performing arts – her passion for acting and dancing already evident. Often, dressed as a fairy or in some other fancy dress, she would fling herself into Max's arms and ask if he liked her outfit. Totally besotted, Max would hug her tight. Cassie, on the other hand, he was always a little afraid of hugging, not because he didn't love her but because of her early upbringing: would she interpret physical affection as potential abuse? Cassie eventually sensed this – and finally put an end to his concerns by saying that she completely trusted him: there was no need to back off, no need to fear her reaction. From that moment on she happily received her fair share of hugs and kisses.

Alex, however, received no physical affection from his stepfather, and scant notice. Max knew in his heart that this was totally unjust, but he could neither help himself nor stop seeing an arrogant von Rittermann in the innocent child.

By now split into two opposing camps, Max's sons and the von Rittermann siblings faced each other uneasily. Cassie, ever the free spirit, flitted from one faction to the other. Alex was the only one with whom she did not really get on, but Amber and the older girl were as thick as thieves, much to the boy's disgust. Well aware, however, that his spirited younger sister was a strong and loyal ally in his verbal battles with the tightly knit and aggressive Rhys and Sebastian, the young baron-to-be reluctantly tolerated the sisters' close friendship. Unable to understand his father's obvious preference for the other four children over himself, Alex clung to his adored and warm-hearted mother and kind great-great-aunt Alicia.

'I'm sorry, Rhiannon, but I think it's time Alex learned the truth about his father. This means that Amber has to be told too, as well as the twins and Cassie; but they're all old enough now.'

Rhiannon glanced up at her aunt, and nodded slowly before turning to her husband. 'What do you think, Max? Perhaps it'll improve relations between you and Alex. As for your little princess, well, she'll have to be told one day that the man she loves so much as her real father is actually her stepfather. Besides, once Alex knows the truth he might begin to understand your attitude towards him.'

'By all means – go ahead and tell the boy. But I'd appreciate it if you'd let me speak to Amber myself while you explain everything to Alex, and show him his father's letter.' Max paused. 'There's something else we need to discuss. Amber's told me about her and Alex's spirit friend, "Daddy Kurt", who no one else can see except you. What's going on? Are you really seeing Kurt von Rittermann's ghost?'

'Well, yes, in a manner of speaking.' Rhiannon glanced apprehensively at a silent Alicia. 'This is his ancestral home, and spirits are often drawn home after death. He doesn't bother anyone, and I don't think there's any harm in his presence. Once Alex knows that it's his father he'll be delighted, whereas Amber will just accept the situation as she usually does.'

'Very true. Now – there's no time like the present. If you could give me Amber's letter and some of the photographs her father took I'll go and have a chat with her while you talk to Alex.'

'Of course . . .'

Rhiannon went to collect together the albums that her lover had compiled, deciding there and then that only Alex, whose discretion she could rely on, would be allowed to see his father's uniform, which she treasured as a precious memento. As for the lock of his greying fair hair, his personal possessions and papers, well, it was safe enough for Amber to see those, along with the will, von Rittermann family documents and pictures.

After handing Max the letter, half the leather-bound volumes and the envelope containing the lock of hair, she went to seek out her youngest son, whom she found in the library, his nose in a book.

'Hello, Alex. We've got to have a little chat . . . about your father. No, not Max, but your and Amber's real father. Baron Kurt von Rittermann; "Daddy Kurt" to you. He died in August 1944, and you may still have some distant memories of him. Amber's with your stepfather at the moment, and he's explaining everything to her. First, though, it's important that you understand that while Amber is your sister, Rhys and Sebastian are only your half-brothers.'

A surprised Alex relaxed. 'That's good. I really can't stand either of them, or Cassie for that matter. Well . . . what was my real father like, Mother?'

'He's the spirit who's present with us in this room even now. When your father died he promised me that he'd watch over us, and he's kept his word. Nor need you worry about keeping his presence here a secret: Amber's told your stepfather all about her mysterious friend. This is your father, Alex: these pictures taken in his office at Gestapo Headquarters . . . and these at his apartment. Don't you remember visiting a tall officer in a grey uniform . . . this gentleman here . . . and being called his beloved boy? He loved me, you and your sister deeply. When he died of cancer aged only fifty we were all at his deathbed. Can you recall anything at all? I know you were only twenty-three months old, but . . .'

'Maybe, Mother. I'm not really sure . . .' The boy shook his head, then solemnly took from her hand the sealed letter bearing his name.

'This is the letter your father left for you after his death. There's one for Amber too. Max is going to read Amber's to her, but you can read this yourself if you want to, or I'll read it to you if you'd prefer that.'

Replying that he would much prefer the latter, Alex snuggled down with his mother in the comfortable old leather armchair, aware of the intensely powerful male presence standing close by. 'My father . . . so you're the spirit of my real father, whose grave we visit every Sunday. And you'll never leave me . . .' Alex smiled pensively at the phantom, then, breaking its heavy red wax seal, passed the letter to his mother and listened in reverent silence as she started to read, her voice shaking with emotion.

Paris, mid-June 1944

My dearest Alexander,
    By the time you see this I will be long gone. Please read my letter to the end before coming to any conclusions, since every story has two sides to it. I'm quite sure that your dear mother will be scrupulously fair towards me when she describes to you the events leading up to your birth and those following it. I'm

your real father: Baron Kurt Alexander von Rittermann.

Since I've already written you a detailed account of my own and my family's history, I don't intend to waste precious time with that now. Instead I'll try to put into words the feelings I have for you, Amber and your mother. From the moment I first set eyes on her in June 1940 at the grand reception at Paris's magnificent Town Hall, I knew that I had finally found the girl I wished to make my baroness, the mother of my children, and spend the rest of my life with. At the time she was standing with your stepfather and his commanding officer, Colonel von Kleiste – your godfather. After a long conversation with this exquisitely beautiful and charismatic young woman, it was quite apparent that your stepfather and the colonel were very keen to see the back of me. Silently vowing to secure this charming red-headed beauty as my wife, I reluctantly left her with the captain.

Alas, winning your mother as my wife was not meant to be. Even if I had succeeded in detaching her from your stepfather, who was living in her home and clearly had a great advantage over me regarding her courtship, my early death would have robbed me of any long-term happiness with her, you and my cherished Amber.

As you and your sister grow up you'll hear many people describe me as an evil war criminal, who committed horrific acts of cruelty. I do not deny that I was responsible for overseeing the torture and execution of numerous members of the French Resistance, and I'm not in the least bit ashamed of this. On the contrary, I was doing my duty towards my beloved Fatherland and Führer, and obeying orders.

When your stepfather finally married the lovely girl I wanted as my own wife, I could only look on with envy and resignation as they went on to have two healthy sons, while I had neither spouse nor offspring of my own. My childless marriage had ended in acrimonious divorce many years before. Then in September 1941, having been diagnosed with prostate cancer, I determined to secure a son and heir to my title, vast fortune and estate, which you, my beloved boy, are to inherit at the age of twenty-one. Your sister will likewise inherit a fortune of her own, and both of you will officially take my surname (and you my title) aged eighteen. Since I could not marry your mother and legitimise you that way, I legally adopted you instead, as well as acknowledging you both as my natural children in my last will and testament.

As I watch my loyal and adored Rhiannon caring devotedly for you and your baby sister, I know that she will love you as my uncaring mother never loved me. The worthy Lieutenant-Colonel Mayschoss will make an excellent substitute father for you and Amber, and whatever your feelings towards him may be later on he is to be respected and obeyed at all times. He stands, along with your mother and Madame Reynard, as a trusted guardian of your inheritance. Once you and your sister come into your majority I hope you will continue to listen to and follow your mother's and stepfather's wise advice. One does not know everything at twenty-one, in spite of what you may both think at the time.

As the days pass I grow ever weaker, and were it not for the blessed company of you all my last weeks on earth would be wretched indeed. I have been blessed in my little family, even if I have only had the great joy of being with you for such a short time, and at the end of my life. The day your mother finally consented to be mine and to bear my child was for me the start of a new and undreamed-of happiness, and after you and Amber were born I knew that my life had not been totally in vain.

Be a credit to me and your mother, Alexander. Study hard at school and university and make a success of your life. As you get older always choose your friends and associates with great care. Try to avoid anyone who might lead you astray. In short, be a son of whom we can both be proud, and, whatever people may say about me, never be ashamed of having me as a father. Might is right, and should the Allies win the war, which I rather believe they will, they will start strutting about and adopting strong moral poses and public ideals; even Stalin himself, who is as ruthless and brutal a leader as any I have seen. Only the defeated enemy is guilty of war crimes, never the victor . . . Ah well, that's how the world works. All is fair in love and war.

Read the documents that I've written out for you and Amber carefully, since they'll provide you with an excellent understanding of both my family and our history right back to the Middle Ages. Likewise study the many photograph albums of our little family, and also my parents and relatives. I hope you will realise that I loved you all dearly, and that we could have been very happy together had fate been kinder.

May God bless you all and protect you, and make your and Amber's lives so much happier and fulfilling than mine was, until you entered my dark and lonely life – blessing me with a deep sense of peace and contentment.

It is on that note that I must end the only letter you will ever receive from me, my beloved son. Love and protect your mother, sister, adopted sister and great-great-aunt Alicia – and always honour my name and memory.

Your loving father,
Baron Kurt von Rittermann

Finishing the last sentence with a sob, Rhiannon looked tearfully at her silently reflective son. 'This evening I'll show you your father's dress and work uniforms, along with his diaries and other personal possessions, and I'll read you his will and family histories. But since your stepfather has no idea whatsoever of the uniforms' existence, and Amber is such a blabbermouth, I ask you not to tell your sister anything about it. This, though, is for you to keep – a lock of your father's hair. Amber's been shown a similar lock, and she'll be given hers when she's older. I own a third – which, like your father's uniforms, is kept very well hidden from your stepfather. They obviously didn't like each other very much, to say the least.

As for your father and godfather, well, let's just say that their relations were a little strained at times, though Baron von Kleiste and his wife Luise – who both like you and Amber very much – generously agreed to be your godparents, and the baron is godfather to Rhys and Sebastian. And if my husband appears to dislike you, Alex, it's only because you resemble your father so strongly in looks and character; whereas Amber takes more after me in appearance and personality. Do try not to hate him. He's always treated you fairly, and has never been deliberately cruel. Your own poor father suffered greatly during his own childhood: his father, your grandfather, regularly beat his children and never showed them any affection. Cassie, too, suffered greatly at the hands of her stepfather, and only learned what love is after Max and I rescued her. So as you can see, Alex, your stepfather is not so terrible after all. You must both try hard, for all our sakes, to be civil to each other – at least. Will you promise me that? Never to deliberately anger him, or show any disrespect, and to avoid baiting your half-brothers?'

'I promise with all my heart, Mother.' The boy gave her a big hug. 'When can I see my father's uniforms?'

'Later today, after we've had a little chat with your stepfather and Amber. We've also got to talk to Rhys, Sebastian and Cassie.'

Finding out a short while later to her great relief that Amber had taken Max's startling news very well, and still loved her daddy just as much as before, Rhiannon called the family together and explained everything. Stunned, the twins promised faithfully never to taunt Alex and Amber on account of their father. After Max and Alex had shaken hands (the youngster solemnly addressing his stepfather as 'Sir' with Max and Rhiannon's full approval), the family promptly headed for the dining room.

'It's certainly been quite a day,' Alicia smiled at her great-niece. 'I hope we'll have a little less civil war now. No one can say that you and Max haven't tried, my love.'

Not long after this remarkable event, during the Mayschosses' summer stay at Bamberg later that year, Cassie, now almost thirteen, slipped slyly away with Otto to a wooded and secluded part of the von Kleiste estate during an al fresco lunch, and willingly succumbed to the young man's amorous advances.

Far too busy looking after their four younger children and chatting to Peter von Kleiste, Klaus von Reinholdt and Heinz Kruger (all three men having been released from their POW camps the previous year) to even notice Cassie and Otto's absence, Max, Rhiannon and Alicia were thus blissfully unaware of Cassie's first enjoyable sexual experience – made all the more so because Otto was always so kind, gentle and considerate towards her. Her passionate love for him was more than enough to sweep away any fears she had about intimate contact. Thanks to Otto, and of course to Max, she had finally defeated the demons that her abusive stepfather had created in her.

Sneaking back an hour or so later to find that no one had missed them, Cassie and Otto grinned at each other and quietly rejoined their families. Thus, unhindered by any family restrictions or suspicions, they continued to meet in secret throughout their two week summer break, and right up until Otto's military service – an earthy and sensuous Cassie as guilty as her older lover in their defiance of moral values and the law.

Chapter Twenty

There's Baron von Kleiste on the telephone asking to speak to you, Mummy.' Bursting into the cool library one hot August day in 1952, her long reddish-gold curls clipped neatly back with a jewelled hair slide, Amber was followed by a wildly prancing Sabre and Storm – two German shepherd puppies purchased to replace Rhiannon's beloved Tiger and Bess, who had finally died of old age. 'Sabre's white fur got really dirty when we took him and Storm for a walk, so Cassie and I decided to give them a good bath afterwards. Alex refused to help, as he had a geography project to finish, and the twins weren't around, as usual. Boys are so lazy. I wonder what my godfather wants to speak to you about.'

'There's only one way to find out.' Putting aside her accounts book, Rhiannon smiled indulgently at the exuberant eight-year-old and stroked the young dogs, Storm's glossy black and tan coat still a little damp from his ablutions. 'Come on, Princess. The good colonel, like most Germans, hates to be kept waiting.'

Life had changed in many ways for the Mayschosses since 1945. Cassandra, Rhys and Sebastian were all doing well at grammar school, while Alex and his sister were likewise excelling. Cassie, only three months off her sixteenth birthday, was far steadier but nevertheless intelligent, her keen interest in languages, English and French in particular, a clear indication of what she would be studying at university. Social ties with the von Kleistes had become even closer, with Rhys and eleven-year-old Hanna von Reinholdt very good friends indeed, and Charlotte, her nine-year-old sister, now Alex's slavishly devoted playmate (although he still preferred the far more stimulating company of his own sister). As for Max's relatives, most of them preferred to give the increasingly high and mighty retired lieutenant-colonel a wide berth, only a devoted Karl keeping in regular contact with his son and his children – who all looked forward to his weekly visits. Like her husband, Rhiannon had also assumed a decidedly superior and aristocratic air, although her natural warmth and sunny nature softened it somewhat. Not to be outdone by their mother and stepfather, Alex and Amber began to adopt airs and graces – while Cassie and the twins silently took note and soon learned to copy them.

Alicia, always accompanied by her four-year-old bichon frise Barney (an ancient Snowy having passed away in 1951), merely smiled serenely at them all, her fond smile hiding an intense pride in her closely knit family – even in seven-year-old Herta and three-year-old Christoph, the dark-haired and brown-eyed children of Christa and Heinz (now employed by the Mayschosses as a seamstress and head gardener). The Mayschosses were loved and admired by their employees, who enjoyed generous wages and excellent living and working conditions, and were treated practically as members of the family.

Otto von Kleiste, his siblings and their parents regarded the von Rittermann estate as their second home. The farm had been turned into a thriving business by Max, while an equally shrewd Rhiannon and Alicia ran a successful conference centre from the mansion itself, along with a luxurious guest house in the grounds. Konrad von Kleiste, taking note of his bourgeois friends' astounding financial success, promptly turned his attention to his own old-fashioned farm and modernised it along similar lines. Adding a small conference centre, on a forward-thinking Otto's insistence, a delighted Konrad and Luise watched their profits soar – while elsewhere in Germany other less enterprising families, the dispossessed von Rittermanns included, saw their ancestral estates fall into disrepair and ruin, with the sale of their treasured property often the inevitable outcome.

Chatting with her old friend Konrad, Rhiannon discovered to her great surprise that Otto, all set to start his BSc degree at Hamburg University in September, and booked into comfortable student accommodation for the duration of his studies, had expressed his strong wish to spend weekends at the von Rittermann estate. As he had a car he could easily make the journey from Hamburg to Celle every Friday evening. 'I'll have to see what my husband has to say about it, but I've got no objections at all.'

'When's Otto coming, Mother?' Trying her hardest not to show her utter delight at the prospect, Cassie looked enquiringly at Rhiannon.

'He'll be staying with us once he starts his course in September, holidays excepted. Alex and Amber are really looking forward to having him as our weekend guest for the next three years or so, but Rhys and Sebastian are rather less enthusiastic. My great-aunt and I both think he's a fine young man. As for your father, well, he must approve of Otto to allow him to stay in the first place. Either that or he's got some mercenary scheme planned – something I'd never put past him.'

Arriving in his well-polished Volkswagen, the dapper twenty-year-old was promptly whisked off to partake of coffee and cakes before being shown his bedroom and private sitting room.

'While Johann sees to your unpacking and puts away your things, perhaps you'd like to join us on a walk round the estate before dinner. Then tomorrow you're very welcome to accompany us to Sunday Mass.'

'Thank you, Mrs Mayschoss. I'd be honoured to.' The affable young nobleman smiled charmingly at his hostess, knowing full well that he and his beloved Cassandra would be spending the first of many nights together. The unassuming but delightful French girl had cast a spell on him even as a child. Quite unlike the spoilt and precious aristocratic young ladies his family was constantly introducing him to, Cassandra was sweet natured and bubbly. Her natural beauty and wit had ensnared him from the start. After enjoying many an amorous fling during his military service (and indeed even long before that), Otto now felt the need for a steady relationship.

The Mayschosses' weekend resident soon became a trusted member of the family – no one suspecting his liaison with sixteen-year-old Cassie, such was their skill in masking their passion with a veneer of innocent friendship. Three years soon passed, and a proud Otto finally left university with a first class BSc, while his paramour gained good grades in her final exams at grammar school. Otto enrolled at medical school, while his girlfriend began a degree course in French and English at Hamburg University, and the stage was set for them to secretly move in together – Otto's devoted grandparents having purchased him a luxurious apartment in an upper-class area of Hamburg.

Later that autumn the young couple received a letter from Rhiannon:

Celle, 20 October 1955

My dearest Cassie,
Yesterday, out of the blue, your father and I received a visit from Adele von Stein and her husband Dietrich. They are Kurt von

Rittermann's detested sister and brother-in-law. Why on earth they suddenly decided contact us now I have no idea, but there you are. Adele reminded me unpleasantly of my late grandmother Perraut, albeit a Protestant version – stiff and starchy, bigoted and intolerant. She's quite tall and thin, with grey hair scraped back in a bun; her sharp features and cold grey eyes, not to mention her severe black suit, give her a most unpleasing air. Her husband's rather plump and of middling height, with white hair and stone-like features which are enough to freeze anyone . . . and neither he nor his wife smiled once.

The first thing Adele did was to ask, or rather order, Alex and Amber to show her their hands (looking for the trademark von Rittermann crooked little fingers, no doubt); then, on discovering that her niece and nephew were being brought up as Roman Catholics, she launched into a furious tirade in which she violently attacked her brother for permitting his children to grow up as 'puppets of the accursed Papist faith'.

As a staunch Catholic, Max was, to put it mildly, absolutely livid, and Alex told her she had no right to insult his father – or his religion. And then Amber weighed in, telling Adele that her father had told her in his letter that she and her husband were detestable and untrustworthy.

Well, after that all I could do was try to pacify everyone – my enraged husband, infuriated children and the mortally offended von Steins. Somehow, I still don't know how, I finally succeeded in restoring a semblance of good-will, then ushered everyone into the drawing room for refreshments. And now, like my late mother, I'm suddenly aware of just how much a woman's diplomatic skills are needed in this cruel world, and also, at the ripe old age of thirty-nine, just how difficult my mother must have found it to rear two lively and disobedient children.

And now, Cassie, awkward as it may be for you and Otto, I must mention something that's rather more serious and important to me and your father than the von Steins' visit or my parents. Max, Great Aunt Alicia and I are fully aware that you're living together, and while we don't object to this in the least, and are quite prepared to pay the rent for your student accommodation (if only to preserve appearances for Otto's family), I ask that you take great care not to become pregnant, or fall behind with your studies. The very fact that you're living together increases the risk of unwanted parenthood, though, and should the worst ever happen we'd expect Otto, as a responsible young man from a good family, to make you his lawful wife and honour his commitments.

I wouldn't want either of you to give up your studies, so I'd be perfectly happy to care for your child at Celle, the only proviso being that you should both be here every weekend. Furthermore, if Otto faces any insurmountable problems with his family as a result of marrying you, we'll be more than willing to finance his studies without expecting any repayment, and offer you and Otto and your family a permanent home here at Celle if you ever need it. Obviously it wouldn't be particularly sensible to become parents at this stage of your lives, but if it happens we'll be solidly behind you, just as long as Otto marries you.

Give our love to dear Otto, keep up with your studies and take good care of yourself.

Your loving mother, Rhiannon

The incredulous Cassie and her lover could only marvel at her family's unexpectedly tolerant acceptance of their living arrangements and relationship. For a moment the two youngsters looked at each other in stunned silence. Taking her courage in both hands, Cassie asked hesitantly, 'Would you marry me, or would you abandon me? I know that I come from a very dubious background, but you've known that from the very beginning. You can't turn round and say that you weren't warned.

God knows, it would break my heart to lose you, but if you intend to leave me if I become pregnant, or want to choose a wife from your own class, then I'd much rather you told me now, so I can get on with my life as best I can.'

'The only girl I ever want to marry is you, Cassandra.' The young man gripped her hand and drew her to him, his blue eyes tender. 'Why do you think I was so keen to stay at Celle while I was studying? So I could see you regularly, as your father and Madame Reynard probably guessed. And if you do become pregnant I'll honour my commitments and marry you there and then, of course, but I'm going to make you my wife whatever happens, even if my family considers it the biggest misalliance in history. Besides, it'll be a great many years before I inherit Grandfather's title and estate, so why should I marry a girl I don't love from my own social class just to please my family? There's no reason for us to be bound by the outdated and snobbish values they're choosing to hang on to. You're going to be my wife one day, Cassandra – the question's not if but when. In the meantime we're very happy together, and that's all that matters.'

Chapter Twenty-One

Well, that's my English essay finally completed. How's your project coming along, Otto?'

'Not nearly as successfully as yours.' A heavy book spread out in front of him, the irritated young medical student glanced enviously at the willowy girl curled up comfortably in the roomy leather armchair, her long chestnut hair and red satin kimono gleaming in the firelight. 'Perhaps I should have studied something easier, like you.'

Cassie smiled sweetly. 'Why don't you just make a rough plan and jot down some notes and headings? Then tomorrow, when you're in a better mood, we can work on it together, now I've finished all my work for the month.'

'That sounds like an excellent idea. Whatever would I do without you, Cassandra?' Otto was painfully aware that life would be very hard indeed without his super-efficient girlfriend organising and helping him with his studies, not to mention overseeing the running of the apartment, keeping him well fed – and warm in bed. 'Right – so what's for supper?'

'How about sausage, pickled gherkins, sauerkraut, potato salad and rye bread, and some of that superb Herrentorte your grandmother sent yesterday?'

'That's wonderful. And tomorrow I rather fancy goulash for lunch.'

'All right . . . did anyone ever tell you that you're an absolute glutton? Your adoring grandparents don't know the first thing about their apparently virtuous grandson, or the scrapes his devoted girlfriend gets him out of. The only reason your anatomy lecturer's still speaking to you after your little . . . mutual disagreement is because I went to see him after lectures and begged his forgiveness. His parting comment was that should you ever tire of me, or me of you, then there'd certainly be plenty of young and not so young men interested in such a charming young lady . . . and since your lecturer and his wife have recently got divorced . . .'

'Well, he'd better look elsewhere for a girlfriend. You're already mine. Besides, he's far too old for a slip of a girl like you.' Deeply grateful, Otto slipped his arm round Cassie's slender waist and kissed her lingeringly. 'And anyway, he and all my other hopeful rivals can forget all about our ever splitting up.'

At the end of November 1955 a horrified Cassie realised she was definitely pregnant, and duly told her lover. Otto immediately gathered together a few trusted fellow medical student friends as witnesses and married her at a Hamburg register office – insisting that henceforth she must officially be known as Mrs Cassandra von Kleiste.

As the Christmas holidays finally arrived, Max and his family welcomed the young newly weds home – the four younger children warned on pain of death not to breathe a word to Otto's still blissfully ignorant family, or any other relatives if they happened to telephone the Mayschosses. Cassie's advanced state of pregnancy at only three months prompted a stunned Alicia to shake her head in utter amazement. 'Good Lord, she must be carrying at least two in there, if not three.'

Rhiannon smiled. 'Either possibility means that I'll need an experienced nanny to care for them. When are you going to tell your family, Otto? They'll have to know sometime . . . though I can easily understand your reluctance to tell them.'

'Oh, maybe after Christmas or the New Year, Mrs Mayschoss – but certainly not just yet.' Aware of his father-in-law's steely gaze, a worried Otto frowned uneasily back. 'Having secretly loved Cassandra for many years, I wouldn't ever have renounced her, but my family's so old fashioned and class conscious. I just don't know how to tell them.'

'Well, you may rest assured that we'll give you all the moral and financial support you need once your appalled grandparents and parents finally learn the truth.' Max nodded approvingly at his son-in-law, knowing full well that Konrad's intensely snobbish wife would be particularly disgusted by her grandson's plebeian spouse – Cassie's criminal family background making the young woman an even more disastrous choice. And Konrad himself . . . would he reject his grandson's wife or show a little more tolerance and humanity?

For the unfortunate Konrad, however, Otto's unsuitable marriage was merely a disagreeable surprise after a sudden, dramatic and devastating family tragedy. Only hours later the stunned Mayschosses and a deeply shocked Otto heard that Peter von Kleiste, just forty-three, had suffered a fatal heart attack while at the wheel of his treasured Mercedes-Benz, instantly killing his mother, wife Katherine and his two teenage daughters.

Quite unable to take in what had happened, a bewildered Otto gratefully drank the whisky that a deeply sympathetic Max offered him, then asked for another, his hand shaking. 'Now my father's dead I suppose I'm Grandfather's sole heir.'

'You are indeed, my boy. Your grandfather knows that you're here, and he's been informed that Rhiannon will take you back to Bamberg, where your Aunt Sophia and her family are comforting him as best they can. I've not told him that Cassie's going with you.'

And, so it was that the next day the deeply apprehensive young couple went off to face the grieving baron – totally unsure what kind of welcome they would receive, and dreading their reception from the bottom of their hearts.

Chapter Twenty-Two

It was getting dark by the time Rhiannon and her two passengers reached Bamberg, having made several rest-stops on the long journey to Bavaria from Northern Germany. Welcoming Rhiannon and Otto with warm smiles, then abruptly taking in Cassie's condition and her and Otto's wedding rings, Klaus and Sophia von Reinholdt could only shake their heads in disapproving shock at the young aristocrat as they ushered the trio into the drawing room for refreshments with Hanna and Charlotte, before facing the unavoidable reunion with the deeply grieving widower, who was cloistered in his study.

'Manfred will take your luggage up to your rooms. So, Otto – when did you get married?'

'Early December. Our child's due in June. You can keep any comments to yourselves. I don't want my wife upset, certainly not in her present condition.'

'But of course not, Otto. I wouldn't dream of saying anything amiss.' Sophia glanced incredulously at a silent and stiffly dignified Cassie, wondering how Konrad would take the news that his beloved only grandson and heir had clandestinely married a commoner.

An hour or so later Sophia accompanied the arrogantly unrepentant Otto, his wife and mother-in-law to where the devastated baron sat slumped at his desk. The apprehensive daughter reverently informed her father that Otto, Rhiannon and Cassandra had come to deliver their condolences in person, then hastily rejoined her husband and children – convinced, as was Klaus, that the wayward young man would now be in serious trouble.

Rhiannon reiterated their condolences, then took a deep breath. 'And now Otto wants to speak to you, Konrad, not just about this tragedy. Please hear him out, and try not to condemn him.'

'Meaning what exactly? That he's given up his studies, or made some common barmaid pregnant and promised to marry her?'

Otto looked indignantly at his elderly relative. 'No, Grandfather, I've done nothing of the sort. I know this isn't a good time to tell you, but by the end of June you'll be a great-grandfather. Cassandra and I were married at a Hamburg register office at the beginning of December, and no, it wasn't a shotgun marriage even though she was pregnant. She told me all about her parentage and family background the first time we met, but despite that she's the only girl I could ever have made my wife. She means far more to me than the finest young lady in the world. I'm very sorry if I've disappointed you, Grandfather – but I hope that we'll prove to you over the years that this isn't all a disastrous mistake, or a renunciation of my social class: I've got every intention of maintaining our fine old family traditions.

'Now that you finally know about this, Cassandra and I would like to get married in church in a proper family celebration. But if you think we're a complete disgrace to you and our family name, we'll leave tomorrow morning and never darken your door again. God knows, it would break my heart to become estranged from you in such terrible circumstances, but if it's what you wish . . .' Otto smiled sadly, his quietly determined manner making it plain that he fully intended to live his own life – with or without his aristocratic family's approval. 'I've said what I wanted to say, Grandfather. If you ever wish to visit your great-grandchild or children at Celle, you'll be very welcome indeed, I know. In the meantime . . .' The twenty-three-year-old paused, then, on receiving no response, shrugged resignedly and headed abruptly for the door, followed closely by Cassie.

Only Rhiannon hesitated for a moment before murmuring almost inaudibly, 'Goodbye, Konrad. I hope you can find it in your heart to forgive dear Otto, and not to break with me and my family. You know where to find us . . .'

'Find you be damned, Rhiannon. Come back here, all of you, and at least give me a chance to reply.' Snapping out of his stupor, the baron regarded the silent trio. 'First of all, I've not said anything about disowning or disinheriting Otto, and I've got no intention of doing either. Secondly, Rhiannon, our friendship's not threatened in any way by my rogue of a grandson's marriage. I should have realised earlier the attraction that Cassandra held for Otto, but I assumed like everyone else that they were just good friends. Dare I ask how old you were when my scoundrel of a grandson seduced you, Cassandra, or would it be wiser for me not to know?'

'Well . . . it all depends on what my husband thinks. If Otto doesn't mind, and it stays a secret between us four, then perhaps . . . I wasn't a virgin when I met Otto, because my step-father had raped me by the time I was three. So, what do you want to do, Otto? Keep quiet or confess?'

'Oh, definitely the former, I think . . . but I'll admit to breaking the law, Grandfather.' The unrepentant young man shrugged nonchalantly. 'But I married her in the end, so there's no need to inform Lieutenant-Colonel Mayschoss . . . Besides, he probably suspects as much but realises that it took two to tango. And since she's now a married mother-to-be, no-one's any the worse for it.'

The baron frowned. 'Indeed. Let's rejoin Sophia and Klaus, and acquaint them with the fact that the prodigal son, or grandson, has returned, and along with his young wife has been welcomed back into the fold.'

There was a quiet but uplifting church ceremony at Bamberg in late January 1956, after the dark and gloomy funeral a month earlier. The young couple smiled contentedly at each other as the magnificently robed priest gave them his final blessing and Max, having led Cassandra up to the altar to be given away, looked proudly on. Heavily pregnant, the smiling bride was pretty indeed in a flowing primrose-yellow and cream brocade dress, her waist-length golden-brown hair falling down her back in glorious curls; a far cry from the shy and timid four-year-old girl with a shaven head who had been received by Baron von Kleiste in his office fifteen years before. That Otto and his family would come to live at Bamberg after he and his wife had completed their studies at Hamburg, the bereaved older man had no doubt. As a junior doctor, Otto was more than likely to find a post at a nearby hospital; while Cassandra could easily study for her MA in French literature at Bamburg University. Meanwhile, until his grandson and granddaughter-in-law came to live with him, Konrad intended to spend much time with Max and Rhiannon at Celle: the very thought of living alone in his lonely and gloomy mausoleum of a stately home did not appeal at all.

Five months later a stunned Otto and his wife were the proud parents of triplets . . . born at Von Rittermann House and delivered by Otto himself, so rapid and unexpected had been their delivery. The delighted great-grandfather was more than satisfied with his two healthy great-grandsons and their slightly smaller but still robust sister.

'So, there you are, Grandfather . . . our first attempt at producing the next generation, not to mention providing sons for the von Kleiste line. Our eldest son is to be named Nikolas Peter, his younger brother Werner Konrad and our beautiful little girl Katherine-Luise Adelaide Emma –

Katie-Luise. Cassandra and I hope that you like their names, which we've chosen in memory of my late family and also to honour you, dear Grandfather.'

'Indeed I do, Otto. Thank you. And now that my great-grandchildren have arrived, with your gracious parents-in-laws' permission I'll continue to live here for the duration of your studies.'

'But of course, Konrad. You know you're always welcome here.' Rhiannon smiled affectionately at her old friend, aware of the intense presence of Kurt close by. 'Well, now that the triplets have arrived safe and sound I suggest that we all go for a celebratory drink downstairs, and allow dear Cassie and Otto some time alone with their brood.'

Issuing orders that a bottle of champagne and some food were to be sent up to the delivery room, Max kissed his happy but exhausted adopted daughter on the cheek, then led the party outside to the Italian garden, where the serving staff had set up a superb cold buffet – Rhys and Sebastian's eyes lighting up at the very thought of it.

'Do try not to snaffle everything, boys. The rest of us would like something, you know.' Alicia smiled amusedly, wondering when her extremely tall great-great-nephews would stop growing. Aged only fifteen they were already taller than their mother – who was no midget herself.

'But of course, Aunt. Oh, wonderful, there's truffle pâté and smoked salmon, Sebastian.' Rhys grinned at his twin, whose plate was already piled high, just like his red-headed brother's.

'Is there indeed? In that case we'd better get some before it disappears. Come on, Amber, hurry up and stake your claim before these two gluttons steal our share.' Eyeing his half-brothers distrustfully, Alex promptly took generous helpings for himself and his sister, while near by an observant Max and Konrad smiled good-humouredly at the four young people and Christa and her family chatted to Rhiannon and Alicia; the robust old lady still going strong at eighty-seven. Christoph Kruger, Christa's eldest son, adored his red-headed benefactress and her family, while Heinz, his father, positively worshipped the vivacious Rhiannon and her dignified husband – the ex-soldier's loyalty and gratitude to his benevolent employers boundless.

Deciding to have their lunch in the summer house, Alex and Amber settled down on the cushions, the twelve-year-old girl's fiery golden-red locks gleaming in the midday sun. Suddenly aware of their father's presence, Amber greeted him warmly. 'I wonder what our family priest would say if he knew that we're watched over by our father's spirit. I rather doubt that he'd believe us.'

'I'm glad he'd with us. If only I could remember something about him, some definite memory, but try as I might I can't. You were only a baby when he died, but I was almost two years old.'

'Never mind, Alex. We know he loved us dearly, and that he's with us now, so why worry? By the way, if you don't want that cheese and salad I wouldn't mind it.'

'By all means, little sister.' Alex passed his plate over, then snuggled up to her affectionately, closing his eyes against the burning sun.

Amber yawned and settled down contentedly next to him, her head resting trustingly on his slim shoulder as they slowly drifted off into a deep slumber.

Chapter Twenty-Three

Six months after the birth of the triplets, now a lively and mischievous bunch who led their nanny, grandparents and great-grandfather a merry dance, but whose radiantly sunny smiles never failed to soften the hardest of hearts, the von Kleiste and von Reinholdt families, and Karl Mayschoss and his wife, gathered to celebrate Christmas 1956 at Celle. Already completely besotted by his angelic-looking but devilishly naughty great-grandchildren, a doting Konrad von Kleiste often, much to their nanny's annoyance, had the babies taken to his private suite of rooms, where he sat and played with them for hours, only reluctantly giving them up when their parents or grandparents wished to spend some time with them.

Celebrating the New Year with a big party and lavish buffet to which many friends of Otto, Cassie and the four younger children were invited, the rambling old mansion was packed to bursting with high-spirited young people.

'Welcome to the five star deluxe von Rittermann hotel.' A tipsy Rhiannon locked the study door and collapsed laughing into her husband's arms, Max likewise having drunk more than was his wont. 'They're even partying in the long gallery – something which should give Alex and Amber's po-faced ancestors plenty to scowl at.'

'Well, let them . . . I never liked those stiff and starchy characters anyway.' Max kissed her lingeringly, his love and passionate desire for his wife as great as ever. 'And now let's mark the New Year in our own special way, Rhiannon.' Slowly unzipping her coffee coloured silk evening dress, he pulled her down on to the floor, his senses flooded with burning desire as they gradually slipped into a deeply sensuous world of their own, oblivious to the joyous cacophony of revellers outside.

Summer 1957 saw the Mayschosses, von Kleistes, von Reinholdts and Krugers, along with Max's father, stepmother, sister, brother-in-law and their three grown-up adopted children spending a holiday together touring Germany.

'Shall we visit the Town Hall before or after lunch?' Rhiannon looked up at her husband.

'Oh, definitely before, I think.' Max glanced admiringly at Lüneburg's impressive pale yellow Baroque edifice. 'I couldn't possibly appreciate such splendid architecture without some nourishment. Besides, it's almost midday. What do you suggest, Konrad?'

'That we take our places in the restaurant over there while there are still tables available.' Accustomed to taking control, the baron promptly led them down the stairs, the two German shepherds and a diminutive Barney following closely at their owners' heels.

'Good afternoon, sir. This way please.' Showing the unexpectedly large party of twenty-nine to their places, the waiter handed out menus and departed. A devious Charlotte von Reinholdt deliberately ended up next to Rhiannon's youngest son, while Rhys and Hanna sat together nearby.

'Just look, Alex. Grandfather was quite right to bring us in so early: any later and there wouldn't have been space. What are you having?'

'Oh, asparagus soup, salmon, then apple tart and cream. And you, Charlotte?'

'Exactly the same I think. As for dear Hanna, no doubt she'll have her boring old favourite: pork, then ice cream for dessert.'

'Never you mind what I'm having, little sister. Just mind your own business for once, while other people mind theirs.' Not particularly fond of her irritating sibling, the sixteen-year-old glared at the grinning younger girl and an amused Alex, then turned her back contemptuously and continued to chat to Rhys.

Charlotte laughed. 'What an unbearable crosspatch. Still, you and Amber have to put up with the terrible twins, so you know exactly what I have to suffer with such a horrid sister.'

'I do indeed . . . but we give just as much as we take, if not more.'

Overhearing, the baron smiled at Otto. 'Well, well, who'd have thought it? It looks as if the sly minx is trying to hook herself a rich husband. As for Hanna, she could certainly do a lot worse than Rhys. Without a title he may be, but that boy could earn an absolute fortune if he perseveres – and becomes a lawyer as he intends. Sebastian's got a promising future too. And Amber, a wealthy heiress and stunningly beautiful, is never going to lack potential suitors.'

After Lüneburg they visited historic old Lübeck, then moved on through a depressingly impoverished East Germany to West Berlin, their convoy of six luxury cars attracting more than a little attention from envious East Germans and Russian soldiers. Rhiannon looked out of the window in disbelief. 'What utter poverty! How ugly the tower blocks are – and the women in their awful old shabby clothes. Do you have any relatives living here, Karl?'

'I do, unfortunately, as has my wife. But given the secret police, I rather doubt the wisdom of contacting them.'

'And to think the war ended in 1945. All that's happened is that it's been replaced by this insidious stalemate between the Soviet Union and the West. It's crazy: the two Germanys sit here as hostile strangers, practically cut off from each other.'

Peering disdainfully through the car window, a hate-filled Alex glowered at the parading Russian soldiers, his grey eyes bitter. 'What sub-humans these Russians are, not to mention the Poles. And to think they actually dared to expel our fellow Germans from Prussia and Pommern in 1946, and annex those prosperous areas to Russia and Poland.'

Karl smiled sadly at his indignant step-grandson. 'We can't do anything about it now. We just have to leave our suffering fellow Germans to their tragic fate and get on with our own lives.'

Alex nodded resignedly, wishing that they were already at their plush hotel in West Berlin.

Finally returning to Celle, the party were not in the least surprised to hear Rhiannon's even more ambitious plans for the next summer: a tour of Belgium, Bruges and Ypres in particular, then Paris and Britain – where naturally they would stay for a few days at Scarborough and visit her parents' and brother's graves. She added that it was a thirteenth wedding anniversary present for Karl and Anna, as well as a gesture of reconciliation towards Maria and Franz. 'Max isn't too enthusiastic about his sister accompanying us, but I felt it would do their children good to see a bit of the world.'

'Not to mention educating Christa and Heinz's children. Your former nanny and her husband are so lucky to have such generous employers.'

'Well, Christa's always been a very good and loyal friend to me, not to mention indispensable for emergency repairs with her needle and a wonderfully efficient organiser. And, of course, Heinz is a skilled mechanic, as well as everything else. Herta and Amber are close friends too, so why not, Konrad?' Rhiannon shrugged nonchalantly, and she and her devoted elderly companion joined the rest of her extended family for dinner.

Receiving in early September a totally unexpected invitation from Kurt von Rittermann's sister and her husband, to spend a few days with them in Hanover at Easter the following year, a frowning Rhiannon shook her head perplexedly. 'What do you suggest we do, Max? Accepting is distinctly unattractive, to put it mildly, but to decline might cause undue offence.'

'Quite.' Her husband grimaced. 'We may as well go, especially since it doesn't interfere with our plans for the summer. Whatever else the von Steins may accuse us of, ill-breeding and bad manners needn't be on the list.'

Chapter Twenty-Four

Seven months after accepting the unexpected invitation, the two Mayschoss cars rolled up outside the once imposing and immaculately cared-for von Stein villa, its white walls and woodwork now desperately in need of a lick of paint. The battered Volkswagen parked in the crumbling drive made the rambling old house seem even more dilapidated than it actually was. The generous portion of the vast von Rittermann fortune that Adele had inherited on her parents' deaths had been spent long ago, paying off her extravagant civil servant husband's debts and in an attempt to maintain the gracious style of living that they deemed necessary for their exalted social status. Now only the villa and Dietrich's salary as a senior government official remained. Kurt, her unimpressed elder brother, had observed with contemptuous disapproval as their finances slowly but surely plunged into the red, and as Paula, his feckless niece, married a penniless fellow aristocrat with equally luxurious tastes. By the time their only child, Caroline, was born in 1940, Kurt had severed all ties with them, disgusted with his family's constant demands for financial aid; even the tragic death of Caroline's young father at Stalingrad in 1943 had not moved him to offer support.

As Rhys and Sebastian got out of their car, speaking together as usual, a girl's wistful face pressed itself eagerly against the window. She watched intently, her pale blue eyes alive with interest as she observed the two tall and good-looking young men and their stunningly beautiful mother.

'Caroline! Come here this instant and show some manners. For an aristocratic young lady brought up with the greatest of care, your deportment leaves a great deal to be desired.'

'Well, what if it does? I think your airs and graces are quite ridiculous, even if we're supposed to be nobility.'

'That's quite enough, Caroline. You'll apologise immediately to your mother, or go to your room and stay there.'

For a moment the rebellious fair-haired girl stared in hostile silence at her sternly disapproving grandfather, then, hearing Rhiannon's merry laughter ring out, muttered an unconvincing apology, determined not to miss out.

Having introduced her daughter and granddaughter to the seven guests, Adele left to see about afternoon refreshments and keep an eye on Ida, the overworked and underpaid maid that she employed – whose diligence and honesty she rather doubted.

Meanwhile a mutually attracted Caroline and Sebastian were already chatting animatedly together on the settee, the seventeen-year-old girl having decided quickly that his gracious and elegant mother was an infinite improvement on her own – and his family likewise preferable. Returning a short while later, an incredulous Adele regarded her suddenly charming and sociable granddaughter with stunned amazement, as did Dietrich and Paula.

An hour or so later, deciding that the three dogs needed a walk, Rhiannon was joined by her children, all four young people finding the stiffly formal atmosphere too stifling for comfort. As she invited a delighted Caroline along, Rhiannon added pleasantly, 'You can show us the easiest route to the park.'

'Oh yes . . . with the greatest of pleasure, Mrs Mayschoss.' The slender and strikingly attractive girl beamed with pleasure, then, pointedly ignoring her family, marched defiantly out of the rather shabby drawing room with her new friends, her head held high.

'We'll be back in good time for dinner, Mrs von Stein.' Rhiannon smiled sweetly, and seconds later had vanished in a flurry of dogs and lively young people, forcing a far less sociable Max and Alicia to keep the artificial conversation alive in her absence.

For Caroline, life began to take on a new meaning: the stimulating influence of Sebastian and his relatives made the bitterly unhappy girl even more determined to break free from her autocratic and repressive family. Their embarrassing poverty was just one more reason in her eyes to sever ties with them and seek pastures new . . . preferably with the charismatic and wealthy Mayschosses and her sympathetic and amiable cousins Alexander and Amber – both of whom felt very sorry for her, as did the twins.

Taking her arm, Sebastian said kindly, 'I'll ask Mother to invite you along for our summer holiday later this year. Alex and Amber can show you round their father's ancestral home, and you'll be able to make the acquaintance of the von Kleiste and von Reinholdt families. Baron von Kleiste is our godfather, and Alex will one day be a baron in his own right. Cassie, our adopted sister, is married to the baron's grandson and heir, Otto.'

'Thank you so much . . . but will your parents allow me to come? There's always my beastly family to consider too.'

'Oh, don't worry about all that. Mother will arrange everything once we've persuaded her and my father to invite you along.' Sebastian smiled reassuringly. 'But in the meantime it might pay to humour your mother and grandparents, and show a little good will towards them even if you don't feel it.'

Caroline nodded thoughtfully. 'I do so wish that I had a mother as wonderful as yours, not to mention a father like Lieutenant-Colonel Mayschoss. My father was killed when I was only two, so I've got no memories of him at all. As for Madame Reynard, well, she's an absolute treasure . . . so kind, but dignified too, without being in the least bit snooty.'

'Even my godlike parents and great-great-aunt have their off days sometimes, so don't go thinking they're as perfect as all that.'

Later in the day, after a quick discussion with Rhys, Alex and Amber, the children approached the unsuspecting Rhiannon and put in a good word on Caroline's behalf.

'Good Lord. You certainly don't believe in beating about the bush do you, Sebastian, any more than your father does.' She smiled affectionately at her charmingly persuasive son. 'I was thinking about this myself earlier this afternoon. I'll talk to her family, if Caroline wishes me to.'

'Oh, yes please, Mrs Mayschoss.'

'Well then, I shall, my love . . . and I'll invite them to stay with us for a week by way of thanks for this visit, not to mention an added incentive to let you come with us on our grand tour. In the meantime, Caroline, I suggest you take good care not to offend your family before they've made their decision.'

Amber grinned wickedly. 'With any luck they'll be so stunned at your sudden obedience that they'll all drop dead with shock. And even if they don't you can still come to live with us once you've left school.'

Caroline glanced up to see how Rhiannon had taken this, and was greatly encouraged to see her smile.

Later, as he and his wife were getting ready for bed, Max listened in amused silence as Rhiannon explained her latest project as she brushed her hair. The name Operation Rescue Caroline immediately struck him as rather apt. 'Just be careful that Paula doesn't plunge a kitchen knife into your back.'

'I'm just trying to get things moving, and prevent Caroline from mouldering here or storming out and then ending up in a mess. I'm not being a bossy organiser, really: I'm just giving people a push in the right direction.'

'Beware of the bossy organiser.'

'I'm not a . . .' Flouncing indignantly into bed, the fiery red-head was promptly caught up in her amorous husband's arms and silenced with a hungry kiss.

Next door a bold Caroline sat on Sebastian's bed and chatted with the twins till midnight. Deciding that she really didn't want to return to her own room, that night or any other while Sebastian was there, she slipped into his waiting arms and bade farewell to her virginity with utter delight – Rhys having obligingly disappearing to the drawing room for a while. His curiosity had already been satisfied with the outwardly prim but unexpectedly passionate Hanna.

Elsewhere in the house, earlier in the evening, Amber and Alex had finally given in to the intense mutual physical attraction that had tormented them since early adolescence. Now almost fourteen, Amber looked and behaved more like a very grown-up eighteen-year-old, while the almost sixteen-year-old Alex could easily have passed for a twenty-year-old, both in appearance and manner. As they sat chatting on his sister's bed, Alex had suddenly, without any warning, passionately kissed her on the lips and pulled her down beside him. The next moment he was sensuously caressing and undressing her. Amber's fiery red hair indicated her passionate nature – and there was no holding them back from breaking one of society's greatest taboos. Totally inexperienced as Alex was, his sister soon realised just how red-blooded he was beneath his habitually calm and dignified public manner. Just like his father, he was more than capable of contemptuously disregarding any irritating moral restrictions – as was the impetuous and head-strong Amber.

By the end of their stay the Mayschosses had changed Caroline's life forever, as the von Steins had willingly accepted Rhiannon's kind invitation of a week's stay at Von Rittermann House – and were quite happy to allow their apparently deeply dutiful and docile granddaughter to accompany her wealthy new friends on their European tour. Only an intensely jealous and suspicious Paula had wanted to refuse her daughter permission to go, but this was soon over-ruled by her parents when they received Rhiannon's generous 'thank you for having us' gift of fine table linen, as well as an offer to pay for much-needed repairs to the dilapidated old villa, and a brand new Volkswagen as a wedding anniversary present.

Adele regarded her satisfied husband with a rare contented smile. 'We've lost Caroline, of course, even though she's so much more dutiful towards us these days, but she probably won't sever all ties with us if we remain good friends with the Mayschosses. That our only grandchild is likely to marry Sebastian and convert to Catholicism seems highly probable, but at least we'll be able to keep in contact with our great-grandchildren, even if they're Papists.'

'I quite agree. I for one can well do without any more battles of wills with Caroline. If she asks us if she can go and live at Celle – and she will – I strongly suggest we let her, on condition that she visits us regularly.'

'As you wish, Dietrich. Now all we have to do is pacify her mother.'

Fully aware, like her spouse, that Caroline had been listening avidly at the drawing room door to the conversation, but proudly preferring not to acknowledge the fact, Adele sighed deeply, then poured herself and Dietrich another cup of tea while Caroline returned to her room, jubilantly beaming. Sebastian having faithfully promised to visit her every weekend until she finally moved to Celle.

Selling their plush Hamburg apartment for a good profit that June, by which time a panic-stricken Caroline had informed her boyfriend that she was carrying his child, an exhausted but very happy Otto and Cassie, correctly convinced that they had passed their final exams with flying colours, were warmly welcomed back to Celle by their family and friends, the mischievous two-year-old triplets greeting their parents with delighted rapture. Just a month later they, along with Konrad von Kleiste and his relatives, finally made the acquaintance of Caroline and her family.

Quite aware that these haughty but impoverished aristocrats had received generous financial aid from Rhiannon, but far too well-bred to let on that he knew, the elderly baron greeted the von Steins graciously. Alex silently observed his revered godfather's punctiliously correct conduct, and immediately adopted it himself.

Adele, meanwhile, felt herself travelling back in time: her wanderings through her childhood home always seeming to end up at her late brother's portrait in the shadowy and echoing long gallery. She could only shake her head in incredulous disbelief at her cold and uncaring brother's deep passion for another man's wife, not to mention his great love for Alexander and Amber.

Adele and her husband finally left Celle, reluctantly on Adele's part, for their refurbished villa in Hanover, leaving behind an indecisive and worried – but still relatively slim – Caroline at Von Rittermann House.

'And now, young lady, it's high time we took you shopping for something more elegant than your present wardrobe, and then have your hair cut and styled.'

Whisked off by Rhiannon and Cassie to tour Hanover's most exclusive shops, an excited Caroline was fitted out with the fine clothes and quality jewellery that she had always longed for but could only dream of – then emerged from the hairdresser's looking like a model, her long fair locks curled and crimped to perfection. Completing the stunning transformation from pauper to princess with some tasteful but effective make-up, Rhiannon and Cassie presented the now almost unrecognisable young woman to her deeply impressed friends and cousins . . . a besotted Sebastian gazing at his magically transformed girlfriend in awed wonder.

Deciding that the time was right, Caroline asked whether it might be possible for her to come to live at Von Rittermann House after their holiday.

'Oh, I don't see why not, providing that your family give their consent.' Rhiannon glanced quizzically at her unsurprised husband and great-aunt. 'There's no reason why you shouldn't attend your present school even if you've moved here.'

Thanking her from the bottom of her heart, Caroline rejoined the rest of the party in the garden for refreshments.

Chapter Twenty-Five

Mother, Caroline and I have got some news for you. You and Father are going to be grandparents in January. We very much want to marry before our child is born. Please can you tell Caroline's family . . . and ask them to grant us permission to become man and wife. I know we've only known each other for three months, but after all, you and Father were parents-to-be only a week after you met.'

Taking the bull by the horns a day or so after their arrival at Ypres on 22 July, the young couple stood resolutely in front of a stunned Max, Rhiannon and Alicia.

'And please don't blame Sebastian for everything. I was the one who made the first move, by slipping into his room on the evening of the very day you all arrived at my grandparents' villa. I'm quite willing to take on the responsibility of caring for a child, but I'd feel happier doing it as a respectable married woman. I'm as sorry as Sebastian for bringing any shame or dishonour to your family, but neither of us wants to consider me having an abortion or giving up our baby for adoption. If you give us permission to marry, I'll ask your family's priest to make arrangements for my conversion to the Roman Catholic faith, and later on to have my child baptised. As they're devout Lutherans I know that my family will be utterly appalled by my decision, but I don't see there's anything so terrible about Catholicism.'

'That being the case, I fail to see any good reason why you and Sebastian shouldn't marry. Your extreme youth's my only reservation. Rhiannon, Alicia . . . do you both agree?'

Rhiannon smiled. 'Of course, Max, but I only hope that Caroline's grandparents and mother will be too.'

'Oh, they will be, once they learn of her pregnancy.' The old lady smiled at her great-niece, then turned to Sebastian's young wife-to-be. 'Welcome to our family, my dear. We certainly didn't foresee you joining us in quite such a dramatic manner, nor so soon, but nothing can change what's happened.'

Informed of the situation later the same day by a diplomatic Rhiannon, Caroline's stupefied family duly agreed to grant the seventeen-year-old permission to marry, their written confirmation of the fact arriving when the large party reached a hotel in Bruges a few days later.

'So now all we have to do is book ourselves in at a register office, and we're man and wife. How does Bruges suit you?'

'Oh, Sebastian, how wonderful. It's such a quaint old town. I love it.'

'In that case Bruges it is.'

The young couple were married at the end of July in an atmosphere of deep relief and general rejoicing. Still unable to believe that those first three blissful nights of passion with Caroline at Easter had resulted in her carrying his child and becoming his wife, a bemused Sebastian accepted the situation – while a shocked Rhys decided to show a good more wisdom in his affair with Hanna, taking every precaution not to end up as a schoolboy father. Alex and Amber, who had been conscientiously using contraceptives ever since their first time together, looked silently at each other, a hint of smugness in their expressions. For Amber, the prospect of having her cousin living at Von Rittermann House was welcome, as the two girls having already become firm and devoted friends. Charlotte was shocked, while Hanna simply shrugged her shoulders, merely thinking that Caroline and Sebastian had been very unlucky. Otto and Cassie, both guilty of the same offence only two years before, vowed to give the newly weds as much moral support and advice as they could.

Moving to Paris and a five star hotel at the beginning of August for ten days, the party split up into family groups to explore the city. Rhiannon and a now two months' pregnant Cassie took a now somewhat plumper Caroline shopping for some stylish maternity clothes – the youthful mother-to-be suddenly very grateful indeed for her wedding ring, as the curious Parisians glanced with a mixture of shocked surprise and curiosity at her obvious condition.

'Why's Paris called the City of Light?' The fair-haired girl picked out a blue and white smock and looked up at her companions.

'Well, probably because it's so lit up at night. Tonight we'll take you,

Sebastian and the other youngsters on an evening stroll, so you can see what I mean. And tomorrow I want you to see some of the sights. Cassie was born in Paris, and I spent four very happy years here during the German Occupation – albeit with some rather unpleasant memories mixed in with the good ones. As well as seeing the usual tourist attractions, I want to show you my former home in the Rue Madeleine. I've also got to visit the convent where my Aunt Agnes lives. I can't believe how the time has flown: she's been there for seventeen years.'

A few days later, gazing up at her still impressive war-time home, Rhiannon turned wistfully to her husband, the forty-two-year-old's memories of her life there as a child and young woman still crystal clear. 'It's such a shame that we can't go in and take a look round – but judging by the suspicious looks we're getting it may not be such a good idea.'

Max stared back at his former neighbours, who had instantly recognised the glamorous red-head.

'Yes, she's still with us, Mrs Mayschoss. But she's gravely ill, and confined to bed with arthritis. But should Sister Ursula wish to see you, you could perhaps visit her for a short while.'

'Sister Ursula? Who's she?' Quite unable to contain her curiosity, a wide-eyed Amber regarded the dignified black-robed Mother Superior. 'My great-aunt's called Agnes, not Ursula.'

'She was once, my child – but we take new names when we become brides of Christ, and Sister Ursula is the name your great-aunt chose.'

'Oh. I don't think I ever want to be a nun. Don't you ever get bored just praying and singing in church?'

'Amber! Do show some manners, please.' Rhiannon shook her head reprovingly at her outspoken daughter. 'Please forgive her lack of tact. She tends to blurt out what she's thinking without considering either her surroundings or to whom she's speaking: I was just the same at her age..'

The elderly nun nodded serenely. 'And now, my daughter, I'll tell Sister Ursula you're here, and ask if she wishes to see you.'

Returning a short while later, the Mother Superior took the little group to a small white-painted room with a disproportionately large crucifix on the wall. A dying Agnes lay in a narrow iron bed.

'Aunt Agnes, it's me: Rhiannon.'

For a moment the dim and hooded eyes looked keenly at the tall and elegant red-head sitting at her bedside, before calmly regarding the five silent young people standing round their mother. 'And this is your family by your Captain Mayschoss?'

'Well, yes . . . all but Cassandra here.'

Giving her older relative a brief account of all that had happened since Agnes had entered the convent, Rhiannon introduced her grown-up offspring and told her aunt that she intended to visit the grave of her grandmother later that week.

'Indeed . . . Well, my life is almost over, and I'll soon be with our blessed Lord. Goodbye Rhiannon, and may God's blessing be with you all.'

'Goodbye, Aunt, and thank you very much for consenting to see us.' Bowing her head respectfully as she left her dying relative, Rhiannon sadly led her subdued children back to where Max, Alicia and the rest of the family waited in the sweet-smelling and peaceful convent garden.

The deeply moving memory of an ill but serene Agnes haunted Rhiannon for the rest of her stay in Paris.

Boarding the Dover-bound ferry at Calais, the convoy of German cars headed for Britain. Their first stop was London, where they intended to spend their first week.

'And after that Bath, Bristol, Oxford, Manchester, York, Scarborough, Newcastle and Edinburgh – along with Ireland, Wales, Devon and Somerset, before retracing our way back to Dover. We'll be missing four weeks of school, but just think of all the fascinating tales we'll be able to tell our friends.' Alex beamed delightedly at Amber; then, remembering that Caroline would not be returning to school but continuing her academic studies with private tutors at Von Rittermann House, he added, 'Never mind, cousin. You'll not be lonely living with us.'

Replying that it was far better not to return to school in her present condition, Caroline smiled contentedly – knowing perfectly well that she would never be lonely again now that she was part of the lively and warm-hearted Mayschoss family.

There had been only one thought in Rhiannon's mind as the ferry approached the white cliffs of Dover, and the native land she had not seen for nineteen long years: Scarborough, and the cemetery where her parents, brother and Magda lay buried. Finally arriving at her cherished destination, the grieving woman knelt alone by the carefully tended graves and wept, while intense memories of her lost family washed over her. Reverently placing her floral tributes, Rhiannon nodded to the rest of her family and friends, who duly came to pay their own respects.

Five months later, in January 1959, a delighted Caroline was safely delivered of a healthy green-eyed baby boy, and immediately named him Siegfried Maximilian, her deeply respected father-in-law's name in reverse, much to a proud Sebastian's great delight.

After giving birth to another fine son, Kasper Ralph, two months later, and still managing to pass her MA in French literature at Bamberg University that summer, a radiant Cassie was presented with the priceless von Kleiste family sapphires as a thank you present from the boundlessly grateful baron – who by now had realised what a utter treasure Otto's lovely wife was. Carefully examining the matching sapphire and diamond necklace, bracelet, and earrings, Cassie looked at the elderly aristocrat with a delighted smile. 'They're beautiful . . . absolutely beautiful. Thank you so much.'

'I thought you might like them, my dear. They're every bit as impressive and valuable as the von Rittermann family emeralds Rhiannon wears on special occasions.' Squeezing her hand affectionately he added, 'It's just a small token of thanks for my four wonderful great-grandchildren, Cassandra. Without them, how would the von Kleiste family line survive into the next century?'

Chapter Twenty-Six

Do hurry up, Herta, or we'll be late. Caroline's already ready to set off for church, and the rest of the wedding party's waiting outside.'

'I'm coming, Amber . . .' Hurriedly joining her friend in the corridor, the bridesmaid smoothed down her long dark blue satin dress and regarded the identically robed willowy fifteen-year-old admiringly. 'You do look lovely. I wish my hair was as long as yours, instead of just down to my shoulders and boring light brown. Your mother must have spent absolutely ages brushing and curling yours.'

The vivacious young red-head laughed affectionately, and linked arms with the awed thirteen-year-old as they dashed through the mansion's endless maze of corridors. 'Well, you look lovely too, so that's that. You haven't see Caroline's dress yet, have you? It's pale blue silk and really stunning. Now that she's a Catholic like Sebastian and their baby she can have a proper marriage service, with music and all the other religious trimmings. And even though her grandfather's a devout Protestant he's agreed to give her away.'

'So he has. And don't forget that my family are Protestants too, and they're all coming along for the occasion.'

Amber shrugged unconcernedly and smiled. 'What does it matter anyway? We're all Christians and worship the same God, and that's the most important thing.'

Escorting his radiant young granddaughter down the aisle later that same day, to where an elegantly attired Sebastian waited for his bride at the altar, a stiffly dignified Dietrich von Stein stared straight ahead, the presence of the magnificently robed Catholic priest at Caroline's religious marriage ceremony still seeming to be an utter obscenity to him. That his Lutheran late brother-in-law could ever have permitted his son and daughter to be brought up as Roman Catholics, then Caroline converting, still deeply appalled Dietrich, his wife and his daughter. But, thanks to the unexpected generosity of the very wealthy Catholic Mayschosses, at least they had an immaculate and luxurious residence worthy of a noble-born family, and Caroline was a respectable married mother. Furthermore, he and his family had been invited with the Mayschosses to the Loire Valley in a few days time – something Adele and Paula were really looking forward to. Naturally enough the von Kleistes, von Reinholdts, Karl Mayschoss's family and the Krugers were joining them.

'And may God's blessing be on you both . . .'

Rhiannon listened to the priest's final pronouncements and hugged a quiet and very well-behaved baby Siegfried to her. 'Now you're a grandfather you'll never know a moment's peace from crawling infants and inquisitive sticky fingers.'

'Oh very funny, Rhiannon. My study door's going to be kept permanently locked.'

'Poor Max. How ever will you cope with all your future grandchildren and great-grandchildren? Little Siegfried here is a good boy, though. He hasn't cried once, and all the other children have behaved themselves ever so well.'

'True – but only because their parents threatened them with the direst of consequences if they didn't . . . just as we did ourselves with our family while they were growing up. But judging by the way the younger generation are behaving, we seem to have lost the respect that our generation automatically gave its elders.'

'Oh come on, Max: things aren't that bad. Do try not to be such a grumpy old man.' Rhiannon shook her head, amused, with an affectionately mocking glint in her cat-like green eyes. 'Anyone would think you men didn't like the children you're so keen to give us.'

For a reluctant Private-Conscript Rhys and Sebastian two months later, life could have been better, however. Having attended the christening of little Siegfried, and enjoyed the last holiday with their family for the next two years, then taking their final grammar school exams at the same time as Hanna and Caroline that June, the two luxury-loving eighteen-year-olds faced a disciplined military existence much less willingly than their father or even Otto had. If Hanna, Rhys's fiancée, had not been attending teacher training college at Hamburg, and Caroline (now a trainee legal secretary), not been staying every weekend with little Siegfried at Hanna's comfortable student flat, the Meredith-Mayschoss boys would have found life quite unbearable. Only the prospect of regular weekly contact with the girls gave the desperately homesick twins something to look forward to for the next two years.

In August the twins were a little cheered by their excellent exam results and very pleased that Hanna and Caroline had likewise passed theirs with superb grades. Rhys and Sebastian welcomed their weekend trips out with the girls, their jealous fellow conscripts enviously watching the twins march away from barracks every weekend to meet up with such good-looking and devoted girls. The brothers' commanding officers merely smiled amusedly as Hanna and Caroline, the latter holding her eight-month-old son in her arms, waited patiently at the gates of the military barracks for their young fiancé and husband to come out, and then embraced the two rookie soldiers with delight.

'Well, what shall we do this Saturday? I propose that we all go for a stroll by the Alster this morning, then go for coffee. After that, lunch somewhere, before we take turns to spend some quiet time in my flat as couples in the afternoon – Caroline and Sebastian first.'

'Agreed, Hanna . . . and then you and Rhys can mind Siegfried while Sebastian and I go out to a night club. If we get back early we'll look after him while you go out..'

'That sounds wonderful. Let's go, girls, and leave this depressing dump behind for a while.' Unaware that his sergeant-major could overhear their conversation, Rhys added decisively, 'And once our military service is over we never have anything to do with the army again, do we, Sebastian?'

'Absolutely not.' Sebastian considered his future: he had recently decided to become an architect, while his brother intended to study law and Alex wanted to be a surgeon.

Noticing the frowning sergeant-major for the first time Caroline stared at him in horror, while the twins grinned sheepishly. Only the resourceful Hanna kept her head and gave him her sweetest smile. 'Oh, hello, Sergeant-Major. You really mustn't take the boys' comments too seriously, you know. They're so terribly immature.'

'I'll try to keep that in mind when I'm dealing with these two rogues later on, Miss von Reinholdt.' Charmed in spite of himself, the officer nodded at a relieved Rhys and Sebastian. 'Off you go and enjoy your weekend. I'd advise you not to have any more confidential chats so near to the barracks, just in case the next officer who overhears you is rather less understanding.'

'Yes, Sergeant-Major . . . and thank you.'

Nine months later, in May 1960, the barracks were buzzing with the news that Private Sebastian Meredith-Mayschoss's wife was expecting her second child, and was four months into her pregnancy. The other conscripts regarded the strapping six foot two nineteen-year-old with awed admiration, while senior officers hoped that the gifted and ambitious Meredith-Mayschoss twins would decide not to leave the army after their military service finished.

Relations improved somewhat between Caroline and her own family when a proud Dietrich and Adele became great-grandparents again in late October. Paula considered her grandmother status with a mixture of pleased satisfaction, but also regret that her late husband was not there to join in the celebrations.

'Benedict Klaus Meredith-Mayschoss – a fine name indeed. How wonderfully kind of Caroline and Sebastian to name their child after my beloved eldest son.' Alicia smiled as the eight week old baby was baptised a few days after Christmas, a ceremony in which Otto and Cassie were appointed godparents.

'Ah well, Rhys, we may have missed out on our holidays this year and last, but at least we've seen the family at Siegfried and Benedict's christenings. Come on, Siegfried, Daddy will get you something to eat. How about some tasty ham, chicken and potato salad?'

'Yes please, Daddy, and some cheese and tomato too . . . and bread and butter.' The fair-haired twenty-three-month-old looked up longingly at the christening party buffet that was set out in the dining room at Von Rittermann House, then at his soldier father and uncle.

'And for dessert there's Black Forest gateau, Herrentorte, and fruit and cream, so don't forget to leave some room for all those.'

Katie-Luise von Kleiste, now a tall and lively blonde four-year-old and possessing, like her fellow triplets, the von Rittermann silver-grey eyes and crooked little fingers, danced up merrily – closely followed by her two boisterous older brothers. 'Granddad's already got a full plate, and so has my father. Do hurry up and get some food, Uncle Sebastian, before it's all gone. Nikolas and Werner and I have already had our first course, but we can't reach the table for the next one. Can you get us something, please, Uncle Rhys?'

'But of course, young lady. What do you want?'

Serving the three hungry youngsters, then piling some food on his own plate, while Sebastian selected his cherished young son's favourite delicacies, the red-headed young man promptly joined his parents and great-great-aunt, his eyes sparkling. 'Well, what do you think of your growing family? By the time Alex, Amber and I have had families of our own, Germany's population will have swelled considerably. As for Cassie and my twin brother, they're going to have at least ten children apiece.'

'I certainly hope not, Rhys. Otto's mentioned six and Caroline four. I for one feel that that's more than enough.' Max shook his head at his wickedly grinning eldest son, and glanced at an animated Alex, Amber, Konrad von Kleiste and Charlotte standing deep in conversation by the roaring fire. 'I'm grateful for all the blessings God's bestowed on us, my boy. Twenty years ago your mother and I were parents-to-be ourselves. Now it's the turn of the next generation.'

Reluctantly returning to the hated army barracks the next day, the twins sat sulkily on telephone duty. Back home at Celle, preparations were well under way for New Year celebrations. Relaxing with Caroline, Siegfried, baby Benedict, Alex (now known officially as Baron Alexander von Rittermann) and Amber in the conservatory over a cup of tea, Rhiannon, sensing Kurt's unmistakable presence at her shoulder, smiled affectionately at him; then told her daughter-in-law exactly what the late baron had said about watching faithfully over his family after his death.

'So the spirit of Great-Uncle Kurt's actually here with us now? He knows that I've married Sebastian – and that he's now got two great-great-nephews?'

'He does indeed, my love. Life has a strange way of reuniting feuding families – or it has in this case, at least. My only regret is that you and your children can't see Kurt or hear his voice.'

'I wonder . . . just look.'

Staring fixedly at the tall and hazy black shape slowly forming by Rhiannon's side, Amber gripped her brother's hand excitedly. 'It's Father, I know it is.'

'Mummy, there's a strange man in the room.' Little Siegfried looked in stunned amazement at the fully formed male figure in black silk dressing-gown and dark-red pyjamas, and reached out to touch it – a puzzled expression on his chubby face as he heard his name called in an amused and friendly greeting.

'Well, they say that the dead sometimes draw their life-force from the living, or at least that ghosts can . . .' Rhiannon regarded her spellbound kinsmen meditatively, and turned with a warm smile towards the now-silent form that was studying them all intently. 'Welcome to your new family, Kurt. Once Alex and Amber marry and have families of their own you'll be a grandfather too, not just a father, uncle, great-uncle and great-great-uncle.'

Celebrating the New Year a day later, a group of thirty or so – the Mayschosses, von Kleistes, all the other families connected to them through marriage, and close friends – gathered in the grand drawing room for a toast after dinner. While Max, fortunately unable to see the black-robed figure standing proudly by Rhiannon's side, surveyed the packed room with a benevolent smile and proposed a toast to the health and happiness of his family and friends, and then to a strong Germany. 'Now please raise your glasses for a third and final toast . . . to my beautiful wife Rhiannon, without whom none of this could have been possible. She's everything I've ever wanted in a wife, and much more. To Rhiannon!'

'To Rhiannon!' As they sipped their champagne, the group roared their approval, while the five dogs barked enthusiastically. As midnight passed and 1 January 1961 arrived, amid a sea of smiling faces and animated conversation Rhiannon looked up lovingly at her husband, all the while keenly aware of a devoted Kurt close by. 'Here's to us, and may we have many more happy years together. Happy New Year, Max.'

Chapter Twenty-Seven

It's mine again, at long last . . . my beloved ancestral home.' The forty-four-year-old Rhiannon wandered dreamily through the empty and eerily echoing early Victorian house, her cat-like green eyes taking in the silent shadowy rooms and great oak staircase as she moved slowly upstairs, memories of the past surging before her at every turn. By her side, in silence, were her two youngest children, eighteen-year-old Alexander and his sixteen-year-old sister Amber – both tall young people, and both possessing the von Rittermann silver-grey eyes and crooked little fingers.

House-hunting in Scarborough during her fortnight's stay at the Grand Hotel, Rhiannon had spotted her former family home for sale, and immediately took a look round with the rest of her family – before buying it back from its elderly owners . . . who had bought Meredith House from her almost twenty-two years before. The property was desperately in need of thorough renovation, and Alicia had sadly shaken her head on seeing her beloved late nephew's home in such a neglected state. Max, Konrad, Otto, Cassie, Alex and Amber were all quick to tell the ecstatic new owner exactly what needed to be done. A dreamy Rhiannon, though, was more intent on reliving the past than paying any attention to what they had to say, and her mind filled with vivid memories as she fondly reminisced to her grown-up son and daughter and to Cassie. Meanwhile, Max commented to his old friend Konrad that he hoped the house was ghost-free, unlike Von Rittermann House – where Kurt von Rittermann's sinister spirit had suddenly appeared to many a family member, various guests, domestic members of staff and estate workers. Loved by some, treated with indifference or even loathed by others (Max and his former commanding officer falling into the latter category), the indomitable baron now visibly roamed his ancestral home and estate with apparent contentment and pride, forcing a perplexed Rhiannon to reassure her employees that the phantom was harmless. To preserve good relations, she announced a wage rise for everyone, along with a yearly Christmas bonus – which immediately ensured that she kept the majority of her staff.

Von Kleiste smiled at his companion. 'Even if it isn't, Max, they can't be any more odious than Kurt von Rittermann's spirit, that's for sure.'

'I suppose we should be grateful that he kept his word so faithfully regarding the protection of us and our families. If he hadn't done so, you, Peter, Klaus and I would never have survived the war.'

'And my late sisters and I would have been denied the great happiness and security of growing up with both my father and your grandfather, so I suppose we should accept his presence gracefully and bury the hatchet. We owe him such a lot.' Otto frowned, then went to join his four children and Alicia in the overgrown jungle of a back garden.

'Ah well, my grandson might have a point, I suppose' was all von Kleiste was willing to admit, but in his heart he knew that without his fellow baron's protective influence his family's safety and survival might have been threatened by the Gestapo.

The next week saw the cheque for Meredith House clear, and the visit of a local surveyor to assess the property's true condition. Over the next few months builders, decorators and finally a professional gardener worked their magic on the forlorn house and its depressingly neglected grounds. Rhiannon's investment soon resembled a building site, full of dust, noise, machinery and workmen.

'It's enough to scare away even the bravest of ghosts – just like the final bills,' Max laughed.

His wife shrugged, and calmly replied that once the house and grounds were restored to their former glory she and her family would be spending long weekends there every month, not to mention the Easter holidays, a few weeks in summer and a week in October. Meredith House would, moreover, be made available for all her family – the von Kleistes included. Rhiannon had long dreamed of buying back her former home, and now it was hers again she intended to turn it into the finest and most luxurious house in Scarborough.

Max nodded. There was no stopping an iron-willed and formidable Meredith female once she had made up her mind to do something.

The rest of the Easter break passed without any further surprises – except for the usual mischief that Cassie and Otto's naughty golden-haired, silver-grey-eyed and deceptively angelic-looking triplets got up to. Everywhere the triplets went they caused absolute mayhem. Otto himself had been wild as an adolescent, his scrapes causing his parents and grandparents to shake their heads in utter despair at his antics; but Cassie had managed to tame him, and had turned him into a model citizen.

This time the triplets decided, aged only four, to slip quietly away from their hotel and explore the town on their own, leaving their family sick with worry until a vigilant policeman noticed them, asking their names and where their parents were. On finding out that the children (who all spoke perfect and accent-free English) bore the aristocratic and distinctly German-sounding surname of von Kleiste – and that they had sneaked away from their parents to have some fun on their own – the policeman returned them to the Grand Hotel, where the desperately worried family were waiting after immediately reporting the trio's disappearance to the police.

The benevolent young police constable smiled good-naturedly at the slim and strikingly attractive Cassie and her handsome husband. 'We don't get many German aristocrats, or any aristocrats at all, come to think about it, in sunny Scarborough for their holidays . . .'

Rhiannon and Alicia duly explained their close connections with North Yorkshire, while the policeman shook his head in disbelief. It wasn't every day that he enjoyed afternoon tea at the Grand with fine nobility – an occasion he would mention to his colleagues back at the station.

Far away in Hamburg an enthusiastic Rhys and Sebastian Meredith-Mayschoss were eagerly looking forward to the end of their hated military service, and Hanna, Rhys's fiancée, to the successful completion of her teacher training at a college there. When they were free the twins planned to return to Von Rittermann House, along with Hanna, Caroline and her two boys until they started at Hamburg University. Rhys still intended to study law, and Sebastian architecture and construction.

Alexander, however, was not nearly so happy, and was absolutely dreading starting his own obligatory military service in late June. It was to Rhiannon, his father's ghost and to Alicia that Alex bewailed his reluctance to leave his beloved home and family to rough it in a military barracks in Kiel for two horrible years. His stepfather Max listened to the tirade with a contemptuous smile. Alexander had, in his opinion, always been far too spoilt, petted and pampered by the deeply indulgent Amber and Rhiannon; Alicia, on the other hand, had always practised a much stricter approach to her youngest great-great-nephew. Max felt he would benefit from a tough and no-nonsense period away from home. Alex and his stepfather had never got on particularly well – in contrast to the close and caring relationship Max enjoyed with Amber, Cassandra, Rhys and Sebastian. This dislike was doubtless thanks to Alex's physical similarity to his father. But, as Rhiannon so wisely commented, enjoying an excellent rapport with four out of five of their children was not so bad really . . . and rather better than some fathers enjoyed.

Not that Alex cared a jot about his stepfather's feelings towards him as he accompanied his family on his last holiday for the next two years: a fortnight in Italy, including an unforgettable visit to Pompeii and a week on the island of Capri). It was a wonderful experience – but also a bitter reminder of what he would be missing. Amber tried to cheer him up by promising to stay nearby at a hotel every weekend, thus allowing them to spend precious time together in comfort and privacy; his mother and great-great-aunt also promised to come and see him for one weekend a month. This had raised Alex's depressed spirits, and even Max noticed the young man's sudden optimism and cheerfulness. On learning of the planned family visits he shrugged, reflecting that even Alicia was spoiling the boy now . . .

Word was getting round Scarborough that the daughter of the late Sebastian and Elisabeth Meredith had bought back her former family home. This prompted much speculation about what she had got up to in Paris during the Second World War, given that she had married a German army officer. Her father had always declared his fondness and admiration for Germany – as had Rhys and Rhiannon; not to mention the fact that they had had a German housekeeper and governess. Despite the suspicions, local trade agreed that it would be good if Sebastian Meredith's daughter returned to her roots: she and her family were reputed to be very wealthy indeed.

Chapter Twenty-Eight

Well, there it is, Sebastian: the old stately home. Let's get out and take a good look at it again.' Rhys, now in smartly casual civilian attire, as was his twin brother, gazed fondly at the high and elaborately monogrammed iron gates. 'I'll race you to the house.'

Ordering the chauffeur of the silver-grey Rolls-Royce to stop, the athletically built siblings climbed out and sprinted up to the grand Baroque mansion, while their wives and Sebastian's two sons were driven up the impressive tree-lined drive in the July sunshine. An army of porters suddenly appeared from nowhere to take their luggage, and they were ceremoniously welcomed by the butler and conducted to a sitting room, where Rhys and Sebastian were already waiting for them.

Otto and Cassie had sent an amusing 'welcome home' telegram, which was duly read aloud and laughed over while exquisitely presented refreshments were handed out. Dark-haired and blue eyed Hanna was in an especially good mood, having passed her exams, and decided to indulge in an extra large portion of cake, as did a much slimmer Caroline – whose lively sons kept her constantly on the go.

Alex was missing, however. Driven to the barracks, with all his close family (Max excepted) there to support him, the young aristocrat had quickly settled into his tough new life. His best friend was a relative of his godfather, Heinz-Ludwig von Kleiste, a rather weedy bespectacled young man, for whose scientific and mathematical genius Alex was full of admiration. In return, the rather timid and hopelessly impractical Heinz-Ludwig worshipped his taller, stronger and more practical protector and helpmate. Whenever he struggled to do anything, his far more capable companion rescued him from his confusion – something that was closely observed by their commanding officers, who noted Alex's potential suitability as an officer and the way all the other conscripts automatically looked to him for leadership. Heinz-Ludwig, who might otherwise have been mocked and mercilessly bullied without Alex's protection and aid, was deeply in awe of his benefactor and was grateful also towards Amber, Rhiannon and Alicia – who had immediately taken the shy boy under their wing and took him out with them during their visits to Kiel. Heinz-Ludwig adored them all, especially Amber.

By the end of July Alex was not just an admired young conscript but a celebrated hero. When a fellow conscript fell into a ravine during a training exercise and broke his neck, the officer who went to his rescue suddenly had a heart attack. Alex promptly had himself lowered down to the victims, told the young and still conscious rookie soldier to keep perfectly still, then used his first aid skills to get the older man's heart beating again. Then the younger victim received the aspiring young surgeon's expert care, before being lifted safely from the ravine by an emergency medical team. Alex's life-saving actions were greatly praised, and the young man's family could not thank him enough for his help, the recovering officer and his family likewise. Alex's relatives, meanwhile, glowed with pride – even Max. The young hero was all the more determined to attend medical school and train to be a surgeon after his military service was over, if his exam results were good enough – which they amply proved to be the following month. Heinz-Ludwig predictably passed at the highest level possible, and had ambitions to become a scientist . . . while Amber, although she still had no idea what she wished to study at university, knew none the less that she wanted to continue her education.

At the beginning of August Rhiannon received the good news that Meredith House was ready for occupancy, and that the gardens were perfection itself. She and her family marvelled at the complete renovation and fresh decoration – her highly imaginative colour scheme bringing the house to life again. All that was lacking was the furnishing of the house. Rhiannon and her daughters never needed any encouragement to spend money on beautiful and luxurious items, and they combed the antique shops of Whitby and Scarborough for the most exquisite Regency and Victorian furniture, paintings and ornaments.

Just two weeks later the house was fully furnished in the grandest style, and the family was in residence and actively seeking a suitable middle-aged married couple (preferably with a well-behaved dog or two to add some life and soul to Meredith House). Within a week a middle-aged couple, with no children but two gorgeous young West Highland terriers, had been interviewed and appointed.

The only fly in the ointment was the news from Germany, with the construction of the Berlin Wall. Max's father Karl and his wife Anna predicted that nothing good would ever come of dividing Germany. Families would be separated and Germany torn apart. Anna had lost her first husband and two sons during the Siege of Stalingrad, and thus had good reason to hate both Russia and its people. Unsure of the future, the elderly couple decided, on Max and Rhiannon's invitation, to move to Von Rittermann House – selling their house in Kassel. Maria and Franz, who lived with them, were to be given half the proceeds (as Maria's inheritance), so they could buy a house for themselves.

By the end of August, as the family's time at Scarborough drew to a close, Karl's house was sold and arrangements were made for him and his wife to move house, while Maria and Franz moved to their new bungalow in Hanover.

Max's elderly father and stepmother were soon comfortable in their new home, undisturbed by the ghost of Kurt von Rittermann – which they had seen so many times before.

Alex welcomed his mother, sister and great-aunt to Kiel that September with the greatest of delight, and Heinz-Ludwig flung himself into their arms as they warmly greeted him.

Chapter Twenty-Nine

Celle, 15 August 1962

Dear Godfather,

Just a note as promised to keep you up to date with my and my siblings' news. I've decided to study economics and business studies at Hanover University for the next three years. Alex is going to study medicine, also at Hanover, when he finishes his military service in June next year, while Rhys and Sebastian are enjoying themselves hugely at Hamburg University – they're even doing a little studying sometimes. Hanna has passed her final exams, as you know, and she's going to start teaching at a Hamburg grammar school. I'm learning to drive, and I'm now the proud owner of a lovely red Mercedes sports car – a present from my family for passing my school exams.

Charlotte's off to a Swiss finishing school in September, for the next two years, and I hope she'll be very happy. The very idea of spending such a long time away learning how to be an accomplished young lady would send me into a blind panic, and I'd be expelled for rebellion and utter ineptitude – but I'm sure Charlotte will flourish.

Your loving goddaughter,
Amber

PS The rest of my family send their love and
best wishes.

The formidable Amber was soon excelling in her academic studies, but also
noticed to her surprise and dismay that her fellow students (she was the
only girl in both her degree subjects) treated her first with amused
contempt, and then, on discovering just how academically brilliant she
was, froze her out – her obviously superior ability, keenly competitive
spirit, larger than life character and striking beauty not being at all to their
liking. Nor did it help that the lecturers and tutors immediately recognised
and acknowledged her genius – thus gaining her even more antipathy and
jealousy. This, however, merely spurred Amber on to ever greater efforts to
succeed, leading to her becoming both the most isolated and the most
brilliant student on her course. She raced ahead of her hostile peers, and
defiantly made it clear exactly what they could do with their attitude.

'Just go for it, sister . . . and when I join you at university we'll join
forces and show them just what the von Rittermann siblings are capable of.
For the moment, though, just stick with it, and don't let the bastards grind
you down.' Alex's fiercely supportive reply spurred Amber on to ever
greater efforts and success.

'Well – she's certainly a stunner, but she's not the kind of girl most
men would dare to take on as a girlfriend or wife. She's a bit too much of a
challenge.' This was the response from Alex's peers when they saw Amber's
photograph and heard from her proud brother about her achievements. All
but one; Heinz-Ludwig von Kleiste blindly worshipped and admired her,
and her brother. Alex determined to keep her to himself for the rest of his
life: no-one else would ever appreciate her true worth or awesome gifts.

Freed from his military service in June, Alex was soon home. The faithful
Heinz-Ludwig had promised to keep in regular contact while he studied at
Bamberg University.

Alex and Amber's sister Cassie had news of her own to announce that
July: she was two months pregnant with her fifth child, much to the great
joy of her husband, his grandfather and the rest of her family. Cassandra
had, reflected Baron von Kleiste, proved to be a truly excellent family
investment.

In January Max's brother-in-law Franz died – but, as is so often the way,
new life arrived soon afterwards, with February witnessing the safe birth of
fair-haired Karl-Otto von Kleiste, Cassie and Otto's fourth son – his silver-

grey eyes and crooked little fingers proclaiming him to be the offspring of a von Rittermann-sired mother.

Later in the month Alex and his sister enjoyed a well-earned week off from their studies at Meredith House in Scarborough, and made one of their rare mistakes. On their first night they got hopelessly drunk, and woke up naked in Alex's bed the following dull and rainy morning with a terrible hangover. Had Alex used a condom during their bedtime frolics? The answer, after much reflection and searching for proof, was a definite no, and the ever resourceful Amber immediately made plans: how could she continue with her studies and arrange suitable care for the baby if she did indeed fall pregnant? Despite the circumstances, there was no way that she would consider an abortion. Immediately sketching out the future in meticulous detail, Amber decided she would continue studying right up until the birth in November, then take time off until January 1965 – with Alex collecting her lecture notes and any other vital information from her professors, so she could continue to study at home. On returning to her studies, her mother and her great-great-aunt would be responsible for the care of her baby during her absence. Incredibly, she even chose names for any child born: Horst Alexander for a boy and Victoria Alice for a girl.

Alex nodded approvingly at his adored sister, and declared her plan to be perfectly workable. Suggesting that they should only tell their mother, stepfather and great-great-aunt that he was the biological father, he said they should let everyone else think that Amber had become pregnant by a fly-by-night lover, but was keeping the child and bringing it up with the help of her family, as any good Catholic mother should. He would play the part of devoted uncle to the child in public, and a more fatherly role in private – all the while giving his sister as much moral and public support as she could ever desire.

Two months later the siblings knew that they were definitely parents-to-be, and approached their beloved mother with the news. Rhiannon was stunned. 'Max and my great-aunt will need to know the truth. She isn't likely to be shocked or angry, but he'll be both. As for the rest of our family, well . . . they'll just have to accept your story and make of the situation what they will. Now let's all hope that your child's born normal and healthy – despite its parents being so closely related.'

As predicted, Alicia raised her eyebrows slightly and only reiterated Rhiannon's hope that the child would be born healthy – while Max reacted with volcanic fury against his stepson, accusing him of corrupting, abusing and shamelessly taking advantage of his younger sister. Only his women-folk's desperate appeals for calm enabled Amber to explain her plans, and add that Alex had done nothing of the kind.

'Can't you see, Daddy? No-one will ever want me but him. Men seem to feel threatened by me, and certainly no-one's going to marry me considering my, well, domineering ways. Alex is my soulmate. He's learned to accept me as I am. And I love him just as much as he loves me. That's how things stand, however shocking it may seem.'

Amber's stepfather nodded resignedly, knowing in his heart that she was probably right.

The rest of the family frowned disapprovingly or shrugged on learning of Amber's pregnancy; their parish priest being the most sternly judgmental of all. Max and Rhiannon informed the university's principal of Amber's condition, and set in motion her plans to keep up with her studies for the two months that she would be away. The principal reflected on how even academically gifted and aristocratic students could come unstuck – but usually managed to pull through thanks to family support.

Soon came the far more pleasing news that a married Hanna and Caroline were both two months pregnant. Amber, meanwhile, now five months pregnant, merely looked somewhat plumper: clever dressing and her slim five foot eleven frame easily enabled her to hide any signs. She could, though, feel the baby (she and Alex had decided it was a boy) moving actively within her, the kicks becoming stronger as the months passed. Alex loved to put his hand gently on her rounded stomach and feel his child's movements before making passionate love to his sister – a red-blooded Amber responding with passion and ardent physical desire.

Chapter Thirty

Well now, he's certainly a whopper – ten pounds and three ounces and a very fine baby indeed, not to mention a rather noisy one.'

'And he's physically normal too, isn't he?' Amber looked anxiously at the midwife, who replied with some surprise that he most certainly was – and why shouldn't he be? 'Oh, no reason in particular . . .' Sitting up in bed, the new mother smiled, then took her loudly yelling son in her arms and tenderly nursed him. By the time Amber's close family were allowed to see mother and son and the nurse had left, little Horst was busily suckling away at his mother's breast. Alex took one look at the hefty, fair-haired and silver-grey-eyed baby and broke into a delighted grin, while Rhiannon and Alicia were all solicitous attention and Max kissed his stepdaughter lovingly on the cheek.

The proud father held his new-born son lovingly, and beamed triumphantly at his family – before passing the child to his mother, and then Alicia. Finally Max, much to everyone's amazement (especially Alex's), insisted on having his turn too . . . and, quite unbelievably, even congratulated Alex on the birth of his baby boy. 'He is, after all, my grandson as well, Rhiannon . . .' Max regarded his wife with a smile, then carefully handed the tot back to his mother.

On his arrival at Von Rittermann House, loving attention was duly lavished on Horst, the most contented child, by Karl and Anna Mayschoss and the rest of the family . . . with the spirit of his grandfather Kurt watching protectively over him every night. For Amber there followed two months of intensive child-care and home study. Her fellow students had been told that she was ill with a virus, which puzzled them somewhat: she had been blooming like a rose the last time they had seen her. Even so, no one suspected her pregnancy. She proved to be the most devoted of mothers, and Alex the most caring of uncles in public and loving of fathers in private. Horst succeeded in enslaving the entire household with his hypnotic charm: this strangely enchanting infant with piercing silver-grey eyes even held the family dogs in a kind of magical spell as they quietly and protectively lay by his side – as if sensing that this was a very special baby boy indeed.

Christened a week after his birth, in the von Rittermanns' private chapel, with Otto and Cassie von Kleiste as his godparents, and the Baron Konrad von Kleiste and his five great-grandchildren in attendance, little Horst proceeded to howl the place down as the decidedly uncomfortable priest anointed him with holy water. He only consented to grant his family some peace and quiet on being returned to his mother's arms.

Christmas came and went, along with the New Year, and finally it was time for Amber to leave her beloved baby son and return to her studies at Hanover University. The young woman serenely rejoined her fellow undergraduates with her usual lofty indifference, and resumed her domination of the academic scene – much to her course-mates' disgust.

February 1965 saw the birth of two sets of male twins: one pair to Rhys and Hanna and a silver-grey-eyed duo to Sebastian and Caroline. Little Karl, Christoph, Klaus and Jurgen caused their families both great joy and great deal of work. By August Amber, Rhys and Sebastian had all graduated with honours, as Hanna had; and by September they had started work as junior partners – Rhys in a law firm and Sebastian in an architect's office in Celle. Having sold their shared Hamburg residence, the two couples moved into adjacent houses.

Everyone seemed content, except Charlotte von Reinholdt, Hanna's still unmarried younger sister. Still a virgin at twenty-two, Charlotte was pious and sweet-natured, with a slim figure of middling height, pretty face, golden hair and gentle blue eyes. She had worshipped Alex since childhood and had, much to her family's consternation, refused several suitable offers of marriage on his account. Deeply shocked by Amber's unmarried mother status, and quite unable to understand her total lack of shame, Charlotte could only wonder how anyone could be so utterly and shamelessly brazen. Alex and his family, however, seemed to be curiously indifferent to Amber's immorality, the young medical student utterly devoted to his younger sister and illegitimate nephew – and also depressingly indifferent to Charlotte's coyly sweet smiles and feminine charm. If only he could, or would, love her as much as he clearly loved his sister and little Horst.

Horst was an intelligent, sturdy, alert and observant child of ten months old – and the apple of his mother's eye, not to mention Alex's pride and joy. Prone to wandering into all kinds of danger, thanks to his adventurous nature, he was followed everywhere he went by at least one of the family dogs and the protective spirit of his grandfather . . . and was watched over constantly by the rest of the family and his nanny. Max devotedly played his part in keeping his beloved Amber's baby boy safe, the deep bond that had developed between Horst and Max being considered something of a wonder by the rest of the family – especially as Max had been the bitterest enemy of Alex and Amber's father. An early talker, Horst was soon able to understand German and English, as could Caroline and Hanna's children.

As Christmas 1965 approached poor Maria, Max's sister, was obviously becoming very ill with breast cancer, and she sold her house and moved to live with her eldest adopted son and his family. By February 1966 she was dead, soon being followed to the grave by Anna, Max's stepmother – leaving a broken-hearted Karl to mourn the deaths of his wife and daughter.

Amid the sad family events. the rather autocratic Baron von Kleiste made it crystal clear to Alex that he wanted to know what feelings, if any, the young baron had for his lovely granddaughter Charlotte.

'Well, she's the most charming person, and, well . . . I'm rather fond of her.' Caught totally off guard during a visit from his godfather, Alex looked a little guiltily at the elderly aristocrat, and wondered just what he should do. Amber could obviously not be his wife, and in the end it was his duty to sire a legitimate male heir – even if he really wanted Horst to succeed him as baron. As a second choice, though, Charlotte was just as suitable as anyone else – so why not marry her, as his godfather so obviously wished him to? Just as long as he did not have to give up his relationship with his cherished sister and lose contact with their son.

Thus it was that Alex and Charlotte became engaged shortly afterwards, and the wedding was booked for early October. An overjoyed Charlotte and her family had finally got what they had so long dreamed of.

By now extremely wealthy in her own right, having inherited a large fortune from her father when she was twenty-one, Amber was reassured by Alex that he would always reserve his deepest love and loyalty for her and Horst. She had decided, on gaining her MA that August, to study for her PhD in medieval European history at York University – and therefore live at Meredith House, with Horst attending a private day nursery. This decision was greeted with approval by all concerned, even her brother realising that it would be unwise to have his wife and lover living in the same house. In order not to risk losing contact with Alex, Amber stated her firm intention of visiting her family at Celle twice a month, and also for a week at Easter and Whitsun – not to mention for a fortnight during the summer holidays and at Christmas. Alex then vowed to spend a weekend each month at Scarborough without Charlotte, causing Max to shake his head at such incredible devotion. Alicia, Max and Rhiannon decided to visit their adored Amber and Horst during the remaining weekend of each month: though far from home, mother and son would still see plenty of their family.

The young couple were married in Munich, Charlotte's native and residential city, at her family church. Dressed in a rich lace-trimmed white satin dress, her long fair hair piled up in a glorious mass of curls and ringlets, Charlotte glided down the aisle on her father's arm with a radiant smile, her deeply emotional parents watching their treasured girl finally become the wife of the childhood-playmate she had loved for so long, and welcoming the family union with the greatest delight. Alex, meanwhile, stood at the altar, his expression unreadable, as he silently wished that it was Amber he was marrying.

Then came the wedding reception at an expensive local hotel, with gourmet dishes – and the breaking of plates for good luck – and after dinner speeches. Horst, predictably, observed all this brouhaha silently, his mother likewise.

As the afternoon turned into early evening the bridal couple departed for their honeymoon in Venice. This proved to be everything that Charlotte had dreamed of – the couple's luxury hotel being a glittering dream of polished marble, shimmering chandeliers and the most exquisitely graceful Greek and Roman statues. Alex was the most considerate of lovers as he gently and painlessly took her virginity, which she had saved for him, on their wedding night. A romantic gondola ride the next day, and an exploration of that glorious city over the next seven days, utterly delighted Charlotte, and even Alex, the secretly reluctant bridegroom. For the moment, anyway, he managed to put on a convincing show of love and romantic feelings for his wife.

Christmas 1966 brought the family together again at Von Rittermann House. Alex quietly commented to his sister that though Charlotte was the most affectionate, loyal and charming of wives, not to mention a highly capable lady of the manor, her conversation was utterly without originality or interest . . . and her company and performance in bed were incredibly boring. Were it not for Amber's twice monthly visits to Celle and his own monthly visit to Meredith House, he confessed that he would soon have been thoroughly fed up with his marriage. Alex even failed to persuade

Charlotte to learn to ride, so afraid was she of horses. Amber, who like Alex was an accomplished equestrian, shrugged; then enjoyed yet another passionate hour of intensely physical pleasure with him, in her private apartment next door to Alex and Charlotte's. A deeply contented and satisfied Alex rejoined his wife with a supremely happy smile – which the innocent Charlotte thought was meant for her.

Amber, meanwhile, had noticed that Englishmen were just as distrustful and wary of her as their German counterparts, and satisfied herself with just a few female friends at York University.

Otto and Cassie had decided to spend some time in Paris with their five children, and duly departed at the beginning of January. Still deeply in love with his charismatic and good-looking wife, the thirty-four-year-old doctor was also utterly devoted to his children – who all thought the world of him.

Horst, for his part, thought the world of the family ghosts that inhabited Meredith House. His ability to see his dignified great-grandparents, his jovial great-uncle Rhys and the stately Magda as they fondly observed that fine residence's many comings and goings, meant that they soon became just as dear to him as any living member of his family. Many a time did a visiting Rhiannon, Amber, Alicia and Max feel these supernatural presences as they chatted together during the day, or relaxed after dinner. Amber and Alex were quite used to the benevolent phantoms' presence as they snuggled up together on the sofa in the evening and watched television, while Horst lay snugly in bed, chatting contentedly away to whichever spirits had decided to watch over him for the night.

Chapter Thirty-One

She had noticed them the very moment they walked into the café that freezing January afternoon – the tall and handsome blond and blue-eyed, early middle-aged man and his beautiful wife, who looked to be in her early twenties. Of about medium height, she had distinctive and strangely familiar silver-grey eyes and crooked little fingers – the latter revealed as she took off her fine black leather gloves and sat down at the next table with her family: five very good-looking children aged from about two to twelve, and all with the same distinctive eyes. The family's elegant and expensive attire, gracious manners and proud bearing were typical of the chic café's usual clientele. The next thing she noticed was that they spoke German among themselves and, in the case of the mother, fluent French with the waiter . . . French of the most educated kind, totally free of any accent. The impeccably dressed stranger with the long and glossy hair hauntingly reminding the slightly built, grey-haired elderly woman in the shabby coat of someone she had known and loved many years before. Her four-year-old daughter, Marie-Claude, had run away only a month before his death to find him – the aristocratic German father she had never known.

Gisèle normally didn't dare to frequent posh places like this, and didn't have the money to do so – but today was so bitterly cold that she really felt like treating herself to a coffee. Not to mention enjoy the wonderfully happy memories of the debonair Ralph, who took her out to grand places like this in the 1930s, when she was still a lovely young woman . . . just like this elegant stranger. So fascinated was she by the family that her staring soon attracted their attention. The lovely young woman gave her a charming smile, then turning away again to chat to her husband.

And then she heard it . . . the name von Rittermann. An overwhelmed Gisèle longed to ask the family about it, but lacked the courage. Suddenly desperate to leave, the next thing she knew she was hunting in her handbag for her purse. It wasn't there. She glanced with a panic-stricken expression at the contemptuous waiter, and, embarrassed, tried to explain.

'I'm sure we can cover the cost for you.' Paying the bill, and giving the appreciative waiter a generous tip, the young woman (whose name was Cassandra, the eavesdropping Gisèle had already learned), added generously, 'And if you're hungry we'll buy you a hot meal and another drink. It's so cold outside.'

After warming chicken soup and another steaming coffee, the deeply grateful Gisèle had learned that her benefactress's name was Cassandra von Kleiste, and her husband was Otto. She was surprised, when she told them her name, to be greeted with stunned expressions – and then to be asked by a suddenly sombre Cassandra her husband's name, and how many children she had.

'My husband was Jean-Pierre. He's been dead since 1945. I had ten children: two are dead now and seven I've lost contact with. One, my dearly loved Marie-Claude, was adopted when she was four by a wealthy German couple during the war.' She pulled some old photographs from her handbag. 'Look – here she is with her adoptive family at their home in Paris . . . and this is me about six years earlier with her father, Ralph von Rittermann. But in August 1944 they left France for good, and I've heard nothing from any of them since.'

Cassandra regarded the older woman with a pensive smile, and reached for her hand. 'Not until now, anyway. I'm that little girl. I was renamed Cassandra Elisabeth by my new parents.'

Gisèle's dark eyes never left her beautiful daughter's face, and the tears silently began to roll down her wizened cheeks.

Having returned to the family's luxury hotel, so they could talk with more privacy, Gisèle revealed that she had been diagnosed with cervical cancer just a week earlier, and had been given about a year to live. She also told Cassandra of the fate of her half-brothers and sisters: the twin boys had been guillotined for the murder of a policeman and three civilians during a bank raid, aged only twenty-two, while their three brothers had all ended up as alcoholics and drug addicts, and had been convicted of violent crimes. Their four sisters had all became prostitutes and petty criminals.

'But you were so different from them. You were the living image of your father – with the same superior air, and a defiant contempt for everything around you. You even told me, your own mother, when you were three and learnt by sheer chance that Jean-Pierre wasn't your biological father, that you wanted to live with your wealthy real daddy instead of with us. This didn't go down at all well with my husband, who beat and abused you all the more. I loved you dearly, but I couldn't protect you from Jean-Pierre's cruelty as he could so easily turn violent. I tried my hardest to be a good mother. With hindsight, I should have done just as your father asked – go with you to live with him, and leave the rest of the family behind – but I didn't have the nerve. I feared your stepfather would go berserk and try to kill us all. Oh, Marie-Claude, how can you – or your poor dead father – ever forgive me after all that I've done?'

Breaking down completely, Gisèle sobbed bitterly, Cassandra giving her a comforting hug while Otto and the five children looked on, bemused.

'Hush, Mother . . . I can and I do forgive you, of course I do. You must come back with us to Germany for the rest of your days. We're leaving in two days' time. We'll sort out all your affairs, and you're to move in here right away.'

Gisèle nodded submissively and wiped her eyes, while her son-in-law silently reflected with an amused smile that his feisty wife was certainly a chip off the old von Rittermann block.

Gisèle's first impression of the vast and impeccably maintained von Kleiste country estate was, inevitably, one of open-mouthed awe – and her first reaction on entering their magnificent home was a stunned look of utter disbelief. The baron himself seemed like a truly celestial being as he graciously welcomed her to his palatial abode, and her luxurious private quarters were a dream come true. She was, however, under strict orders from the very beginning never to call her daughter Marie-Claude in public, or whenever the baron received visits from friends, family or acquaintances. Officially she was to be her offspring's aunt, not her mother – as her daughter's fictional parents were both long since dead, and had been the very rich French friends of her adoptive family. Rather than risk embarrassing her cherished offspring, Gisèle wisely remained silent, much to everyone's relief.

Dining with the family was a nightmare at first – with so many sets of cutlery that she was completely confused. Marie-Claude came to her rescue, and always sat next to her in order to advise her . . . and thus Gisèle gradually became accustomed to and appreciative of the sheer magnificence of the meals and her surroundings, as well as greatly enjoying the time she now spent travelling round Europe with Marie-Claude and her German relatives.

Gisèle's own story began to slip out bit by bit. She had been born in

1900 to a fairly well-to-do middle-class French family in Paris, her father, Charles Dupont, by profession a senior town hall clerk. In 1914, when war broke out, he was conscripted into the French Army and sent to fight on the Western Front, being killed in action in April 1915. Georges, Gisèle's beloved elder brother and only sibling, was likewise killed in action. Gisèle was devastated. After she left school the girl went to work in a jeweller's shop, and then, after a series of vicious rows with her mother, with whom she had never really got on, she had moved in with and married Jean-Pierre Jacques. She was already two months pregnant. Jean-Pierre, a young man she had been dating since the end of the Great War, had cunningly avoided conscription by faking extreme myopia. Three years her senior, and a railway guard, he found no favour whatsoever with his new wife's mother or bourgeois family, who disowned her. Living in a working-class suburb of Paris, Gisèle and her husband had seven children in quick succession.

Then, in 1932, Jean-Pierre lost his job, through drinking, and turned to crime. Gisèle reluctantly resorted, with her husband's ready approval, to prostitution in order to pay the bills and keep their family fed . . . and met and fell madly in love with one of her punters, the charming and generous Ralph von Rittermann. When Jean-Pierre was sent to jail for three years for petty theft in late 1933, an utterly besotted Ralph gleefully reserved her entirely for himself, becoming her only customer.

Then, out of the blue, Gisèle had become pregnant with Ralph's child, and gave birth to a daughter just before her husband's release from prison.

The rest Cassandra knew – and she was able to fill in some gaps for her mother. 'The officer who interrogated you at Gestapo Headquarters was my father's first cousin, Baron Kurt von Rittermann, deputy head of the Paris Gestapo. My adoptive parents weren't relatives of my father at all, but Kurt's Anglo-French married lover and her German army officer husband.'

Gisèle smiled sadly, and handed her daughter a solid gold heart-shaped locket and matching chain. 'This is for you to keep when I die . . . it's the only valuable thing I still have from Ralph which I managed not to sell or exchange for food when the Allies took Paris. I too was beautiful once – as these pictures taken with your father show . . .

'My time with you all is slowly but surely coming to an end. At least I'll die happy, having finally got to see you again. To know that you'll be the next Baroness von Kleiste . . . Your poor dear father would have been so incredibly proud, I know . . . just as I am.'

Cassandra smiled gently and gave her mother a warm hug . . . her heart too full to say anything in reply.

In August 1967 Amber received the glad tidings that she was the proud possessor of a doctorate, and was in a wild and celebratory mood . . . so much so that she requested another child from Alex . . . and was duly given ample chances by him to conceive, during her two week stay at Von Rittermann House and afterwards. Charlotte still knew nothing of her husband's incestuous relationship, her in-laws never intending to enlighten her.

By October both Amber and Cassandra were two months pregnant – with Horst being told by his mother that Alex was the father of his unborn sibling. She instructed her little boy to remain completely silent, and he solemnly promised to obey – having first informed Amber what he had seen 'in his head': that she would have a healthy baby boy and Cassandra would have female twins, while Charlotte and her unborn baby would be dead by February . . . A deeply shocked Amber immediately made him promise not to repeat this to anyone, but didn't doubt the truth of his prediction. Horst was proving to be a remarkably psychic child, predicting events with an unbelievable accuracy. His ability to see ghosts and spirits was becoming ever more evident . . . as was his rather worrying gift of being able to guess what other people were thinking, or even read their minds . . . a perplexed Amber was not quite sure which yet. His grim prediction put her mind at rest on one point – that she would never see a legitimate son of Alex's by Charlotte replace Horst as the next Baron von Rittermann.

A still barren Charlotte, meanwhile, eyed her far more fortunate sister, Hanna, as well as Caroline, Cassie and Amber, in an increasingly jealous and resentful manner, something which did not make her the most pleasant of companions to her husband. But then, in November, she finally managed to achieve her long-dreamed-of ambition, began once again to look forward to the future with a joyous heart. But then, during one of Horst and Amber's visits on a bitterly cold morning in mid-February, she was found in a lifeless state by a grim-faced Alicia in the Italian garden, and declared dead on arrival at hospital – victim of a massive brain haemorrhage.

'Which now means that you'll be my beloved wife and baroness in all but name. I'll adopt Horst as my own son – so he'll inherit my title and entire baronial estate and three-quarters of my fortune. Our second child will inherit the remaining quarter, and all your fortune – and will also be adopted by me straight after birth. Any other details can be agreed later, and everything will be legally ratified as soon as possible. Charlotte's loss is no loss at all . . . rather a blessed relief, in fact, since our marriage couldn't have remained amiable for much longer, given our total incompatibility.

This way she'll never know that I never loved her, and didn't even want to marry her in the first place.'

Amber and Alex regarded the intense grieving of Charlotte's parents and grandfather with a detached air; Hanna, Max and Horst likewise not appearing remotely affected or grief-stricken. Amber was far too busy taking advantage of everything that Charlotte had now lost to feel the slightest interest: a generous personal allowance from Alex and the right to wear the spectacular von Rittermann heirloom emeralds were uppermost in her mind as she leisurely took her pick of her deceased sister-in-law's valuable collection of jewellery. Most of the remaining items, on Alex's orders, were to be shared between Hanna and Charlotte's mother, with both Rhiannon and Caroline receiving a few pieces each, at their request, in memory of the dear departed.

The Requiem Mass was held early the following week, with Charlotte being duly interred in the spacious von Rittermann burial vault with honour, pomp and ceremony, as befitted the wife of a wealthy German baron. All the while Amber could feel her baby son kicking inside her – as if he longed for the day when he would take his allotted place as a member of the illustrious von Rittermann family. 'Your time will come, my darling boy, I promise. Just try to be patient for a little longer.' She patted her swollen stomach with maternal pride and affection, all the while aware of her family's silent and deeply caring scrutiny. This was what it was like to be truly loved.

Chapter Thirty-Two

Congratulations, my dear. You're the mother of a fine baby boy – and an unusually fiery-headed and hefty one.' The Hanover Hospital midwife regarded an exhausted Amber with a brisk professional smile, then handed the delighted mother the red-headed and silver-grey-eyed tot. It had been a long and agonising birth, and the twenty-four-year-old Amber silently vowed not to have any more children. Her wonderful son was everything she had wanted.

Horst was soon allowed in to see his mother, and regarded the new-born baby with an intense curiosity and interest before snuggling up to her affectionately and receiving a loving smile and kiss in return. An ecstatic Alex held his younger son in his arms and beamed delightedly at his sister, before Rhiannon, Max and Alicia were allowed to hold the child. 'And I assume, my love, that we'll be calling him Daniel Kurt, as we agreed?'

'But of course. So, Horst, what do you think of your baby brother?'

The little boy smiled at her and gave the baby a warm and brotherly hug in reply.

The following day Cassandra was the happy mother of beautiful non-identical twin girls named Isabella Gisèle and Victoria Gisèle – the former lacking the von Rittermann silver-grey eyes (having inherited her father's blue ones) but still sporting the crooked little fingers; the latter inheriting the silver-grey eyes but not the distinctive fingers. Hanna and Caroline Meredith-Mayschoss had already completed their own families of two and four sons. The issue of godparents was neatly solved by Amber and Alex becoming Isabella and Victoria's, and Otto and Cassie baby Daniel's godparents – the latter couple closely observing the young baron's paternal behaviour towards his two nephews and exchanging a meaningful glance, but with no intention of saying a word to anyone about their suspicions.

In early June Gisèle Jacques finally passed away, her daughter grieving deeply for her loss but grateful, nevertheless, that they had at least been able to spend a final year together. Gisèle was buried after a very moving and well-attended Requiem Mass, her grave in Bamberg's main cemetery henceforth visited weekly by her devoted daughter, who regularly wore her mother's prized gold locket with pride. That the terminally ill Gisèle had managed to live long enough to hold her twin granddaughters in her arms and also attend their christening was deeply appreciated by both mother and daughter.

By late December Daniel was becoming ever more active and mischievous – as a somewhat bemused Konrad von Kleiste found out when he invited the von Rittermann family to Bamberg for Christmas. Apart from watching the toddler, who with his brother had now been formally adopted by Alex, and thus called him Daddy, he managed to spend much time walking with his beloved Rhiannon, or enjoying cosy chats with her at home – having been more than a little in love with her ever since he had made her acquaintance back in June 1940. Being the perfect gentleman, though, he had never given a hint to anyone of his feelings towards her – and he never would.

A thorny question that worried Alex and Amber deeply was their children's future education, as the state system did not impress them in the slightest.
    'So why not set up your own school on the von Rittermann estate? You could base it on the traditional English system.' Rhiannon regarded her younger children, who nodded thoughtfully, her idea rather appealing to them. And after this single comment it was all systems go. Hanna immediately offered her services as headmistress, while Otto and Cassie requested weekly boarding places for their four elder children, and quite a few von Kleiste relatives in Bavaria showed a definite interest too – as did many of Max's kinsfolk, Sebastian and Caroline, and Rhys and Hanna.
    Thus it was that the Von Rittermann Academy, taking pupils aged three to nineteen, came into existence in September 1969. All pupils wore a dark red and green uniform, their blazers proudly sporting the von Rittermann coat of arms on the top pocket. Otto and Cassie's children, and those of their von Kleiste kinsmen, lived at Von Rittermann House with their titled relatives – but Alex and Amber only allowed their relatives to pay a nominal fee one term in advance: the school was nothing more than a legal way of educating their own sons exactly as they chose.

Educational standards were high and discipline strict, with all pupils encouraged to do their very best and seek to excel. The curriculum, naturally enough, covered exactly the same subjects as West German state schools, but added some more interesting and unusual elements as well, such as riding and swimming lessons, karate, archery, animal care and theatre studies.

Word began to get out locally about this innovative and select new school as its teachers, pupils, parents and families enthusiastically praised it; and gradually more pupils were enrolled – paying a full fee.

By mid-November 1969 the aged Baron von Kleiste's health was beginning to fail, and he moved into Von Rittermann House to be near his four elder great-grandchildren and Rhiannon. Otto realised he had to give up his profession as a doctor and, along with Cassandra, take charge of the running of the von Kleiste estate – with his ailing grandfather's full blessing.

Alicia, aged a hundred and one, was in unbelievably good health for her age, and still completely mentally alert. Horst and Alex adored her and she them, with an equally devoted Rhiannon dreading the day her seemingly immortal great-aunt finally passed away.

Karl Mayschoss, like Konrad, was becoming decidedly frail – but was nevertheless the most contented of men as he watched his adored son's family grow up around him in such prosperity, health and happiness.

Christmas 1969 and the New Year were to be spent by the extended family at Von Rittermann House, with Otto and Cassie bringing their three younger children along, and Sophia and Klaus von Reinholdt joining their children and their families. Perhaps this large and joyous family gathering would prove to be the last at which Karl, Konrad and Alicia would all be present.

Chapter Thirty-Three

Life, reflected Amber, as she left a happily playing Daniel at the von Rittermann crèche and took five-year-old Horst to school (where he attended lessons with children aged ten, such was his ability), could sometimes be unbelievably hectic as a working mother – especially when her position was so demanding: she was now managing director of the von Rittermann Business Park, a prestigious position she had occupied since 1969, after working as Rhiannon's deputy for nine months. Rhiannon was now in charge of the school's pastoral department, while the capable Caroline was head of school administration and Hanna, her sister-in-law, was still headmistress.

Both Caroline and Hanna's twin sons attended the von Rittermann Academy as pupils – as well as its after-school club. Max was in overall charge of the farm, along with the care and management of the estate. His deputy was Hans Mayschoss, one of his relations, whose ambition, industry and skill meant that he would one day succeed Max as estate grounds manager. Alicia helped out in the school's pastoral department as a valued and experienced counsellor, while many other members of the Mayschoss family worked on the estate and at the mansion, along with a number of von Kleistes and even quite a few North English-born and bred Merediths – who had recently made contact with Rhiannon after about thirty years of utter silence.

As a trip down Memory Lane, Donald Meredith, a retired police inspector, and his cousin Paul, with their wives Florence and Mary, had visited Scarborough to see their cousin's former residence. To their surprise they had discovered that the house was once again in the possession of

Sebastian's daughter, and that she visited every month. A delighted Donald and Paul, who were now Sebastian's only surviving cousins, Barry having recently died, had duly left their names, addresses and phone numbers with the housekeeper. Rhiannon was more than happy to renew contact, and arranged a meeting between the two families at Meredith House that Easter.

Meeting their German cousins for the first time were the two English Meredith girls:

Donald's cherished five-year-old granddaughter, Damara, and the nine-year-old Jessica, Barry's granddaughter. The former was slightly built, black-haired and blue-eyed, with a quiet but determined nature, while Jessica was her complete opposite, with long golden locks, green eyes and vivacious spirits – not to mention a cheeky grin. Both cousins were adored as the only girls born in their generation, and were thoroughly spoiled and pampered.

After this emotional family reunion, at which Alicia had been welcomed warmly back into the Meredith family, quite a number of German-speaking Merediths who had trained as teachers asked if they could come and work at the Von Rittermann Academy, which now boasted three hundred pupils, while others were given employment elsewhere on the estate.

Konrad and Karl were by now extremely frail, and Horst predicted their deaths within a few months. The two men were the best of friends, and loved to put the world to rights as they reminisced over a cup of coffee or glass of wine. Max's beloved father was the first to die, his bad summer cold rapidly turning into pneumonia, while just a few weeks later Konrad had a massive stroke in front of his family, leaving everyone in a state of shock and grief. Both Requiem Masses were well attended by family and friends alike, with a pensive Alicia regarding her dear old companions' passing with a pensive smile, all too aware that she had outlived not only them but also so many younger members of her own family, her husband and their six sons included.

The summer holidays brought Rhiannon and her family back to Scarborough for yet another family reunion. Otto and Cassie were now the new Baron and Baroness von Kleiste, while Amber was Baron Alexander von Rittermann's wife and baroness in all but name – and sporting the von Rittermann emeralds at all important social occasions as if she were indeed the baroness. Amber thought the world of her brother Alex, and could not imagine life without him . . . and Alex felt exactly the same about her. Adored by her sibling-lover and two sons, the beautiful young red-head ruled supreme over her brother's country estate. As Max said to Rhiannon one day, 'Sometimes I wonder just who the true baron is . . . the indomitable Doctor Amber von Rittermann, who manages this estate with such brilliance, or her brother: he's just not showing any interest in what his father's left him.'

If Karl's last will and testament had been utterly straightforward and without surprises, Baron Konrad von Kleiste's had most certainly not. His grandson Otto had inherited his title and the entire baronial estate, and all but an eighth of his vast fortune – which went to Sophia, Konrad's beloved daughter and only surviving child. The surprise was the sealed letter that Rhiannon received, as well as some of his personal belongings and papers, and a magnificent old Ruby-set gold-filigree tiara, necklace, earrings, bracelet and ring that had belonged to his grandmother, and which he had given to Rhiannon a month or so before his death as an early birthday present.

'So when are you going to read it, Rhiannon?' Max regarded his wife quizzically.

'Oh, I really don't know. Perhaps after all this has finally sunk in.'

'I wonder what he has to say . . . perhaps how much he adored you, and couldn't bear to be parted from you in his last year or two of life, not to mention just how exquisitely beautiful and desirable he found you from the very beginning. And you needn't look so shocked: even I could guess his true feelings, even though he was obviously trying to keep them secret.'

'Oh, well, in that case, Mr Sherlock Holmes, I'll let you read it too, when I eventually decide to open it.'

'You're a truly remarkable woman, Rhiannon. Do you know that?'

Rhiannon smiled at her husband. She had long ceased to wonder at life's strange and unfathomable twists and turns, and now accepted them as part of that mysterious thing called Fate.

After outstanding exam results at the Von Rittermann Academy, Alex, Amber and the family decided to go ahead with expansion, and to accept a maximum of two hundred more pupils, something which still left a long waiting list and a lot of disappointed parents.

Soon preparations were being made for Max and Alicia's joint birthday party in November 1970: Max was to be fifty-eight, Alicia one hundred and two. Physically frail as she was, Alicia had lost none of her invincible spirit, quick wit or razor-sharp faculties. She stood proudly beside her great-nephew-in-law as the rest of the family sang Happy Birthday to them in English and German.

Rhiannon finally read her letter from Konrad von Kleiste, as did Alicia and Max. The baron indeed declared his undying passion, devotion and love for Rhiannon, as Max had so accurately predicted. But there was so much more.

Celle, 3 January 1970

My dearest Rhiannon,
First of all may I state my heartfelt thanks for your welcoming me so warmly to your home and into your family for what I know are my final months of life. Just to be near you is a delight in itself, and also a comfort in my old age . . . not to mention a real ray of sunshine. Max too has been the best and most loyal of friends to me and my family, and I bless the day I sent him to be billeted with you back in June 1940, thus bringing two such well-matched young people together. My own deep gratitude to you, Rhiannon, for using your influence with Kurt von Rittermann to protect me and my close family from Gestapo arrest is something you already know. And though neither Kurt nor his former commanding officer had the authority to prevent my arrest, they did at least ultimately secure my official release from custody, saving me from any further torture, and execution.

Moreover, I have loved you passionately for many years now, not to mention desired you greatly. But out of my loyalty for and friendship with Max I have said nothing to either of you, nor acted on my feelings.

Regarding Alex and Amber, I have come to realise just how deeply devoted and physically close my two younger godchildren are – with young Horst and Daniel the probable results. No wife could ever hope to compete successfully for Alex's affections. My poor little Charlotte was, on reflection, a most unsuitable match for your youngest son, both in intellect and personality. On the other hand, Alex and Amber are one of the most perfectly matched couples I have ever seen – and have two extremely fine sons. Your Amazon of a daughter has turned out to be a truly wonderful mother, and Alex the best and most loving of fathers. I have no option but to forgive the guilty pair and wish them the very best of luck, not only in raising their family but also in the future management and running of the von Rittermann estate. They will, however, have to be extremely careful if their unlawful relationship is not to become public in the future, as both you and they are doubtless aware.

May God bless and keep you and your family always, Rhiannon.

Your eternally devoted and ever grateful old friend,

Konrad

'Ah well, I didn't really think he was so naïve as to remain ignorant of Alex and Amber's guilty secret' was all Max said when he read the letter, while the wise old Alicia only smiled at her great-niece. She too had long realised that Konrad had harboured deep feelings towards Rhiannon, but had prudently chosen to remain silent.

One hot and humid night the next July, Horst heard his beloved elderly relative calling his name, then stared up at her smiling figure as she bid him a final loving goodbye, her small white dog clasped in her arms. Not in the least surprised, the six-year-old boy listened in reverent silence as she bid him always to be a credit to the family and true to himself, before invoking her last blessings on him and his clan. Gradually her form faded, leaving the child spell-bound for a minute or so, before he bolted from his room to inform his mother what he had just seen and heard. They immediately went to check on the old lady, and discovered that she and her cherished old bichon frise had both passed away peacefully in their sleep.

Alicia's will was more straightforward than Konrad's: she had made Rhiannon her one and only legatee, and left instructions to her great-niece to decide exactly what she wished to give to other family members as keepsakes.

Following a deeply moving and majestic Requiem Mass later in the week, the red and white rose covered coffin containing both Alicia and her dog was interred with ceremony and honour in the von Rittermann burial vault. Broken-hearted Rhiannon sobbed on Max's shoulder as she bid farewell to her cherished great-aunt, only to dream that very night of the old matriarch, her little dog held lovingly in her arms, waving a radiantly happy farewell before vanishing into a misty tunnel with a glowing entrance. This dream reassured her that Alicia's spirit had passed safely over to the other side – and her insight was confirmed when Horst told his family the next day that he had seen exactly the same in his dreams.

Alicia's death marked the end of an eventful and often traumatic era – and only precious family memories and memorabilia remained to evoke those years.

Chapter Thirty-Four

S o, have you had any thoughts yet about further education, Nikolas?' Otto regarded his eldest son intently. Nikolas's siblings had already made detailed plans – Werner to study engineering and applied mathematics, the artistic Katie-Luise art, design and fashion, Kasper economics and geography, and the devoutly religious Karl-Otto adamant that he was to enter the priesthood.

Nikolas took a deep breath. 'I want to do a BSc at Bamberg University, and live at home as the others are planning to do, then do military service. But I don't know what to choose as my career. Perhaps medicine . . .'

His ex-doctor father smiled approvingly. 'Take all the time you need to make a decision. Now, before you go there's something I've got to tell you. Young Jessica and her family are going to spend the first two weeks of August with us, and then she's staying on for another fortnight – so she can come to France and Switzerland with us. Damara, with her parents of course, is going to spend a fortnight with Sebastian and Caroline, and then go to the Loire Valley for a week. Jessica's even been having German lessons in England for the last year or so.'

A week later Jessica arrived at the von Kleiste estate. And then, suddenly, the sun wasn't shining any more – with the devastating news of the tragic deaths of her father and mother, Richard and Jennifer, and her three brothers in a house fire. The Meredith family was plunged into a state of deep shock and mourning. Jessica was noticeably quick to ask her generous and warm-hearted hosts if she could live permanently with them – and become their adopted daughter. The answer was an automatic and heartfelt yes, since they had taken to her just as much as she had to them, but only if her English relatives had no objections, which they soon proved not to have. Her education would be at the Von Rittermann Academy, so she would spend the week in Celle, then return for the weekend along with Nikolas and his siblings to Bamberg. The orphaned girl willingly accepted this.

'You must make the most of your new life with Baron and Baroness von Kleiste . . .' Rhiannon regarded her relative earnestly, her green eyes serious. 'Your parents, brothers and grandparents, along with my own parents and brother, will, I know, be looking down on you. They'll be very happy that you've found such a caring new home and a wonderful new family. Just show them all what you're capable of.'

A tearful Jessica nodded back, then sobbed brokenheartedly against Rhiannon's shoulder while Max looked sadly on. Rhiannon's wise words made a lasting impression on the bereaved girl.

Katie-Luise, Isabella and Victoria were utterly delighted to have Jessica as a friend and adopted sister. The other von Kleiste siblings were likewise pleased to welcome her into their large and easy-going family, Nikolas especially: he found himself caring more deeply for the girl than he had realised was possible. An overwhelmed Jessica suddenly found that she had acquired a brand new set of kinsfolk in the place of her lost family. Lonely she most certainly was not. Her adoptive siblings, Horst and Daniel, soon formed a circle of loving and supportive friendship around her, and many other new schoolmates likewise became her good friends as she settled into her exciting new life as Jessica Meredith-Von Kleiste – the adopted daughter of Baron Otto and Baroness Cassandra von Kleiste, and part of a wealthy and well-respected family. Max, Rhiannon, and the rest of their family gave her all possible support as she grieved, and as the days turned to weeks and the weeks to months it began to seem as if she had always lived and studied among the von Kleistes and von Rittermanns. Time would surely, as her wise Aunt Rhiannon had said, soften the grief.

The following August, 1972, pupils at the Von Rittermann Academy were celebrating their truly brilliant exam results – with Nikolas and his fellow triplets, Siegfried and Benedikt Meredith-Mayschoss and Kasper among them. Such academic success was a mixed blessing for the Academy, as it was immediately and completely snowed under with applications. The result was that Alex and Amber, in a joint venture with Otto and Cassie, decided to set up another school on the von Kleiste estate in North Bavaria. Named the Von Rittermann and Von Kleiste Academy, it was to be run on exactly the same lines as their first school, the only difference being that the uniform badge was the von Kleiste coat of arms, on Otto's insistence.

By January 1973 the new school was built, staffed and running – and Jessica, Karl-Otto and Kasper all transferred to it. As with its sister school, the Academy had a maximum quota of five hundred pupils, as well as an extremely long waiting list, while the teachers and other staff were drawn to some extent from the von Kleiste, Mayschoss and Meredith families. Several male Meredith teachers had married local, von Kleiste or Mayschoss girls – and were now raising families of their own, having taken out West German citizenship.

Cassie gazed at her mother and twelve-year-old Jessica, who were looking at family photographs together, and reflected how all this had been set in motion back in 1940, when Max had met and married Rhiannon in Paris.

By 1977 a great many changes had occurred. Max retired from his position as managing director of the von Rittermann estate and Agricultural Production and Export in November, and handed over power to Hans, his ambitious and capable deputy. With no intention of twiddling his thumbs, Max became a part-time counsellor in the Academy's pastoral department, and was much valued.

Jessica passed all her exams with flying colours and in September the next year she started a degree course in French and German at Bamberg University. The medical student Nikolas married her in December, after her eighteenth birthday.

Chapter Thirty-Five

Goodbye Grandma, and I love you too.' Jessica put down the phone and smiled at her husband as she recounted her grandfather's latest DIY disaster. Nikolas, as always, was puzzled: why didn't the old couple have the job done professionally and be done with it – since they could so easily afford to? Like his granddaughter, though, Thomas Morton was stubborn and independent. The young aristocrat shook his head at this typical English eccentricity: his wife's maternal relatives were decidedly fiery – but not always able to distinguish what was possible from what wasn't. The Meredith family was far more down to earth and logical – as well as having a definite tendency to swim with the tide rather than against it. Despite her Morton traits, Jessica was an archetypal Meredith who could charm the birds from the trees – her golden beauty, charisma and sweet-as-honey smile able to reduce the hardest of hearts to putty.

One day Jessica would inherit her late mother's half-share of her grandparents' estate. Damara, on the other hand, had no such generous inheritance to look forward to, but she obviously still had great ambitions – studying hard at her English grammar school, perfecting her German, and carefully and skilfully courting the von Rittermanns, making it clear that she had decided on Klaus Meredith-Mayschoss as a future husband and would stop at nothing to secure him. The deeply adoring thirteen-year-old Klaus cheerfully allowed himself to be dominated by the quiet but formidable Damara, who was just a year older than him, without the slightest complaint – and showed no desire whatsoever to resist her plans.

Three months later, in April 1979, it was the turn of Werner, Nikolas's brother, to tie the knot with his long-term lover Elisabeth Mayschoss, while Katie-Luise married her bank manager fiancé, Ludwig von Kleiste – a distant relative on her great-grandfather Baron Konrad von Kleiste's side of the family. The high-spirited and flirtatious Katie-Luise had merrily played the field for a good six years before finally deciding aged twenty-one to settle down and marry her far more serious boyfriend. Her family was amazed, but utterly delighted, that this worthy and devoutly religious man would consider taking her on as his wife.

Kasper, Katie-Luise's bookish and bespectacled younger brother, reluctantly served his military service in Cologne alongside the equally reluctant and aspiring future lawyer Siegfried Meredith-Mayschoss. Siegfried, unlike Kasper, had no girlfriend – nor had he ever shown the slightest interest in the fairer sex, unlike his three brothers and two cousins. He had, though, numerous close male friends and acquaintances, something that did not give his worried and ultra-traditional Roman Catholic parents very much comfort or hope.

The Academies continued to be successful, and in 1980 a third was set up, this time in Düsseldorf. Like the others, it was soon heavily oversubscribed. The pupils sported the von Rittermann coat of arms on their blazers, since it was not in South Germany.

Werner and Elisabeth's first child, Gunter, was born in late February, Otto and Cassie's first grandchild. Katie-Luise gave them their second in the form of Miranda Gisèle just a few months later, but this was the only child she was destined to bear: a cancerous tumour was found in her womb immediately after the birth, and a hysterectomy was necessary to save her life.

Katie-Luise's devoted husband reassured her. 'My darling, we've got one precious child to cherish. But most important of all, the cancer's not spread: you're going to be all right.'

After making a full recovery, the young mother returned to her job as a fashion designer – her little daughter slumbering peacefully in the most luxurious of cots as she worked close by.

Meanwhile, Benedikt Meredith-Mayschoss, Sebastian and Caroline's second son, passed his degree in pathology with first class honours, but was refused for military service, much to his delight. A slightly damaged lung was cited as the reason – the young man having suffered a serious bout of TB as a child. He immediately sought a position as a junior pathologist, and soon found a suitable post at Hanover Hospital, with the influential help of his surgeon uncle, Alexander von Rittermann.

Alex and Amber's pride and joy in their beloved elder son knew no bounds as they observed his astounding academic progress and obvious contentment with life. They were utterly convinced that they had made the right decision in setting up a private school for his benefit. Horst, predictably enough, had sailed through his school exams, and in September 1980 began to study for a BSc at Hanover University aged only fifteen.

Nikolas, meanwhile, was still immersed in the world of medicine, not to mention celebrating the safe birth of his first-born son, Kurt-Siegfried, in December. The baby was everything his proud parents had hoped for, and a third grandchild for his overjoyed paternal grandparents. Jessica still had seven months of her degree to complete, and duly returned to her studies the following January – before easily attaining a first class degree, and taking over as her son's carer – as well as working full-time as a translator in the von Kleiste publicity department.

Kasper, too, was riding high. His military service completed, he took up a post as a bank clerk in Bamberg, with the sure hope of future promotion. Nikolas was likewise doing well in his medical studies, while Siegfried had landed a coveted post as junior solicitor at a successful Nuremberg firm . . . but even this was not enough to please his family. By now they had realised that he would never have a girlfriend, marry and have children, as 'normal' people did. Unable to understand or tolerate his homosexuality, his parents rejected their gifted eldest son, his siblings likewise ostracising him. But Max and Rhiannon, his paternal grandparents, remained as deeply devoted to him as ever, and flatly refused to condemn him: he was still their beloved grandson, and they would always be there for him. The equally tolerant Mayschoss, Morton and Meredith families were not at all shocked by Siegfried, while the von Rittermanns and von Kleistes made it clear to him that he would always be very welcome at their homes with his partner Rolf Mayschoss, with whom he now shared a luxury rented flat. Karl-Otto alone in his family declared the cohabiting male lovers to be a sin and sacrilege in the eyes of God – but was told by an unimpressed Otto and Cassie to show more tolerance and humanity.

By mid-March 1982 Jessica was two months pregnant, and was the proud mother of a second son, Wolfgang (immediately nicknamed 'Wolfie' by his family), seven months later. After six months maternity leave, she returned to work.

An equally contented Karl-Otto, like Benedikt, had been rejected for military service, because he had a slight heart murmur, and was thus free to follow his dream and enrol at Munich Theological College as a trainee priest.

By now Damara was armed with three excellent 'A' level passes, and was attending a teacher training college in Hanover. She was living at Von

Rittermann House – her studies being paid for by Alex and Amber. The ambitious young Englishwoman had also applied for West German citizenship. Her future plans included studying for an MA and taking up a teaching post at the Von Rittermann Academy. Klaus had not been forgotten by her, and he was now her adoring lover: determined not to lose him, she had faithfully promised to visit him every weekend during his military service the following year.

Rhiannon's four twin grandsons, naturally enough, all had grand future plans of their own, with Klaus and Jurgen hoping to attend dental school after their military service, and their cousins intending to study engineering at Hanover University.

By summer the following year both sets of Meredith-Mayschoss twins were doing their military service at Hamburg, knowing that they had passed well enough to follow their chosen vocations. A cheerfully resigned Klaus had now had his wings well and truly clipped by becoming engaged to the quietly dominant Damara, while the other three boys were still unattached and sowing their wild oats with a vengeance.

Werner and Elisabeth von Kleiste were more interested in presenting their delightful new-born silver-grey-eyed baby girl, Henrietta, to the world in early September, their second and last child. The young mother decided to give up work until her daughter reached the age of six.

Kasper, now a senior clerk, finally married the girl of his dreams in the form of Antonia von Kleiste, a distant relative, and their first child, Alexa, was born in mid-October 1984. Nikolas too had something important to announce: that very summer he graduated from medical school with first class honours, and soon afterwards, thanks to his father's influential contacts, found a position as junior doctor at Nuremberg Hospital. He and Jessica decided, much to Otto and Cassandra's joy, to make the von Kleiste estate their permanent family home. After this momentous decision had been taken, a contented Otto decided to continue giving his eldest son half the monthly allowance he had been enjoying since he had started his degree studies, especially since Werner and Kasper had both been bought homes by their father when they married.

On Otto's death, however, Nikolas alone would inherit the estate and his father's entire fortune, along with the title of Baron von Kleiste. Isabella and Victoria were to have the choice of money or a small house or flat in a few years' time – and Otto's six younger children would only get a few valuable keepsakes, along with more personal possessions. Young Jessica had quite enough money of her own – now that Thomas and Joy Morton had died and she had inherited her mother's half-share of their estate – as well as her parents' entire estate. Looking further ahead, she would also be sharing in Nikolas's wealth later on, as his baroness – and consequently also be sporting the von Kleiste family sapphires.

Horst should have been starting his military service at Hamburg in July 1984, but had broken his arm in a rather rough and tumble wrestling game with an equally physically powerful Daniel. By the time it had fully healed, Horst and sixteen-year-old Isabella were lovers, and had decided to marry as soon as she was eighteen. Daniel had chosen Victoria as his lover, and she had decided to study psychology at Hanover University. In contrast, Isabella had chosen to study English and French; with Daniel taking a degree course in law.

'All of which means, Amber, that we'll have Daniel, Vicky and Isabella living with us for the next four years – with Horst receiving regular weekend visits from Isabella in the meantime.'

Amber smiled gently at Alex, her heart rejoicing at just how perfectly family affairs were turning out.

Chapter Thirty-Six

Our commanding officers couldn't wait to see the back of us, as we'd played so many practical jokes on them in those two years. Our fellow conscripts enjoyed it all enormously – and we were damned lucky not to be caught red-handed. Although the officers always suspected that the formidable Meredith-Mayschoss quads, as we were known, were behind everything, they couldn't prove anything.'

Karl Meredith-Mayschoss grinned at his fellow twin Christoph, first cousins Klaus and Jurgen, and Damara, now Klaus's wife, as the family celebrated the four young men's return home at Rhys and Hanna's large and luxurious house in the outskirts of Celle.

'I rather doubt that the German army would have considered you as potential officer material, given behaviour like that.' Max regarded his four younger grandsons in bemusement. 'But then again, your fathers were just as unsuited to and bored with army life, so perhaps I shouldn't be surprised.'

'With Horst, Daniel and everyone else preferring to take up civilian professions instead of the army, you'll be the last military professional in the family for a long time to come.' Hanna nodded fondly at her father-in-law, with whom she enjoyed an excellent rapport.

'The army hasn't exactly benefited from our family over the generations.' Caroline sipped her champagne serenely and shrugged.

Rhiannon smiled cheerfully at her daughter-in-law, and changed the subject. 'It's so wonderful to have Klaus and Damara living with us at Von Rittermann House, and for you to have Jurgen back at home with you again.'

'They'll all be terribly busy, won't they?' Caroline considered the twins' engineering and applied mathematics course at Hanover, Klaus and Jurgen's dentistry studies, not to mention Damara's teacher training. 'In the meantime I hope Jurgen and his cousins meet some suitable girls, and bring them home to meet the family.'

Rhys smiled approvingly at the gifted young Englishwoman of whom he and his kinsfolk were so fond. True, Damara was no great beauty like Jessica, but what did that matter when she had so many other fine qualities?

Paula and Dieter, Caroline's mother and stepfather, sat back in their chairs and surveyed the cosy family gathering with contented smiles. For Dieter, Caroline had long been his daughter, and Caroline's four sons the beloved grandchildren he had never been blessed with. He had even left the four brothers equal shares of half his estate, with Paula inheriting the rest.

The totally unexpected death of Paula in a hit and run accident while shopping a few weeks later, however, changed Dieter's plans, and his death from pneumonia in September left the four Meredith-Mayschoss boys with more than enough money. Klaus and Damara were all set to buy an old house in Celle once probate was completed, and Siegfried planned to use his share to invest in a luxury flat in Hanover with his partner Rolf, the latter contributing a large part of his considerable savings. Benedikt, now engaged to Anna von Kleiste, intended to buy a generously sized house in Celle, while Jurgen decided to save the bulk of his inheritance and enjoy the rest in good living, while still residing with his parents.

Other family members were busy romantically, with Daniel becoming engaged to his adored Victoria, and Horst to Isabella the summer of the following year. Back at home, and all set to start his veterinary studies, Horst and Isabella, with an enthusiastic Daniel and Victoria, enjoyed a ten day trip to the Bahamas – courtesy of the ever indulgent Alex and Amber. With marriage the next inevitable step for these young couples, as well as Benedikt and Anna, they all got hitched in great style in December 1986.

By now a fully qualified teacher, Damara was busy with her MA studies – and more than happy with her privileged life in West Germany.

A few months later the extravagant Adele and Dietrich von Stein passed away only a month or two apart, leaving Caroline their modest savings and their elegant mid-nineteenth-century villa in Hanover. Their grand-daughter immediately put the property up for sale, only to find that the highest interested bidder was none other than her estranged eldest son. She consented to accept Siegfried's generous offer, and thus it was that he and

Rolf became the proud new owners of his great-grandparents' spacious former home, renaming it Meredith-Mayschoss House.

At the same time Kasper, by now promoted to the position of deputy bank manager, and Antonia became the stunned parents of fine twin sons, Marius and Maxim, who completed their family of four children.

By late December, moreover, Isabella was two months pregnant with her first child, and glowing with maternal joy and the best of health.

The following year proved to be as eventful as the previous one – with Benedikt and Anna's first son, the dark-haired and light-grey-eyed Damian, making his appearance in May, and Kurt-Alexander, Horst and Isabella's eagerly awaited first child, following in July. Light-brown haired and silver-grey eyed, he weighed in at a hefty ten pounds, and delighted his third-cousin parents.

Daniel and Victoria, on the contrary, found nothing to celebrate in Daniel's obligatory military service now that he had completed his law degree. The good news that he had passed with first class honours hardly raised a smile. His colour-blindness, alas, was not enough to gain him exemption – despite his desperate protestations. Daniel, the doctor declared, was as fit and healthy a young man as he had ever seen, and such a minor disability was no reason at all to excuse this powerfully built young giant.

Victoria, having gained a degree in psychology, was studying hard for her MA in childhood development studies at Hamburg University and renting a small but comfortable flat in the city. Thus Daniel lived in two worlds: a grim and military army camp during the week and a luxury flat at the weekend.

Horst, in contrast, rather enjoyed his military service. Admired by his fellow conscripts and commanding officers alike, he was sometimes decidedly strange in his manner – not to mention gigantically tall and possessing the most unnervingly hypnotic silver-grey eyes.

A silver-grey-eyed baby Damian was proving to be the most placid, lovable and well-behaved of tots, while Kurt-Alexander was the opposite. Lively, always hungry and ready for a feed, as well as the most vocal of babies, Horst and Isabella's first-born was also the most demanding of infants: his furious howls of rage if he thought no-one was paying him enough attention soon caused his fondly devoted great-grandmother Rhiannon to comment that he reminded her of Alex, Kurt-Alexander's paternal grandfather, when he was a baby. Alexander was not remotely amused. Despite his challenging and often difficult behaviour, the young parents were utterly devoted to their baby son. The ghost of his great-grandfather, Kurt von Rittermann, was likewise completely enraptured, and was often seen talking fondly to the keenly alert little boy.

All was not well in Kasper and Antonia von Kleistes' household by late August, as two-year-old Gabrielle, their second child and younger daughter, lay stricken with meningitis and fighting for her life. Desperately willed on by her devastated parents, grandparents, and the medical staff, her once happily smiling face was a mask of contorted agony and her once strong body a writhing wreck of pitiful weakness. Her death a few days later plunged the von Kleistes into the deepest of mourning – and at her funeral a heartbroken Antonia and grief-stricken Kasper sadly walked behind her small snow-white coffin.

Death, however, is followed by new life, and a sandy-haired and green-eyed baby Mathias amply proved this point when he was safely delivered in mid-December 1989 – a delighted Benedikt and Anna Meredith-Mayschoss celebrating the birth of their second son.

At about the same time Jurgen and his fiancée, Luisa Mayschoss, became man and wife, and bought the old house next door to Klaus and Damara that had just been put up for sale.

The auburn-haired and silver-grey-eyed Victor Kurt arrived in early January 1990, making Horst and Isabella the proud parents of yet another healthy baby boy. The two other babies born that year were Rebekah Luise to Jurgen and Luisa in mid-June and James to Klaus and Damara the following month. Equally cheering to the family was that Daniel and Victoria were back at Von Rittermann House by mid-August, having spent a fortnight with her parents, Otto and Cassandra, at their fine old Baroque mansion in North Bavaria. In October, moreover, a delighted Daniel found employment as a junior partner at the solicitors' firm in Hanover where Siegfried worked, and Victoria took up a position as psychologist at a Hanover children's clinic.

Two years later Victoria was the proud mother of Max-Fabian, with the blond Christian completing Horst and Isabella's family a week or so later – both children possessing the von Rittermann silver-grey eyes. Not to be outdone, Benedikt and Anna also produced their third son and final child, Martin, a month later – and Karl and Christoph finally decided to tie the knot with their fiancées – Johanna, a lovely black-haired nurse, and her identical twin, legal secretary Klara. Klaus and Damara also added to their family with a second son, David, and vowed to have two more children before calling it a day.

A very large house was duly bought in Celle for the inseparable Karl and Christoph and their wives by their immeasurably proud parents, Rhys and Hanna. The two young wives soon fell pregnant simultaneously, and Karl and Christoph were taken on by a local engineering firm.

Damara too had plenty to smile about, as she was appointed as Hanna's deputy at the Academy. Horst, meanwhile, was nearing completion of his veterinary course and had been promised a job on graduation at Hanover Zoo as junior vet.

The birth of Susanna to Karl and Johanna Meredith-Mayschoss and Thomas to Christoph and Klara Meredith-Mayschoss only a few days later completed Rhiannon's family for that year – giving her and Max great satisfaction.

Once again, Damara was with child by her remarkably virile husband. The arrival of identical red-haired and blue-eyed twins, Charles and William, both possessing the family crooked little fingers obliged her to take her third and final maternity leave. Then in June 1996 Leo, the second son of Daniel and Vicky, made his appearance. This fine baby boy completed their family, but was not the daughter they had so longed for.

Chapter Thirty-Seven

The lavish christening celebrations at Von Rittermann House that followed little Leo's birth two weeks later were in full swing. A beaming Arabella and Alicia, Karl-Otto and Rosa's deceptively angelic-looking three-year-old twins, romped with the elder von Rittermann boys as their elegantly dressed parents looked smilingly on. A happily married man and proud father of two children, soon to be three, Karl-Otto had changed greatly since he had briefly attended the Roman Catholic seminary in Munich as a trainee priest. This rather timid, unassuming and devoutly religious young man had felt a vocation to the priesthood from childhood, but unfortunately this became more and more difficult to pursue because of his enduring love and adoration of Rosa von Kleiste, his charismatic third cousin. Never having found the courage to declare his feelings, and genuinely believing that they were God's way of testing his faith and intended vocation, Karl-Otto had done his best to ignore them. But it did not help when attractive females of about his own age, more than a little attracted by his boyish good looks, curly fair hair and dreamy silver-grey eyes, smiled sweetly at him as they passed – and inflamed all the more his burning desire for Rosa in particular and young women in general. For ten months Karl-Otto tried unsuccessfully to suppress his deep longings, but finally concluded that the priestly life was not for him.

Rosa was, understandingly enough, known to both the von Kleiste and von Rittermann families as 'the man-eater' and the 'lascivious honey-trap', thanks to her promiscuous ways and rather risqué taste in wealthy married men, and not just well-heeled and upper-class bachelors. She was a good-looking, cultured and intelligent brunette, slim and curvaceous, with come-to-bed green eyes. As the only child of wealthy parents, she had been brought up with every indulgence and luxury that money could buy and family love provide.

Cruelly torn between his desire to enter priestly orders and the starkly opposing longing to pursue a far more worldly life, after much deliberation Karl-Otto decided to abandon his priestly ambitions before he had completed his first year of study. This decision was greeted by the seminary teaching staff with relief, as they never really felt that he could make the grade: he didn't have the right qualities for such a disciplined vocation. Training as a teacher instead, given his love of learning and keen intelligence, was an ideal future career; a view expressed by his parents and a wise old Max and Rhiannon as well.

As he studied, Karl-Otto – though not averse to the occasional love affair – always kept a longing eye on Rosa, who was a student at the same institution. The friendship that developed between them became ever deeper as time passed.

Graduation arrived for both of them, and teaching posts at the same Munich grammar school. Rosa had long nurtured hopes of marrying Karl-Otto, whom she secretly adored – never quite believing that he would consider taking on such a moral reprobate as herself. Karl-Otto, meanwhile, still hesitated to declare his love, for fear that she would reject him as not being good-looking enough for her tastes.

All this, though, changed dramatically after the tragic deaths of Rosa's parents, at which point Karl-Otto became an emotional rock for the deeply grieving young woman. After finally declaring his true feelings for her and receiving assurances of her love in return, they embarked on a passionate and whirlwind affair. After a year of living together they decided to become engaged, and their marriage took place six months later.

No longer remotely timid or shy, the reserved Karl-Otto positively radiated self-assurance and happiness; his three more aggressive and powerfully built elder brothers regarded their magically transformed sibling with stupefaction and respect, which had been denied him during their childhood.

'It's incredible . . . our weedy kid brother is a real man now. He's even conquered the affections of Rosa.' Werner was stunned.

Cassandra's comment to Otto, on learning that her youngest son had left the seminary, was far wiser. 'I never really believed that, as your child, he could ever have been a successful priest. But that was something he had to work out for himself. Now all he and Rosa have to do is to give us grandchildren – once they've satisfied their wanderlust and finally decide to settle down.'

'Be assured they will, my love. In the meantime, let's leave them in peace. They deserve their happiness together.' Cassandra heartily concurred with her husband's sage reply.

In November 1992 Otto and Cassandra became the delighted grandparents of identical twin granddaughters. Rosa had no wish whatsoever to return to formal teaching, and decided to work as a private tutor once Arabella and Alicia were fully weaned.

A couple of years later Alex and Amber inevitably made a play for the twins and their aristocratic parents, with the offer of a luxurious grace and favour apartment at Von Rittermann House, well-paid part-time teaching posts at the Von Rittermann Academy for both Karl-Otto and Rosa, and free places at the Academy for their precious offspring. The delighted couple enthusiastically accepted, selling their flat and moving into Von Rittermann House to take up their new professional responsibilities.

Rhiannon, meanwhile, finally decided to hand over charge of the Von Rittermann household to a much younger Isabella. She also felt it was the right time to divide half her fortune equally between Cassandra, Rhys and Sebastian as an early inheritance. The trio received their very generous cheques with the greatest of thanks. Klaus and Sophia von Rheinholdt, Hanna's parents, likewise handed their daughter a considerable early legacy, then sold up, left their native Bavaria and moved into the comfortable granny flat that had been built onto Hanna's house in rural Celle. Still in the very best of health, as were Max and Rhiannon, Klaus and Sophia continued to live life to the full, delighting in close and regular contact with their daughter's tightly knit family.

In October 1996 a third (and final) child was born to Karl-Otto and Rosa. Karl-Otto held his new-born daughter in his arms and gazed at her lovingly, a proud smile lighting his serious face. 'What a little beauty she is, with her rich auburn hair! Just like her sisters, little Lucilla Rhiannon's got the von Rittermann silver-grey eyes and crooked little fingers.'

'And who will you choose as Lucie's godparents? You've got so many brothers and sisters . . .' Alex settled himself into a comfortable armchair.

'Oh, Isabella and Victoria, I think – along with their husbands, of course – so we'll only run the risk of offending Karl-Otto's five other brothers and sisters, and their spouses!' Rosa laughed, and relaxed against the dark blue satin pillow. In reality she wasn't particularly concerned if they were offended or not.

Amber, too, was delighted by Lucie's arrival. 'She's going to be another very welcome female playmate for our five grandsons – and possibly a highly suitable wife for Leo. Rebekah and Susanna, along with Arabella and Alicia, will likewise, God willing, make equally suitable wives for Leo's elder brother and three cousins – and the von Rittermann lineage and name will survive and thrive through their offspring, our great-grandchildren. I think we can congratulate ourselves on a job well done!' She looked triumphantly at her brother, to whom she had for so long given her heart, body and soul.

Alex smiled at his sister's flight of fancy. 'Even if we've achieved it by risking public disgrace and prison . . . But you're the only one I've ever truly loved. Marriage to Charlotte was a serious error of judgement, I admit, utter disloyalty towards you and Horst. If she'd lived it would have been a disaster: she'd have figured out our true relationship in the end. Rightly or wrongly, we were destined to be together – and everything has ultimately worked out for the best.'

Chapter Thirty-Eight

It had been Arabella's question that had first got Rosa wondering about how grown up the twins had become for their age. 'Does Baron von Rittermann love his sister, Mummy?'

'But of course he does. Why on earth shouldn't he?'

'No, Mummy, you don't understand. We mean really love her, as Daddy loves you, and Granddad von Kleiste loves Grandma.' Alicia looked insistently at her bemused mother, an intensely curious expression on her little face.

'Well, no, girls, I shouldn't think so – he's her brother. But even if he did, it's certainly no business of ours.'

'That settles it then – he does. So his sister's sons are his sons too, aren't they, Arabella?'

'And their sons are the baron's grandsons.'

'And you two are going to be utterly silent, or else. You've got absolutely no proof, children. And anyway, as I said, it's none of our business.'

'No, Mummy, but . . .'

'No buts, Alicia. It just isn't, that's all.' Suddenly livid, Rosa glowered at her daughters, who abruptly dropped the subject and never dared mention it again.

Rosa considered their perceptive comments, which struck her as pointing towards a distinctly possible truth . . . Aged only four, the twins were growing up too fast for their own good – which was only accelerated by their being so often in the company of the mature von Rittermann boys, not to mention the equally precocious Rebekah and Susanna

Meredith-Mayschoss, and their brothers and male cousins. Arabella and eight-year-old Kurt-Alexander had become utterly inseparable, as had Max-Fabian and Alicia. An equally besotted Viktor and Christian were the passionately devoted beaux of Rebekah and Susanna, but Leo and Lucie were still far too young to show any such preferences – but might become childhood sweethearts later on, thought the perceptive Rosa.

In 1997 the whole extended family, along with the rest of Germany, grimly followed the news, as yet another victim of a paedophile rapist and murderer was discovered. Victoria, now a criminal profiler, and Benedikt, a pathologist, were deeply involved in the macabre investigation – as was Horst, his awesome psychic powers having been brought to the police superintendent's attention by his relations. It was his instructions that directed the police to where the next victim could be found. The trio's holiday plans were put on ice until the perpetrator had been discovered and arrested – while Alex and Amber jetted off to Stockholm and Copenhagen, and Karl-Otto and his family slipped away to Meredith House with Max, Rhiannon, Rolf and Siegfried, before spending some time with his parents at Bamberg. Back home, Victoria, Horst and Benedikt's efforts were given a new sense of urgency after the death of a postman's seven-year-old son in Celle at the hands of the psychopath. It was Horst who finally succeeded in nailing the paedophile.

'To cap it all, the police have put Horst on the payroll as a casual employee, as a consultant criminal psychologist rather than as a psychic, to avoid adverse publicity.' Alex was enthralled by his relation's gifts. 'I've learnt so much from Horst about the supernatural.'

Rosa regarded her assembled relatives with a smile, her glossy dark hair hanging loosely around her shoulders. 'Horst's told me that he's foreseen a family reconciliation in the next few years, and another dramatic life-changing development. He's refused to say any more, and says we've just got to be patient.'

Horst nodded composedly, before attacking his breakfast with a keen appetite. It was quite pointless, he thought, to enlighten his family – especially as there was nothing to fear.

Chapter Thirty-Nine

Little Lucie was growing up as the most delightful and charming of little girls, with appealingly sweet manners, her delicate Celtic beauty contrasting with her sisters' Nordic good looks and colouring. But she was certainly no pushover when it came to asserting herself against the formidable united force of her devoted siblings. This flame-headed great-granddaughter of Ralph von Rittermann also benefited from the adoring Leo's staunch support when she needed it most. Usually together, and often hand in hand, these first cousins would make the most perfect married couple – or so thought their close relatives.

Arrangements were well under way for a family holiday to America. A party of fifteen was planning to visit Salem, Miami and New York.

'Mr and Mrs Mayschoss are going. He's taking an electric wheelchair so as to get about more easily. Then there are Baron von Rittermann and his sister, Rolf and Siegfried, Karl-Otto, Daniel and their families. Horst and Isabella are taking charge at Von Rittermann House. He's needed at the zoo as it's so busy during holiday time, and he's also helping the police with a murder case. The family dogs will be cared for here by us. The Meredith-Mayschoss clan is off to Australia, and Baron and Baroness von Kleiste are going to New Zealand with various members of their family, leaving Werner and his wife Elisabeth in charge at their house.' The von Rittermanns' well-informed butler nodded at the head cook, who silently took everything in, then spread the word to the domestic staff and estate workers.

'New York really has quite a buzz, hasn't it?' Max carefully steered his wheelchair along the teeming pavements.

'We're keeping an eye on you, Granddad, so we don't lose you in this horrendous crowd.' The red-headed young giant gripped the arm of his step-grandfather's wheelchair, his steady pace never breaking step with the elderly man's vehicle. Victoria followed closely behind with their two sons. Amber was talking to Rhiannon, while Alex was protectively close behind his cherished mother and sister. Karl-Otto and his family followed along behind, the twins hanging tightly on their mother's hands, and Lucie perching on her father's shoulders, her face alive with glee.

The family headed for the exclusive Italian restaurant so highly recommended to them by their hotel receptionist, and sat down to a truly excellent meal. Speaking English, as they had agreed to do, their cut-glass accents and refined manners soon attracted the attention of the other diners, a nearby family of wealthy and noisy Texans in particular. A lively conversation between the two groups was inevitable, and they eagerly swapped family details. The Texans, who owned an oil well and refinery or two, mentioned an even wealthier and more successful oil baron friend of theirs, Herbert Meredith – a widower, who was an English expatriate. 'Is he a relative of yours, Mrs Mayschoss? You said your maiden name was Meredith.'

'Indeed he is: he's a cousin on my father's side. We grew up together in Northern England. When I left for Paris I lost contact with him and his family. I had no idea he'd emigrated.'

'We'll mention you to him tonight. We're going to his house.'

The oil baron was as good as his word, and he and his family told their keenly attentive friend about the fascinating European aristocrats whom they had met, and were staying at the Park Central Hotel. Rhiannon's name in particular caused his heart to skip a beat.

Born in 1920, Herbert had been rejected for military service, after childhood polio, and had studied at the University of York, taking a junior post at the London Stock Exchange on his graduation. Marriage was closely followed by the birth of their first son, after which the family emigrated to the USA, where the couple had a second son.

Then in 1998, out of the blue, came utter disaster. Herbert's first son, Frederick, with his wife and four children, were all killed in a plane crash – when the family jet crashed into the mist-covered French Alps during an electrical storm. Then, as if this was not enough, Herbert's wife Kathryn died of cancer eighteen months later, and his second son Roger from a stroke a matter of weeks after that. Herbert, devastated and grief-stricken, had only his two beloved Pekinese left for company.

The moment his dinner guests left, Herbert phoned the Park Central Hotel. Talking to Rhiannon for an hour or so, they fondly reminisced about the past and attempted to catch up with all that had occurred over the last sixty years. And thus it was that the bereaved Englishman renewed his links with his Meredith cousin – with whom he had once been more than a little in love.

Herbert advanced with a lurching heart towards Rhiannon and her family, and warmly embraced her, the tears rolling down his withered cheeks.

'And now you must make the acquaintance of Max and our son – and the rest of our clan.'

His two armed bodyguards looked on impassively as he greeted everyone, before sitting down for an unusually hearty lunch – his insistent request that they should have dinner with him that very evening being bowed to with all possible good grace.

And what a magnificent dinner Herbert served to his highly honoured guests. Even the normally self-assured Alex and Amber were bemused by his treasure-house of a mansion, and stared disbelievingly at the many Old Masters that adorned its walls.

'But none of this can ever make up for what I've lost. Do remember that before you're too over-awed.' Herbert looked grimly at the baron and his sister, who nodded seriously and reflected on his words. Their shrewd distant relative studied the devoted siblings with a keenly attentive expression, rapidly realising that they were, in all likelihood, husband and wife in all but name. Herbert smiled to himself as he talked to Rhiannon. Not that it was any business of his . . .

As the evening progressed the lonely business magnate seriously began to consider adopting Rhiannon's family as his own – especially after his research that afternoon into their business dealings, and his confidential enquiries to an influential and trustworthy contact in the German business world, who had expressed nothing but praise for the von Rittermann and von Kleiste families, and their richly deserved reputations for business integrity, reliability, efficiency and competence. All of this helped to convince Herbert that the von Rittermanns would make the perfect inheritors of his business empires – as well as his massive personal fortune. His yacht, along with much property, had already been sold, but there still remained his private jet, luxury apartments in Paris, London, Vienna and Berlin, a lovingly restored manor house in Normandy, a villa in Sorrento, a château in the Loire Valley and his New York residence. All these had to be as appreciated and cherished by their new owners as they had been by his family – and the von Rittermanns were truly worthy.

The first thing a distinctly bemused Rhiannon knew about all this was when Herbert asked if he could move to Von Rittermann House as soon as possible, along with his two dogs and a small retinue of personal staff and bodyguards. Shocked, she listened to his plan to make her family his trusted business partners, and cede the ownership of half his shares in Meredith Oil and Meredith Enterprises to them, renaming them Meredith-Von Rittermann Oil and Meredith-Von Rittermann Enterprises – along with his medieval manor house, four luxury apartments and half his fortune. If the partnership was satisfactory, Herbert added, he would transfer his remaining business shares to them, along with his private jet, three other properties and most of his remaining fortune. If they founded another school it was to be known as the Meredith-Von Rittermann Academy. And yes, he would dearly love to pay a visit to the von Kleiste estate and Meredith House as soon as possible.

Alex and Amber, downing a large double whisky each, silently vowed to give their elder son a flea in his ear for failing to warn them of this financial bombshell. Unsurprisingly they were quick to agree to everything Herbert proposed.

Inevitably, the time came for the family to pack their suitcases and return home to Germany. A deeply upset Herbert waved them off at the airport, avidly counting the days until his own arrival in that country. His heart rejoiced at the thought that he had, so unexpectedly, been given a second chance of happiness with a new family.

Chapter Forty

It was September 2000, and Herbert, his two dogs and staff had been residing at Von Rittermann House for four months. No longer lonely, the elderly gentleman's health had fully recovered, and he had become far more optimistic. It was as if someone had suddenly waved a magic wand over both him and his equally perky Pekinese, the vibrant and caring presence of Rhiannon and her family seemed to have woken him from a drugged sleep.

'Let me assure you, you've got well over ten years of life ahead. Do you still want to hand over the rest of your assets, or would you prefer to hang on to them? I think the latter makes most sense.' Horst regarded the older man intently. 'You can take my prediction as the absolute truth, Herbert. As a family we're not out to defraud you or take advantage of you financially – whatever our other moral failings may be.'

'I'd never consider you and your family capable of such contemptible behaviour. My decision still stands – especially as, according to you, I'll be around for a while to advise and guide.'

Despite his admiration for the Meredith-Mayschoss family, Herbert found it hard to tolerate their continuing rejection of Siegfried. 'Listen to me, all of you . . . I'm near the end of my life, yes, but not without having made my peace with God and my nearest and dearest. You should take the chance to let bygones be bygones and welcome Siegfried back into your midst, while you still can. If you don't you might regret it later. Siegfried's gifted, successful and someone to be truly proud of. All I ask of you is that you reconsider your attitude, and find it in your hearts to take back the prodigal son.'

Herbert's appeal to the four Meredith-Mayschoss elders was successful, and an utterly delighted Siegfried was soon fully reconciled with his close family. Once Sebastian and Caroline relented, so did everyone else. Max and Rhiannon were unable to hide their disbelief and their heart-felt joy, and Herbert his jubilation.

Otto and Cassie and their family were likewise more than satisfied with this development – as they were by the news that their newly married grandson, Kurt-Siegfried, and his wife Miranda (the only child of Ludwig and Katie-Luise) were to be parents, and wanted Karl-Otto and Rosa as godparents.

One problem for Baron von Rittermann was that this sudden wealth and additional business assets to manage meant that he had no option but to take early retirement on his fifty-eighth birthday from his beloved profession as a neuro-surgeon, so he could assist his sister back home. His colleagues at Hanover Hospital were glad to see the back of him, as he had been extremely domineering, albeit a highly skilled surgeon and an efficient head of department.

Way back in 1968, soon after Charlotte's death, Alex had installed a secret entrance, hidden by a revolving bookcase, to directly connect his apartment with Amber's next door, meaning that the siblings could, unseen and unnoticed, spend the night together. Horst, of course, knew all about this, but had also, on his parents' orders, kept silent – as had Daniel when he found out about it.

The birth of their first child to Kurt-Siegfried and Miranda at Easter 2001 added yet another member to the ever-expanding von Kleiste family. Reinhart-Max Herbert Otto made a very happy and proud Otto and Cassandra great-grandparents.

Later in the year Rhys, Sebastian, Hanna, and Caroline all retired, the two last being replaced by their trusted deputies, Damara Meredith-Mayschoss and Isabella von Rittermann.

Daniel and Siegfried, meanwhile, decided to form a partnership under the business name von Rittermann and Meredith-Mayschoss, Solicitors, and made their plush business headquarters in the suitably enlarged and converted Meredith-Mayschoss House, also Rolf and Siegfried's home.

Horst was promoted to the rank of head veterinary surgeon at Hanover Zoo, and Victoria to the position of criminal psychiatrist at Hanover police station, the first woman ever to combine this post with that of criminal profiler, and indeed the first to be appointed to either post.

A fourth Academy (duly named as Herbert had requested) was

flourishing in Berlin, with its pupils proudly sporting the Meredith coat of arms on their blazers. The astounding success of the school encouraged Alex and Amber to set up two more, in Hamburg and Munich.

Herbert could not have been happier. Whenever he visited Meredith House all the North Yorkshire Merediths and Mortons descended on that fine abode, to pay homage to their illustrious relative. Rhiannon's extended family also got back in touch, with her Irish paternal relatives, the O'Donnells, having inaugurated yearly visits. Even some opportunistic Perrauts (Rhiannon's French maternal relatives) and Duponts succeeded in forging close links with the vastly complicated family network. Rhiannon had long ago made her peace with the Perrauts ,while Cassandra finally found it in her heart to forgive her mother's family for their harsh treatment of Gisèle.

'Just as I have made my own peace with God' was an approving Herbert's comment. This deeply religious, tolerant and fair-minded man contemplated everything around him with a contented smile and serenely joyful heart.

Chapter Forty-One

There was nothing quite as satisfying, thought Heinz-Ludwig von Kleiste, sitting with his wife Renata and chatting to Alexander and his family over afternoon tea, as catching up with old friends' news. As a senior science lecturer at Munich University, and the proud father of two sons and three daughters, who had gone on to give him fourteen grandchildren, well – he had not done at all badly.

The quiet and reserved Heinz-Ludwig was visiting Von Rittermann House with his wife for a week. For years he and Renata had puzzled over Alex and Amber's strangely married air, preferring to keep such thoughts and the dark suspicions that they raised to themselves. What the siblings did in private was absolutely none of their business.

An equally perceptive Herbert, meanwhile, listened to his friends' animated conversation as he sipped his favourite Earl Grey tea, his dapper form comfortably settled in a plush leather armchair.

'So Cassandra finally decided to forgive her maternal Dupont relatives, did she? That was a very generous gesture.'

Alex smiled. 'It was inevitable, given Cassie's generous nature. Remember, Heinz-Ludwig, my mother buried the hatchet with the Perrauts. We're all getting together, the O'Donnells too, for a big reunion in Paris.'

Renata glanced up. 'And the von Kleistes are so very pleased about the Meredith-Mayschosses finally taking poor Siegfried back into the fold . . . I mean, who'd have thought it possible after so many years?'

'I rather think Sebastian and Caroline were starting to feel more than a little guilty about the long-standing estrangement. All that was needed was the right person to get them to act.' Amber smiled affectionately at Rhiannon.

'We're deeply grateful to you, Herbert.' Rhiannon gave her cousin a warm hug, all the while aware of a ghostly Kurt von Rittermann in the shadows.

The conversation turned to the younger generation: Rebekah's hopes to become a veterinary surgeon, Victor's intention to study civil engineering, Kurt-Alexander's determination to study at Hanover University – as well as Kurt-Siegfried's excellent progress in his medical studies and his wife's flourishing career as a fashion designer. Wolfgang and Octavia were likewise doing very well indeed in their dental and teacher training studies, and their younger relatives also being considered a real credit to the family.

Horst sat in reflective silence and silent grief – knowing that his beloved parents would die in a tragic accident in autumn 2014, but unable to see how and when. Otto would be dead from a stroke in 2009 and Klaus and Sophia von Reinholdt would both pass away the following year, as would Max, Horst's step-grandfather. Rhiannon, though, had many years left to live: she would easily outlive them all.

In the ever reproductive von Kleiste family, family births were the more cheering domestic news during the next four years: Kurt-Siegfried and Miranda produced two more fine sons, as did Wolfgang and Octavia. Quads were born to Gunter and Alexa, while baby Eleanor delighted Kurt-Siegfried and Miranda: she was their fourth child and only daughter. Henrietta and her husband, Hugo Meredith, were proud to announce the arrival of their twins, whom they named Maximilian and Sebastian.

Kurt-Alexander, Horst and Isabella's elder son, excelled in his chosen university studies, and had also made an utterly besotted fifteen-year-old Arabella his secret lover. Viktor and Rebekah, Christian and Susanna, and Max-Fabian and Alicia were all likewise involved in the most intimate and physical of relationships. A mutually devoted Leo and Lucie were left to enjoy their far more innocent kisses and cuddles.

Chapter Forty-Two

'Viktor, I really think you ought to know . . . I'm pregnant.'

'What! But you can't be, Rebekah . . . I mean . . .'

'Well, I am, I'm afraid. Your father's told me that we're expecting a son, along with insisting that you make an honest woman of me and ensure that our child is born a legitimate von Rittermann, preferably well before his birth.'

'I'm sixteen and you're seventeen, so why not? I mean, we can't disappoint our mothers, can we . . . or our sentimental old great-grandma. And yes, before you ask, I do love you, and would have married you anyway – sooner or later.'

'Later rather than sooner, no doubt, but never mind.'

The news in late June 2008, following Viktor and Rebekah's April nuptials, that Kurt-Alexander, aged nineteen, and Arabella, four years younger, were also expecting a child, was not nearly so well received by their respective families.

'But I was always very careful, I swear. I'll marry Arabella as soon as she turns sixteen, in November, so that our baby will be just as legitimate as Victor and Rebekah's.' The young roué looked fondly at his intended, who snuggled lovingly up to him and nodded enthusiastically at everything he said, her eyes shining with happiness. Nor did she object when told by Horst that she would have to be educated by private tutors, keep away from Mass, and attend a private clinic in Hanover, to receive the most discreet ante- and post-natal care. That his rogue of an elder son had fathered her baby would be kept a close family secret until the time came to register the fact officially, when he was married to Arabella.

All this was agreed to by the parties concerned, Karl-Otto and Rosa not wishing to upset or offend their relatives, and also more than happy to see their beloved elder daughter marry into the fabulously wealthy von Rittermann family.

Otto and Cassandra were utterly delighted by the idea of their lovely granddaughter, Arabella, becoming a future Baroness von Rittermann, and likewise kept silent about her pregnancy; their own conduct as illicit (and in Cassandra's case underage) lovers many years before did not permit them to judge the young couple.

A month later, and the silver-grey-eyed Friedrich made his grand entrance into the world. His godparents were Benedikt and Anna, and Christoph and Klara Meredith-Mayschoss, their names picked out of a hat by Max to ensure absolute fairness.

The normally very slim Arabella had become somewhat plumper as she entered her sixth month , but was still not noticeably pregnant as she larked around with her husband-to-be. Soon, though, her high spirits gave way to serious and responsible reflections on her fast approaching motherhood, and Kurt-Alexander began to indulge in long and ardent discussions about marriage and fatherhood with his parents and great-grandparents. When they became man and wife just after Arabella's sixteenth birthday, the increasingly serious and mature young couple began to assume dignified and grown-up airs and graces, much amusing their von Kleiste relatives – who gently reminded them that there would be plenty of time for all that later.

The baby, of course, cared nothing for any such notions and, frustrated, kicked away inside her mother. With a spectacularly quick delivery by Alex and Horst, in mid-December, as Isabella and Rosa held her mother's hands, the tot's arrival took everyone by surprise. Arabella's brief screams of pain gave way to delighted shouts of joy when she first beheld her red-headed and silver-grey-eyed daughter. Little Annabelle Amber Rhiannon, as Arabella and Kurt-Alexander decided to name her, was a welcome great-grandchild and also, declared a delighted Amber, was the first von Rittermann female born since 1944. This meant that Karl-Otto was the only male in a family of six, not a prospect that dismayed the reserved and serious-minded aristocrat, so deeply did he love his wife and three lively daughters. Little Annabelle proved to be every bit as feisty and full of her own importance as her close female relatives.

An immensely proud Kurt-Alexander cradled his new daughter lovingly in his arms, and announced that her godparents were to be Viktor and Rebekah – along with Kurt-Siegfried and Miranda von Kleiste.

Kurt-Siegfried and Miranda were in need of this good news. They, and the rest of the von Kleiste family, took in the depressing news that Otto had suffered a stroke and had almost died. Vowing to survive, Otto made a surprisingly rapid recovery, even cutting down on all his favourite high-fat foods and on alcohol, as well as losing weight. But none of this, reflected Horst, would save him in the end . . . and in November 2009 the old man died, aged seventy-seven, from a second massive stroke.

Nineteen months later Otto's deeply grieving widow met the widowed, childless and heirless eighty-year-old Count Alfred von Aalen, and became his wife. The elderly aristocrat adopted Werner, Cassandra's second son, as his heir, inviting him and his family to make Castle von Aalen their home and legally making him the next Count von Aalen. A stunned and delighted Werner learnt that he would also be inheriting Alfred's large fortune, and his castle and estate in Baden Wurttemberg. All this, as foreseen by Horst, was due to fall into his possession eight years later.

Max, Horst's cherished step-grandfather, lived on until just after his ninety-eighth birthday, dying of pneumonia in early December 2010. Rhiannon mourned his passing for a year, before becoming the wife of an ecstatic Herbert for the next six years – when he died peacefully in his sleep, leaving her a deeply grieving widow for the second and last time.

Of Alex and Amber's ultimate fate Horst was still none the wiser – his vision of his parents' deaths restricted to a confused and vague impression of 2014, and stormy autumnal weather.

Horst shared this, sometimes heart-breaking, secret knowledge with his ghostly late grandfather, who listened to his beloved elder grandson with a reflective expression, then tried to comfort him with words of grandfatherly wisdom as the rest of their huge family made all the usual preparations for the forthcoming Christmas and the far more ebullient New Year celebrations. 'You and I, my boy, will now join them in these uplifting celebrations, living in the far more cheerful present rather than the sometimes sad family future that only you can see. It will come when it's meant to, and not before.' The two of them entered the festive banqueting hall, and von Rittermann proudly watched his son and daughter make toast after toast as midnight approached, before joining in Auld Lang Syne and welcoming 2009 with enthusiastic cheers.

'Well, here's to us, Alex. May we celebrate many more such events in the years to come.'

'We'll never be parted, Amber – not even in death.'

'Oh, I'll drink to that, and much more besides. Happy New Year, Alex.'

The sixty-four-year-old red-head smiled lovingly at her brother, who took her hand in his and held it tightly as he affectionately returned her greeting. Horst reflected meditatively on all this and much more as he regarded the fireworks. What did it matter if these unorthodox sibling parents had broken one of society's biggest taboos by becoming husband and wife in all but name? All you could do was look at their dynasty and judge if it had been worth it. Their life-long love and loyalty spoke to him directly. Such were his parents, and such were his feelings as he observed them, his heart stirring with the deepest of filial devotion.

Lightning Source UK Ltd.
Milton Keynes UK
11 September 2010

159751UK00001B/14/P